PHILIP PARIS

the Italian Chapel

BLACK & WHITE PUBLISHING

First published in the UK in 2009
This edition first published in 2018 by
Black & White Publishing Ltd
Nautical House, 104 Commercial Street, Edinburgh, EH6 6NF

A division of Bonnier Books UK
4th Floor, Victoria House, Bloomsbury Square, London, WC1B 4DA
Owned by Bonnier Books
Sveavägen 56, Stockholm, Sweden

A CIP catalogue record for this book is available from the British Library.

ISBN: 978 1 78530 164 3

5 7 9 10 8 6 4

ALBA | CHRUTHACHAIL

Typeset by Ellipsis Books Ltd, Glasgow
Printed and bound in Great Britain by Clays Ltd, Elcograf S.p.A.

MIX
Paper from
responsible sources
FSC® C018072

www.blackandwhitepublishing.com

Acknowledgements

During this quest to tell the story of the Italian Chapel, strangers have become friends, while others have remained strangers. But they have all offered help, information and advice without hesitation and for that, I am eternally grateful.

John Andrew (Balfour Beatty), Chris Asher, Graeme Bowie, Father Antony Collins, Claudio and Paola, Balfour Hospital, Guido DeBonis (ex POW, Orkney), Gina Ellis (daughter of Sergeant Major Fornasier), Letizia Fonti (daughter of Domenico Chiocchetti), Gary Gibson (Kirkwall artist), Bryan Hall, Dave Hover, Lesley Jeffreys, Rosemay Johnstone (daughter of Bill Johnstone), Primiano Malvolti's family, Lesley McLetchie, Sam Moore, Society of Jesus, Willie Mowatt (Orkney blacksmith), John Muir (Italian Chapel Preservation Committee), Tom Muir (Orkney Museum), National Gallery for Scotland, Orkney Library, Renato and Giuseppe 'Pino' Palumbi (son and grandson of Giuseppe Palumbi), Norman Sinclair (son of Orkney photographer James Sinclair), Tom Sinclair (owner of Lamb Holm), Manuela Re, Francis Roberts, Anne Simpson, Alison Sutherland Graeme (daughter of Patrick Sutherland Graeme), Rachel

Stuart, Sheena Wenham (granddaughter of Patrick Sutherland Graeme), Gale Winskill, J Wippell & Company, Wendy Young, Fiona Zeyfert (granddaughter of Major Buckland).

There are two special thanks I must give. One is to Coriolano 'Gino' Caprara, whose enthusiasm for the story and phenomenal ability to remember minute details of the period he spent as a POW in Orkney provide an invaluable insight into the lives of the Italians. The other is to my wife Catherine. Her love, encouragement and common sense are the rock to which I steer the course of my life. In return, I have taught her more about the construction of a Second World War Nissen hut than she thought it was possible to know.

This book is dedicated to Domenico Chiocchetti, Giuseppe Palumbi, Domenico Buttapasta, Giovanni Pennisi and the other men who defied great hardship, hostile weather and the limitations of a WW2 prisoner of war camp, to create a monument of hope and peace that can reach out to us more than sixty-five years later and move us to tears.

Prologue

Spring 1946

That morning, the silence that had enveloped Camp 60 since the Italians left was shattered; destroyed violently, like the gates, as they were flung apart by a huge bulldozer. Hut after hut on the tiny Orkney island was torn down in a frantic race to erase all traces of war. As the work progressed, the demolition team moved ever nearer to the little chapel.

The contract was clear. Nothing was to be left.

Inside, the Madonna watched the entrance over the gates of Giuseppe Palumbi's rood screen . . . and waited.

In the recreation hall, the three billiard tables that the Italian prisoners of war had made out of leftover concrete each had a neat triangle of balls set up for the next game. It had been eighteen months since the hut resounded with the ruckus of men laughing and cheering.

The screech of tearing metal was followed by brilliant daylight flooding across the tables, as a bulldozer ripped off part of the corrugated iron wall. The operator edged the machine forward, raised the bucket and brought it down sharply in the middle

1

of the nearest table. It cracked cleanly in half and balls scattered across the floor to be crushed, returned to dust. Speed was everything; the destruction relentless.

The demolition crew started a fire just outside the camp, where the Italians had once burned the wood that could not be used in the huts' pot-bellied stoves. Scenes of Italy, skilfully painted backdrops for plays and performances, were reduced to ashes. Domenico Chiocchetti's hard work was discarded, its value unrecognised.

While the flames raged and buildings crashed to the ground, the Madonna stared serenely. Eventually the door of the chapel opened, creaking in protest after being closed for so long.

Two men entered, wearing hats and overalls. Heavily built and tough, they were used to being obeyed without question. The immediate tranquility took them totally by surprise. They walked along the nave, astonished at how realistic the imitation stone and brick walls appeared, until they stood before the rood screen.

The gaffer, an Irishman, placed his hands on the wrought-iron work, appreciating the skill required to turn scrap metal into an object of such delicate beauty. He wondered about the man who had dedicated so much effort to such a task.

Removing their hats, the two men entered the chancel to stare at the paintings of saints on the windows, angels and evangelists, the Madonna and Child above the altar. The gaffer picked up one of the brass candlesticks. He had spent more than thirty years putting up and taking down buildings, but had never been moved by one . . . not like this. Something deep within him stirred and he wasn't sure why.

'What are you thinking, Pat?' asked the other man eventually.

His friend did not answer, the peace he had felt moments

earlier eroded by waves of emotion; anger at the bureaucrat who had written the orders without checking what was on the site, fear that a different gang might have followed those orders, the chapel pulled down like a worthless hut.

'I'm thinking,' he said, barely controlling his feelings, 'that I'll not be the man who has to stand before God on Judgement Day and explain why I allowed such a dedication to His glory to be destroyed.'

'There's certainly some skill here, but you know what our contract says. The land restored to how it was before the war.'

'No, this is more than craftsmanship, Jack. Men put their souls into this and left a part of themselves behind.'

'There'll be a price to pay if we leave it.'

The Irishman replaced the candlestick so that the surrounding dust remained undisturbed.

'You know, this Nissen hut, *this* was the Italians' escape. They didn't dig a tunnel . . . they built a chapel. It's a symbol.'

'Of what?'

'Hope. Tell the men, Jack, to leave the chapel and the statue. Make sure nobody misunderstands what I'm saying.'

'You're the boss.'

Alone in the building, the Irishman studied the paintings closely, poked his head into the vestry and then walked slowly back to the door, marvelling once more at the curved walls as he went. When he reached the entrance he looked back at the chancel.

'Made out of scraps,' he said, closing the door quietly behind him.

Back in the open, the pace of work was frantic. Wooden purlins were hurled on to the fire, while machines and men competed to eradicate what had been home for more than 500 Italians. There was no pretence to finesse; speed was the aim.

A few men stopped briefly to look at the statue of St George slaying the dragon, just outside the impressive façade of the chapel, but neither was touched.

By the end of the day it was over. The huts were demolished. All that was left were the concrete foundations. A couple of men stacked the fence posts and made neat rolls of barbed wire for the landowner or local farmer to use. Anything else that could not be burned had been loaded on to the back of trucks.

The noise and activity stopped just as suddenly as it had burst upon the camp that morning and the chapel was alone again, still and silent.

This time there was no fence to keep people out.

1

The Madonna's face swayed. Domenico Chiocchetti held the image in his hands as he sat in the bowels of a packet steamer, which had left Aberdeen that afternoon. The constant left-right motion was interspersed with a twisting action as the ship not only rode the waves but yawed from side to side. The rancid smell of vomit, unwashed bodies and cigarette smoke hung in the air alongside anger and despair, loneliness and dread. Domenico looked down at the picture and thought of his family and home . . . and Maria.

He was thirty-one. A quiet, kindly, humble man. An artist, caught up in a war just like the other 1,200 Italian prisoners of war, captured during the North African campaigns, now being transported to some unknown destination. There was a rumour they were going to an island north of Scotland, but few believed such a place existed. Even if they had been told its name, it is doubtful any of the Italians would have heard of the tiny Orkney island of Lamb Holm. He had no idea his life would be bound to that island and to the image in his hands.

As he looked at the picture of the Madonna and Child, men around him murmured, coughed and retched. One or two wept in silence and several prayed because the journey was as terrifying as the battlefield. They felt helpless, at the mercy of the British army and the violent waters of the Pentland Firth. If the latter didn't sink them, which seemed increasingly likely, there was a good chance that a German U-boat might.

'Hey, Domenico. What's that card you're looking at? Domenico!'

Domenico looked up. He wasn't smiling, his mind still in his home village of Moena, where life had been simple, safe and wholesome. He stared blankly at Aldo; the easy-going, happy-go-lucky wheeler-dealer, whose cheeky grin made him look about sixteen. But Domenico sensed the vulnerability in the younger man. He thought the real Aldo Tolino was yet to be revealed to the world.

'You've been gazing at that card all the way from Liverpool.'

Domenico's face cracked into a smile.

'Since Durban before that, Egypt before that and Libya before that,' he replied, handing over the card.

Sergeant Giovanni Pennisi had been sitting with his eyes closed in an attempt, not to sleep, but to ignore what was going on around him. He looked down with eyes that were only half open and spoke for the first time since the ship left Aberdeen.

'It's one of a series of paintings of the Madonna and Child by Nicolò Barabino.'

'You know paintings, Sergeant Pennisi?' said Aldo, surprised both at being spoken to and the content of the comment.

'That's because,' said Domenico, 'Sergeant Pennisi is a man of culture, a man of significant artistic talent. Something of which I suspect you, young Aldo, know little.'

Domenico and Pennisi shared a common bond in their

burning desire to paint, but few of the other men knew of this or their friendship.

'Hey, I admit my talents lie elsewhere, but why do you treasure this card so much?' Aldo persisted.

Pennisi opened his eyes fully out of respect for his friend, who was about to speak of something close to his heart.

'My mother gave it to me just before I left. Sometimes I feel if I look at the picture, I don't have to look at the horror around me. It gives me strength at moments when the future looks bleak. And it reminds me of my mother.'

Aldo was not untouched by the honest explanation.

'It's beautiful,' he said. 'You can show it to her again when you return to Italy.'

Domenico laid the prayer card carefully in an empty tobacco tin and pressed the lid tightly closed, before tucking the tin safely into an inside pocket of his jacket. It was almost a ritual.

'At least for us the war is over,' said Aldo.

'There will be other things to fight Aldo,' answered Domenico. 'Boredom, loneliness, loss of hope . . .'

The ship listed heavily and men grabbed frantically at what they could, including those next to them. The tension in the air vied with the smoke for space. With an agonising effort the ship gradually straightened and 1,200 Italians let out their breath.

'Someone said we're being sent to an island off an island and that it's so small if you turn around suddenly you will knock someone else into the sea,' said Aldo. 'The British must really fear that we are going to escape to send us to such a remote area . . . like that place in America. What's it called?'

'Alcatraz,' said Pennisi, now committed to the conversation.

'That's it. They're sending us to Alcatraz,' said Aldo, his boyish enthusiasm making him sound almost excited at the prospect.

'I think the British must have some purpose in mind to transport us to this remote island. I don't believe it's because they're worried that a few hundred weary Italian prisoners of war will escape en masse and overthrow their country,' said Pennisi.

A figure rushed past them to stop several yards away where the man was sick into a fire bucket. Pennisi closed his eyes. Aldo looked on with fascinated disgust.

'Wherever we're going we'd better get there soon,' he said. 'If there's a fire we'll be throwing vomit instead of sand.'

Pennisi replied without opening his eyes.

'Ah, but good Italian vomit,' he said.

2

Disembarking had been a nightmare of confused shouted orders, darkness, cold and resentment. The little stone pier that had been hurriedly constructed on Lamb Holm wasn't suitable for the ship to dock, so the men had been forced to climb down with whatever kit they possessed into two tugs that had drawn up alongside.

At first no one understood what was happening, but as part of the disembarking procedure men were split into two groups. It appeared they were being sent to two camps, on completely separate islands, because when full the tugs had set off into the darkness in different directions, returning sometime later to pick up the next batch. Those still on deck were tossed about roughly, while the men who had landed stood around on the exposed shore becoming ever more frozen. As fate would have it, Domenico was put in one tug and Pennisi another. The loss of his friend was a bitter disappointment.

For as long as they could remember the prisoners' lives had consisted of a series of increasingly miserable situations and as the Italians trudged doggedly through the icy rain, it was difficult to decide whether they had been better off on the ship. Armed British soldiers walked along the outside of the column; vague indistinct figures, probably no better off themselves. Domenico wondered why they were there; escape was the last thing on anyone's mind. Some men staggered from the after effects of being on such a rough sea for so long and as the gut wrenching sickness receded it was replaced by hunger.

The gale beat at them mercilessly like an angry Norse god who resented their presence; a malevolent viciousness, which whipped off hats into the night and slapped capes against thighs with the force to sting. There was no pretence of marching or of order. This was a line of men so wretched and wet that they had not one single dry item between them.

'Hey, Domenico!' Domenico squinted into the rain to see the short, stocky figure of Dino, whose beautiful tenor voice had enthralled people in countless camps during the previous months. 'The priests had it wrong.'

'Do they ever get it right?' The reply was from Aldo, shouting from Domenico's other side. He ignored the comment, which irritated him.

'Why have they got it wrong?' Domenico's words were almost inaudible.

'They said Hell was a place of fire and burning. It's not. It's a place of fierce rain and biting cold . . . and we've just arrived.'

They walked on. Near the back Giuseppe Palumbi stumbled along in a grim silence that had become a habit. Giuseppe had expressed communist views at a time when promoting such beliefs was a dangerous activity in Italy. One morning a friend had dragged him into a corner of a café, where he told him his outspoken opinions had put his life in great peril. Giuseppe was a hopeless romantic but not a foolish one. He went home, said goodbye to his wife, kissed his baby son and joined the

Italian army; Mussolini's fascist army. He had lost a great deal that day and since then had kept to himself.

Eventually, almost unnoticed, they passed a large sign that read 'Camp 60' and moments later entered their new home. The men crowded into an ever larger group as those at the back of the line filtered into the camp. There seemed to be some confusion and shouting going on ahead but Domenico and those around him couldn't work out what was being said. However, men started moving quickly towards the huts around the compound.

'Come on,' Aldo shouted at Domenico. 'We've got to claim a hut.'

Aldo fixed his eyes on a building further down the camp and shot off, head tucked into his thin chest, arms and legs pumping with desperate determination. Domenico and the men nearby followed as fast as their stiff legs would carry them.

They were instantly slipping and sliding uncontrollably in every direction. Mud, so deep it would have stopped a tank. Halfway to the hut Domenico felt his legs slide ominously and he began to fall backwards until someone behind gave him an almighty push that almost sent him sprawling the other way. They lurched onwards. Aldo reached the hut first and burst through the door, stopping dead at the stark sight that greeted him.

'Christ, it's colder than my granny's corpse.'

The men were out of the rain but they looked in dismay at the bunk beds, squashed together down each side of the hut. There were a few chairs and cupboards and a table with two benches, standing just beyond a stove, whose black stack rose up to the roof in the very centre of the building. It was as cold as the Pentland Firth they had just crossed.

The men moved quietly around, laying down bags and

belongings on the floor. Aldo claimed a bottom bunk near to the stove and Domenico took the one next to it. Dino and Carlo had taken beds near the stove on the other side of the hut. They were cousins but more like brothers and wherever you found one you found the other.

Carlo set about getting the stove going, which he did quite quickly, but it didn't make a lot of difference unless you were standing near. Before long, hooks and pegs were covered with an assortment of dripping clothes, while several pieces of long stout cord appeared from the bottom of rucksacks for makeshift washing lines.

Domenico shivered as he removed his shirt. It was only as he was drying his hair with the towel that he spotted the British sergeant and private standing just inside the doorway, watching. They might have been there for several moments, but no one had actually noticed.

'Alright! Listen up. My name's Slater . . . Sergeant Slater to you. You're going to get to know me well, and I'm going to get to know you. But I don't want this thought to give you nightmares. Better men than you have had nightmares at the idea of being my friend.'

The Italians were silent and sullen. Only a few had a sufficient grasp of English to understand the essence of what was being said, but all anyone wanted was to get into bed and try to get warm. Sergeant Slater resumed his speech.

'Work hard, keep your noses clean and you'll be alright.'

He fell silent, staring as if trying to memorise their faces. The sergeant looked hard but Domenico reckoned he was probably the same with his own men and his comments were standard 'sergeant speak'.

'Why does he want us to keep our noses clean?' whispered Aldo.

'He means keep out of trouble,' said Domenico, who had taken off his vest and was drying his chest and arms.

'Don't they speak English on this island?'

Before Domenico could speak, if indeed he thought the comment worthy of a reply, Sergeant Slater started again.

'Now, settle down and get some sleep. As you've all had a long day you can lie in tomorrow. Reveille won't be until daylight.'

This comment created a moan from those who had followed what was said.

'Don't worry. I believe it's going to be a nice day, so you'll want to make the most of it.' He paused for a moment, but no one spoke. 'Lights out in fifteen minutes.'

Sergeant Slater left, followed closely by the private who slammed the door behind him. The door wasn't locked. A few men quickly put back on their coats and boots and went out to find the latrines. Everyone else hurried to get ready for bed. Aldo had disappeared under the coarse blankets. Exactly fifteen minutes later, the hut was plunged into darkness.

Exhaustion overwhelmed Domenico, but the sleep he craved didn't welcome him. He lay there, hungry and cold, trying to block out the noise made by the rain on the corrugated iron roof above his head. It reminded him of machine gun fire. He thought about Maria; sweet, gentle Maria. He had not seen her since leaving home eighteen months earlier to work on the decoration of a church in Laste. While there he had been called up, put in an anti-tank regiment and sent to fight in Libya.

Dino and Carlo had also been there, the three of them only fighting for six months before they were captured by the Australians. There had followed a confused round of different POW camps, during which it had been almost impossible to keep in touch with family back home; never staying in one place long enough for letters to catch up. Since leaving the camp in Egypt they had been travelling for months, and Domenico was weary to the bone, uneasy at what the future held in this strange and wild land.

3

Nothing had dried. The concrete floor was wet where clothes had dripped throughout the night and everything was still damp. Men were forced to climb back into shirts and trousers that sucked the heat from their bodies and made them shiver and swear.

Daylight came much later in the morning than any of the men had imagined. No one had experienced an Orkney winter and many were baffled by it. Domenico and Aldo left the hut carrying their towels, soap and shaving gear and joined the stream of men making their way to the wash block. Men scrubbed at their bodies as if trying to wash away the memory of the previous day's journey and, to an extent, they succeeded. But there was one thing they were more in need of than cleanliness and that was hot food.

The mess hall was by far the biggest building and could feed all of the men in one sitting. It was half full when Domenico and Aldo entered. Murmured voices were accompanied by the sound of metal spoons on metal dishes. Joining their third queue of the morning, they entered immediately into conversation.

Someone had heard that British guards had woken half the

occupants of one hut whilst it was still dark, marched them to the huge kitchen ranges in the mess hall and told them to start preparing breakfast. Some of them had never even boiled an egg before and apparently the commotion in the wash block had been nothing compared to the mayhem in the kitchen. Aldo well believed the story as he reached the serving area and looked down suspiciously at a vat of a bubbling, watery, lumpy substance.

'What's that?' he asked of the Italian on the other side of the table.

A guard standing nearby overhead the question.

'You'll not get a good nourishing meal like porridge in your country, laddie. You start eating that every day and it'll make a man of you.'

The Italian ladled porridge into Aldo's dish. He moved along and was given two small slices of bread, a cube of butter and a spoonful of jam. The last thing he collected was a mug of hot but weak coffee. Aldo and Domenico found places at a table opposite Dino and Carlo, but the men barely spoke apart from the occasional mumbled curse aimed at the substance in their bowls.

Domenico studied the faces of the men on the other side of the table, hoping it was not too obvious. Faces fascinated his artist's soul. Dino and Carlo were both in their early thirties and each had two small sons back home near Bergamo in the north of Italy. In appearance they were very similar, their round, dark-skinned faces topped with a cropped hairstyle that Domenico thought made them look like Roman centurions, and yet their personalities were as different as possible. As well as an exceptional singer, Dino was gifted at sketching. He was always scrounging paper, constantly filling sheets with birds and animals, drawings for which he had a natural ability. Carlo, was as talented with mechanical, practical tasks as his cousin was with art.

As he stood on the parade ground later that morning, Domenico thought that Sergeant Slater had been right. In its own way it was a beautiful day. The cloudless blue sky mocked the storm of the previous night and there was only a slight breeze. However, the men shivered as they stood in line. A British corporal walked up and down, counting. Aldo and Domenico were near the back, separated by a large Italian of about forty. When the corporal had walked past and was well out of hearing range he held out his hand to Aldo.

'I'm Domenico Buttapasta.'

'Aldo Tolino. Better known as Mr Fix-It. If you need something, you let me know; alcohol, cigarettes, gambling, equipment. Anything you want and all for a good price.'

'That's an impressive list,' said Buttapasta, amused by the boast.

'It's all a matter of time,' continued Aldo, unabashed. 'I simply need to set up my channels of supply. Just give me time.'

'Well, you'll have plenty of that,' replied the big man. He turned and held out his hand to Domenico.

'Domenico Chiocchetti,' said the artist, taking the strong hand in his. 'I would normally say I'm pleased to meet you, but I don't expect you're any happier to be here than I am.'

'There'll come a time when we won't be in such a strange place my friend then we'll show the British what a proper Italian greeting is.'

'Agreed,' said Domenico.

'I think I understand what Aldo does, but what about you?' asked Buttapasta.

17

'I guess I paint.'

'Paint? Walls or pictures?'

'I studied the art of painting statues as a student and was working on the decoration of a church when I was called up. If I wasn't painting, I sometimes tried my hand at sculpture.'

'An artist. I like that.'

'And you?' said Domenico.

'Oh, I'm a simple man. I just work with cement, that's all.'

'You'll have plenty of opportunity for that,' said Aldo from the other side. 'They say the British want us to hold back the sea . . . to create a huge dam and stop the tide. And they think they will win the war? They're more insane than my uncle Fabio and he thought he was a buzzard . . .'

'Buttapasta.' Domenico was suddenly alight with interest. 'Not *the* Buttapasta, the artist with cement and stone?' Buttapasta shrugged. 'Your work is famous throughout Italy. It would give me great pleasure to talk to you later.'

'And I look forward to it,' said Buttapasta graciously. 'Although for now I think we are both about to do some listening.'

He indicated with his head and they turned to face a British officer as he walked towards the front of the lines.

'Attention!'

The order came from Sergeant Major Fornasier, the most senior Italian in the camp. He was standing facing the men, a few yards from a wooden crate. The British officer stepped on to this and when he spoke, his voice was crisp, authoritative.

'Stand at ease. My name is Major Yates and I am in command of Camp 60 on the island of Lamb Holm and also of Camp 34 on the island of Burray.'

Whispered translations went up and down the lines.

'The nearest land is mainland Orkney, which is also an island.

18

You will know from your journey that we are a long way from Italy. You're all here to do a job, to help build a unique set of barriers between mainland Orkney to the north and between the islands to the south of Glimps Holm, Burray and South Ronaldsay. Four barriers in all. It will be a big job, but you won't be alone. In addition to your fellow Italians in Camp 34 there is a large contingent of civilian workers and experts from the construction company Balfour Beatty, as well as admiralty engineers and local Orkney men. 'I understand some of you may feel this is a bleak place, very different from your home- land, but the sooner you get working, the quicker this project will be completed. I know you will do your best. Your day-to- day orders will come from Sergeant Major Fornasier. He will liaise directly with Major Booth, the deputy camp commander, and myself. His staff will organise you into work groups with specific tasks. Before that, however, you will need to have your uniforms . . . updated.'

Major Yates did not intend, it would seem, to elaborate on what this entailed.

'Thank you, Sergeant Major.'

Sergeant Major Fornasier stood smartly to attention and barked out an order with a volume that would have made Sergeant Slater proud.

The men on the parade ground snapped once more to atten- tion.

When Major Yates had walked away the men were dismissed and the noise on the parade ground switched instantly to excited babble. By mid-morning the washing lines that had festooned the inside of huts had been strung up outside. Camp 60 consisted of an assortment of Nissen huts contained within a high barbed- wire fence. Apart from the mess hall and the accommodation huts there was a canteen, which contained a small shop, and

19

an administration hut, where the British officers worked. The wash and latrine blocks were the only brick buildings. Just outside the camp, in its own enclosure, was the concrete discipline block. The camp had a feeling of emptiness and desolation.

A large number of POWs stood silently along the west-facing fence, stunned at the sight before them. The number of destroyers, cruisers, battleships, dreadnoughts and other vessels were staggering to behold; an armada the like of which they had never seen before. Scapa Flow was unique for the opportunity it provided to sail west into the Atlantic or east into the North Sea.

Domenico, Buttapasta and Aldo walked to the fence facing mainland Orkney. Aldo spoke in a voice almost hushed with bewilderment.

'Where are all the trees?'

'The wind is too strong and too constant across the islands to allow trees to take root,' guessed Buttapasta.

'And people live here?' said Aldo with awe.

When the 230 civilian construction workers had arrived in May 1940 on board the liner *Almanzora* to put in place the first stages of the barriers' creation, Lamb Holm had consisted of nothing other than rock and soil. The first men rowed ashore in dinghies, with nothing more than crowbars and muscle power to build the small pier, which was needed before anything else could be landed.

Every single item of equipment had to be transported from the *Almanzora*, including building materials, food, water, fuel, lighting and power generators, cranes, lorries, railway track, plus the steam and diesel trains to run on them. A great deal was lost overboard before it could be transferred safely from the liner to a barge, and then from the barge to the pier. One of the trains had even slid into the sea during the transfer and had to be recovered later. Most of the smaller items that had fallen overboard were simply washed away.

But the Italians knew nothing of the enormous effort that had taken place before their arrival, nor of the toil and hardships men had endured just to get the materials onto Lamb Holm to build Camp 60 alone. Most knew nothing about Scapa Flow, more than 120 square miles of sea encased by Orkney islands, nor of the 833 men who had gone down with the battleship HMS *Royal Oak*.

The British forces had tried to seal every sea entrance to Scapa Flow with a combination of sunken discarded ships, anti-submarine mines, nets and thick steel booms. But during a particularly high tide on the night of 13th October 1939, German U-boat U47 had slipped past the defences, only hundreds of yards from where Camp 60 now stood. In around fifteen minutes, the 29,000 ton *Royal Oak* sank where she was anchored, and the U-boat made its way silently out to sea, through Kirk Sound.

Winston Churchill, then First Lord of the Admiralty, ordered the eastern approaches to Scapa Flow to be sealed completely, which meant the creation of huge barriers between the islands; Churchill's Barriers, a phenomenal feat of engineering that would require vast amounts of money, time, materials, skills and men.

4

Later that morning, six long lines of chattering and shivering Italians stood before six British army privates. Each private sat at his own table, flanked by two armed guards. On the tables were large piles of circular red cloth, either twelve or five inches in diameter.

'Your jacket,' said the private, holding out his hand to Aldo, who was at the front of one line.

'Why does he want my jacket?' he asked. Domenico and Buttapasta looked back blankly, equally at a loss. 'Why do you want my jacket?' said Aldo in halting English.

'Look, mate,' the Cockney accent became even stronger, 'just hand over your jacket and you can have it right back. You'll hardly have time to feel the cold.'

'Hand over your jacket Aldo, or they'll simply take it from you by force,' advised Buttapasta.

Aldo muttered noisily in Italian, took off his coat, gave it to Domenico, and removed his jacket, which he reluctantly handed to the private.

The soldier turned the garment over in his hands then, quite casually, produced a pair of scissors and began to cut a large hole in the back. Aldo cried out and took a step forward but Buttapasta laid a powerful hand on his shoulder as one of the guards levelled his rifle.

'What the hell are you doing? Are you insane? He's cutting up my jacket. Stop it! You've no right. No right!'

This was shouted by Aldo in an agitated mixture of English and Italian, directed at both his friends and his enemies. The private, ignoring the expected outburst, carried on and expertly cut a circular hole then a smaller hole on the outside of one arm. Moments later he held out the jacket to Aldo, who grabbed it angrily and examined the garment as if he couldn't quite believe what he had just witnessed. The soldier seemed amused, which infuriated Aldo even more.

'Now, so that you don't get a nasty draught blowing through those holes in your jacket, His Majesty's British Government has kindly provided these circles of cloth,' said the private holding out a large piece of cloth and two smaller pieces. Aldo took them warily.

'And His Majesty's British Government has also kindly provided the needle and thread to sew them on with. You may keep the needle and thread for future repairs, such being the generosity of His Majesty's British Government.'

After a moment's hesitation Aldo snatched the small bundle and was about to storm away when it dawned on him he had three circles but only two holes in his jacket. He turned back to face the soldier.

'Why have you given me three pieces of cloth?'

'Ah, that mate, is because now I want your trousers,' said the private with a grin.

An hour later Domenico and Aldo were sitting on their beds sewing. Domenico's artistic eye and hand producing neat, even stitches. Aldo sat bare-legged opposite, rather clumsily sewing a target disc over the hole in his trousers, his face a mask of indignation. The other men were busy with the same occupation and there was a hushed concentration in the hut. Aldo could hardly contain his anger.

'Why should we help the British shoot us if they want to? It must be against the Geneva Convention. It must be against some convention. Anyway, can't they shoot straight?'

'Aldo, we're prisoners of war,' said Domenico, trying to calm him down. 'We have no choice in most things but to do what they tell us.'

'I know,' replied Aldo rather petulantly, 'but I'd looked after my jacket.'

Domenico grinned, although he tried to hide it from his young friend. At that moment the door opened and someone shouted into the hut.

'Hey everyone, Sergeant Major Fornasier wants us on the parade ground in fifteen minutes to organise the work groups.'

'You'd better hurry Aldo or you'll be on the parade ground with no trousers,' said Domenico.

'Very funny,' muttered Aldo, swearing loudly as he stabbed his finger.

It was lunchtime before the men were ready to leave the camp, having been fitted out with a variety of heavy overalls, oilskins, Wellington boots and gloves.

In order that every accommodation hut contained an Italian corporal or sergeant there was some movement of men. Domenico's hut already had Sergeant Primavera. However, the result was far from perfect and it was impossible to completely separate men from the north and south who, on the whole, did not want to share huts, owing partly, though not entirely, to practical reasons. Two men in hut number three, from Calabria, had ended up surrounded by men from north of Venice and had already complained they could not understand a single word being spoken.

Those who claimed to have cooking experience were given jobs in the kitchen, but it was discovered over the next few days that a few POWs had exaggerated their kitchen experience so they could get what seemed easier, and certainly warmer, work.

Around thirty men were selected for other tasks and not to work on the barriers. These included the cooks, who were considered to have full-time jobs, and men whose skills ranged from shoe-making and barbering to the camp doctor, Gerbino Rocco. In addition to supplying these services to the other POWs, this latter group was made responsible for maintenance and cleaning of the camp. This included the task of travelling, under escort, once a week to the army supply depot near St Mary's on the south coast of mainland Orkney to pick up food, supplies, cleaning materials and cigarettes.

The men from Domenico's hut, along with about 160 others, were destined for the quarry. No one knew what to expect. When the POWs finally walked through the gates they were accompanied by armed guards. The British soldiers kept their distance in every respect and in their defiance the Italians ignored them.

Having holes cut in their uniforms then being given the undignified task of sewing on target discs – so the guards could shoot them more easily if they tried to escape – had hurt the men to the core. They had fought for their country and been captured. There was no dishonour in that. Their resentment was like a physical presence, which enveloped the group and followed it along the road . . . waiting for the chance to reveal itself.

It only took one person to be the catalyst, and when someone shouted out 'Viva il Duce!' the cry was taken up immediately like an infectious chant. Nearly 100 men had joined in when it was shouted for the fourth time. Many held out their arms aggressively in a classic Mussolini salute.

Halfway down the column, the Lee Enfield in the hands of eighteen-year-old Private Kemp shook visibly. He had never fired the rifle other than on the practice range. He looked frantically up and down the line, trying to see an officer. Instead, he caught the eye of the next private further along the column, but the fear on his face brought Kemp one step nearer to panic. 'Viva il Duce.' He brought the rifle down from across his chest. 'Viva il Duce.' The Lee Enfield swung around slowly.

Several of the POWs who hadn't joined in the chanting watched with growing horror at the events unfolding around them. They didn't know how far the guards could be pushed but they understood how dangerous frightened men with rifles could be.

It was a sign of the power of Dino's voice that when he started singing he could be heard by all those around him. It seemed like a beacon of sanity and an increasing number of Italians started to sing with him. For a while the singing and chanting competed while the life of the original trouble-maker hung in the balance. Unknown to him, Private Kemp had levelled the rifle at his head.

More men joined in the song until the chanting eventually died away. The tension dispersed with it, and by the time they reached the quarry the group were walking along in silence and Private Kemp was once more carrying the rifle across his chest.

'Heaven help us,' said Buttapasta to Domenico beside him, 'it looks like something from Dante's *Inferno*.' The quarry was a combination of noise, dust, cold and confused activity. Mechanical diggers and excavators appeared locked in a dual of strength with the rock face, while around them trucks full of stones crawled away in low gear, whining with the effort, as empty lorries almost raced into position to be filled.

In the centre of it all was a steam train to pull loaded wagons from the quarry to the barriers. A feeling of foreboding descended upon the Italians. Sergeant Slater appeared before the group, accompanied by six civilian workers in hats and overalls. He used his parade ground voice to be heard above the noise behind him.

'Someone from Balfour Beatty is about to speak to you. He knows what he is doing so listen carefully to what he has to say. Then make sure you jump to it.'

Sergeant Slater stood back a few paces to let one of the civilians move forward, although the man seemed rather reluctant to do so. Before him stood 200 Italians. He was nervous.

'You are at the Lamb Holm quarry,' he shouted as best he could. 'What we are doing here is supplying stones to be crushed to make concrete blocks, and stones to fill bolsters . . . large steel nets . . . which are being dropped into the sea between the islands. Eventually, when we've sunk enough bolsters, the islands will be linked by solid barriers. It's mainly manual work here and you'll operate in parties of forty with your own NCO, along with a Balfour Beatty engineer and a guard. I believe you've already been allocated into your working groups according to your hut numbers, so could huts one and two please make their way forward.'

The Balfour Beatty man stood back a little, not quite sure if anyone was actually going to do what he said. But then about eighty men started moving away from the main body.

'There Aldo,' said Buttapasta, 'it's not all bad. We'll get lots of fresh air after being cooped up travelling for so long.'

'Fresh air! I've never known such cold. I think you and

27

Domenico are sadists, not artists,' replied Aldo.

Buttapasta laughed and slapped him on the back. Despite his protestations, Aldo stuck close to the older men and they ended up in a gang, dropping stones from a high ledge into the back of a lorry. The men were covered in dirt and dust. Domenico and Buttapasta struggled with a boulder between them. Domenico was considerably shorter than the big man, but years of skiing and rock climbing had made him extremely fit and he kept up the pace easily.

'Not the usual sort of stone you're used to, Domenico,' said Buttapasta. The two men hated idleness. The quarry might be strenuous, but it was better than the claustrophobia of a ship and preferable to the inside of a hut while the weather stayed dry.

'I wonder how many months we'll be doing this.'

'I think we might be looking at years.'

Aldo joined them, just as Domenico uttered this comment, and threw a rather small stone into the vehicle below.

'Did you say years?' asked Aldo aghast. 'I can't do this. It's slave labour.' He looked down at his hands as if he could actually see that they were cut and bleeding under the heavy material of the gloves. 'This is not what I was built for. It's a crime against nature.'

The two older men exchanged a glance and Buttapasta put an arm around Aldo's shoulders, steering him gently back to the rock face.

'Come, Aldo. Just consider how good the exercise is for you.'

Aldo stopped dead, his dusty face a mask of misery.

'I thought you were my friend.' Buttapasta and Domenico burst out laughing.

By mid-afternoon, daylight was failing. There were no defiant shouts or singing on the return journey, just a line of silent, dirty, weary Italians. The wind picked up, drops of rain began to fall and by the time they reached the camp the washing that had been left out on the lines that morning was soaked.

The cold hit the Italians hard. The Orkney winter weather was something alien and the following few weeks were a nightmare of cold, rain, mud and gruelling work.

By mid-February, the mood in the camp had changed from being resentful to rebellious. The Italians' only escape came in writing to loved ones back home. Dino lay on his bed one evening, writing to his wife of the events of the last few days.

. . . I think the guards are basically decent but there is a great deal of misunderstanding on both sides, because none of them speak Italian and those of us who speak some English are often completely confused by their accents.

Domenico lay resting on his bed, trying to ignore the complaints from Aldo a few feet away.

'Everything in my body hurts. I have hurts where I don't have body. If I was religious I would believe I was being punished for past sins.'

Domenico sat up on his bed.

'You are religious Aldo. You just fight against it.'

'Religious! Not me. No offence Domenico. Every man to himself and all that. But I've seen too much, perhaps too much of the wrong thing, and you can't forget what you know.'

'Every man has the capacity to see the right things and follow the right path. You just have to be able to open your eyes to it,' said Domenico. This conversation had been coming for a while. Domenico was frustrated by Aldo's cold materialistic streak. Aldo was already establishing himself as the camp's wheeler-dealer and the only time he wasn't moaning about the conditions was when he was involved in some deal.

'My eyes have seen enough,' said Aldo.

'My young friend, I think you look, but do not really see.'

Aldo was about to reply but at that point the door was suddenly flung open and an Italian stepped inside.

'Quiet everyone. Quiet! We're not working here anymore. Everyone is on strike, so stay in your hut when the British come around in the morning.'

The men were stunned.

'Is everyone going on strike?' asked Sergeant Primavera.

'They'd better, Sergeant,' replied the man at the door. 'If we all stick together the British can't make us do anything.'

No one else spoke and it wasn't until the man had left that the men in the hut broke into excited murmurs.

'Ha, there is a God,' said Aldo, his complaints suddenly forgotten. 'We don't have to get up early. No work. No more stones. I feel better already. It's a miracle.'

'It won't end at this,' said Domenico, who was concerned at this development.

'They can't force us to work. What can they do? Sack us? Refuse to pay us? Send us to a prison camp?' Aldo was becoming more elated with each point he made.

'Well, we'll see what the morning brings,' said Domenico. 'But I have a bad feeling about this.'

5

The rain fell lightly against the window in Major Yates's office. He sat at his desk, a mug of tea in his hand, ploughing through a list of figures that compared the actual usage of consumables such as food, fuel, water and medical supplies with what had been estimated. The amount of coffee drunk during the period was staggering.

'Enter,' he bellowed in response to a knock at the door.

'Sorry to bother you, sir, but the prisoners have gone on strike,' said Sergeant Slater, as if he was simply making a comment on the menu for dinner. The effect was dramatic.

'On strike! What the devil do you mean they've gone on strike?' Major Yates slammed down his mug, spilling tea over his papers.

'There's a small delegation of them, sir. They say the camp is too near the Scapa Flow base, which means they are in danger should there be an air raid, and the barriers they are being asked to construct are works of a war-like nature,' said Sergeant Slater, the latter point being quoted from a letter he produced while speaking and which he now kept in his hand. 'Both of which contravene the Geneva Convention.'

'The Geneva Convention!'

'Sorry, sir. That's what they say. They've written it down.'
He laid the letter on the desk and took a step back to let Major
Yates read, which he did with a growing rage.

'They want to be transferred to another camp. Do they think
they're in bloody Butlins and can be moved if they don't like
the entertainment? Tell my orderly to get me someone from
the War Office on the phone.'

The following week, Domenico and Aldo were sitting side by
side outside their hut. The weather, something the Italians had
given up trying to predict, was currently clear and bright and
whilst Domenico sat quietly with his eyes closed, Aldo was
complaining. It seemed to be a regular scenario.

'Three days on bread and water. How can we survive,
Domenico? I'm so hungry.'

'Normal food tomorrow, Aldo.'

'Yes, but then it's back to bread and water for the next three
days. How long can this go on?'

'I told you the British wouldn't let us get away with this,'
said Domenico, looking at his friend.

The call by Major Yates on the first day of the strike had
resulted in the Inspector of POW camps making the long journey
from London to Orkney. It had taken nearly two days. Negotiations had then begun and the men told they were subject to
the same regulations and laws as the armed forces of the
detaining country. However, their complaint had been passed
to the relevant Swiss delegation, the 'Protecting Power' in
London, for further investigation. In the meantime, they were
all to go back to work.

The Italians had refused and the British had imposed punishment rations — three days of bread and water with standard
rations every fourth day.

A couple of Italians retaliated by leaving all the taps running in the wash block. The sudden increase in water usage was quickly noted and spring-loaded taps were then fitted to every sink. The Italians tied these down with whatever came to hand and so the guards had to go around the wash block several times a day and free the taps, making relations between the two sides even worse.

There wasn't sufficient coal to keep the stoves burning all day so men pooled their fuel and occupants from several huts crowded into one building. The air became so thick with cigarette smoke that when the door was opened it looked as though the hut was on fire. The gates were firmly locked. If the weather was fine men walked around the inside of the perimeter fence for exercise or stood about in small groups. They were subdued. No one seemed to have any purpose.

'Anyway,' Domenico continued, 'I thought by now you'd have secured some extra supplies.'

'Domenico, even a genius of my abilities can't achieve miracles when feeling so weak with hunger. It affects the efficiency of the mind.'

'Nonsense! It should sharpen up your efforts, not muddle them. Do you think anything great in the world was ever created by a fat man sitting around eating?'

The two men sat in silence. Aldo didn't understand Domenico's ability to ignore his surroundings by taking his mind to a place where he could explore, plan and calculate what could be made with the materials to hand. It was one of the reasons Domenico stayed, in his own quiet way, stubbornly cheerful.

After a while, Buttapasta and two other men appeared from behind a hut. Buttapasta was taking large strides, as if measuring distance, while the other men took notes on scrap paper.

'What's he doing?' asked Aldo. 'Has he gone mad already?'

'Several of the men want to build concrete paths between the huts and they've asked Buttapasta for help. You've got to admit it would be nice not to slide around in the mud.'

It was one morning in March, when the head count had been completed and the Italians were waiting to be addressed or dismissed, that rumours of a change in the camp spread throughout the parade ground.

'Hey,' said Aldo, 'I hear there's a new camp commander.'

'What's happened to the other one?' asked Micheloni, who was in Domenico's hut and had become friendly with the artist.

'Now only running Camp 34.'

'So who have we got?' said Buttapasta.

'No one knows but they say the men who started the strike idea were moved off the island first thing this morning.'

'I think we're just about to find out,' said Micheloni.

A new British officer walked on to the parade ground.

'Attention!' shouted Sergeant Major Fornasier.

The men snapped to attention and were immediately silent. When the camp commander started to speak there was a moment of whispered surprise. He spoke Italian.

'Stand at ease. My name is Major Buckland and I am the new commander at Camp 60. I'm sorry things have got off to a bad start. None of us want to be here. We all have loved ones, wives and families back home who we would rather be with. Unfortunately, for now, we are all here. Fate has decided we should end up together on this little Orkney island. You might have noticed it rains a bit more than in Italy. I'm told that it does stop and, after all, it is March. But just as I can't make you any promises about the weather, I can't make you any promises about how long we will be on the island. We are all married together.'

This latter comment caused some amusement. Major Buckland's Italian was far from perfect and he knew he hadn't said what he meant to. However, he smiled at his mistake and the men found themselves liking this rather fatherly figure, addressing them in their mother tongue.

'I know some of you have concerns about the position of the camp to Scapa Flow and about the work you have been asked to do. We seem to have reached a stalemate in recent weeks. In order to resolve the matter I have asked Sergeant Major Fornasier to meet with me this afternoon, along with the Swiss delegation that provides guidance on the living and working conditions of prisoners of war. They should arrive here from London later this morning. In addition, I have invited the Provost of Kirkwall, the main town on Orkney, to join us, because he can give a local and civilian view of the work being carried out. I hope this meeting will clear up any misunderstandings that may have arisen.' Major Buckland turned to Sergeant Major Fornasier, who was standing nearby. 'Thank you, Sergeant Major Fornasier.'

The Italians stood smartly to attention. Major Buckland and Sergeant Major Fornasier exchanged salutes and the British officer walked off the parade ground.

'Dismissed!'

The men instantly broke up into little groups.

'Well, he seems different,' said Buttapasta.

'And he speaks Italian,' chipped in Micheloni.

'Call that Italian!' said Aldo.

'He tried,' said Domenico, 'and that's all you can ask of any man.'

'What now?' asked Micheloni.

'Well I'm going to start laying some paths,' said Buttapasta. 'There are men sitting around with nothing to do and they all like the idea of paths between the huts, so I'm going to see if Wooden Leg will let us have some tools and help us get some cement from the blockyard. There's plenty of it.'

'Wooden Leg?' asked Domenico.

'One of the British sergeants,' answered Aldo, 'the one with the limp.'

'He lost his leg in France, but he's a good man . . . for a sergeant,' said Buttapasta. 'What about you Domenico?'

'I don't like this lying around. I've an urge to make something.'

'There speaks a true artist . . . driven by a desire to create,' said Buttapasta.

'What are you planning to make?' said Aldo. 'There's nothing here except mud and huts, but now we might have some cement.'

Domenico's face took on an almost dream-like appearance. 'Yes cement. Cement . . . and barbed wire. It's perfect.'

'Barbed wire!' Aldo was irritated by talk of creativity, unless it could be turned into money and he doubted that was what Domenico had in mind. 'We're surrounded by it, Domenico. I'm sure the new British major won't mind if you take some from the fence, as long as you explain it's because you're feeling creative.'

'I'll come with you to see Wooden Leg,' said Domenico to Buttapasta.

'What about you, Aldo?' said Micheloni.

'While we've not been working some of the men have been making things, taking ordinary items and turning them into something else. And if they have products to sell then they need buyers. All it takes is someone to put the two together.'

'And make a profit in the middle,' said Buttapasta.

'That's what life's about,' said Aldo.

'You've a lot to learn, Aldo,' said Buttapasta with a sigh.

6

The men went back to work. Wooden Leg helped them obtain the materials and tools they needed to lay concrete paths between the huts, so that particular cause for unrest was removed. However, there was a last incident of rebellion inspired by the weather, which had been particularly cold and wet for more than a week. That morning, the men in one hut simply refused to get out of bed. When the others went off to work they remained where they were, venturing out only to go to the latrine block or mess hall.

The British left them alone until that night, when soldiers burst into the hut in force and made the inhabitants stand outside while they conducted a 'search'. Of course, they didn't find anything, so the men were let back in. An hour later, the process was repeated. It went on throughout the night, with the Italians barely warm in their beds before having to stand outside again.

Like so much in Orkney, destiny was determined not by men but by weather. The following morning dawned clear and bright. The Italians got up, had breakfast and went to work like everyone else. Each side had made its point and the British made no more of the incident.

As the temperature rose so did the general mood and during the spring they transformed the camp by creating flower beds and vegetable plots. Huts competed with each other to have the best borders. The effect was stunning and the camp lost some of its desolate feel. Many of the flowers came from the grounds of nearby Graemeshall whose owner, Patrick Sutherland Graeme, also owned Lamb Holm. He had taken a keen interest in the Italians on his land and small groups had been escorted over several times to gather bulbs and flowers from his own garden. During their visits they had met his daughter Alison and occasionally, to their delight, his small grand-daughters Sheena and Elspeth when they were visiting Orkney.

Men took up hobbies and a variety of groups were formed. They built a stage at one end of the mess hall and most Sunday evenings there was a performance of music from the camp band, which grew in size and stature. A large Nissen hut had been erected within the camp for recreational use and the Italians constructed a billiard table and balls out of leftover concrete. They smoothed the surface of several blankets with razorblades then glued them to the top of the table, using tightly-rolled blankets for side cushions. The POWs also created a concrete bowling alley, whilst several different sporting activities became regular pastimes, as long as they could be carried out within the confines of the perimeter fence.

Every few weeks a selection of books, both English and Italian, arrived from the Red Cross, so an increasing number of men were able to read in their spare time. Some of them used it as a way of trying to improve their English, and Aldo became an avid reader of thrillers. Otherwise, men picked up the language from the construction workers, which left many with a bizarre mixture of slang and swear words, but no understanding of grammar. The POWs also started to receive parcels from their families in Italy. These provided a small source of items that were difficult to obtain from the camp shop and, more importantly, they always contained letters and photographs.

Throughout much of May and into June, Aldo entertained those around him at the end of each working day by bringing back as much gorse as he could carry. Sometimes he could hardly see where he was walking, and as he trudged through the camp gates amidst the other Italians, it looked as though a bush had magically become mobile and set off to explore the land. The guards knew what he was up to but decided to ignore it.

Between the huge pile of stacked wood and the coal bunker at the end of his hut, Aldo made himself a little shelter and he could be found there most fine evenings, happily pulling the petals off the bushes and putting them into a bucket. Along with Dino, who was working in the kitchen, and with some practical advice from Carlo, he had converted a tea urn into a still. At any one time, on the floor by the kitchen ranges, there were several tubs of fermenting liquid containing gorse petals, yeast from the bakery, some of the camp's valuable sugar ration, plus a few other items that Aldo refused to reveal.

Domenico sat with him one evening, reading a copy of *Il Corriere del Prigioniero*, one of two regular newspapers printed in London by the British government for the tens of thousands of Italians held in camps around the country. News of what was happening in Europe was readily available as the mess hall contained a radio they could listen to whenever free of work. The battle lines in Africa seemed to shift constantly backwards and forwards. During June the Germans had retaken the Libyan port of Tobruk, capturing thousands of Allied troops. It was the very place at which many of the Italians in Camp 60 had been taken prisoner the previous year.

In other ways the Italians on Lamb Holm were isolated.

Physical contact with outsiders was normally only with the guards or Balfour Beatty workers. No communication was allowed with their fellow Italians in the Burray camp and, apart from those fortunate to be given a rare trip to Graemeshall, there were few opportunities to meet Orkney people other than the locals working on the causeways. Aldo chattered away, apparently unconcerned that he was getting no response from Domenico.

'I hope you're going to try my gorse spirit when it's finished. According to one of the guards, this year has been particularly good for gorse on the island. However, Dino and I need to improve the output of our still. It's too slow. Maybe we should get a second one going. I'm already getting orders from other huts, including one that wants to buy the entire stock. I tell you, it's becoming quite a business.'

Domenico listened with half an ear. He thought Aldo was happy enough talking to himself.

'If you give it all to one hut there's a chance they will get too drunk and the British will probably only ignore your little venture as long as men aren't incapacitated because of it. Also, you'll annoy people in other huts who may not be keen to buy from you in the future. They might even start their own stills.'

The latter possibility, which Aldo had not considered, caused him a moment's concern and he paused in his petal picking.

'You're right. I'll only allow so much per hut and if I run out it will be the turn of the other huts the next time. I'll keep a list.'

Aldo kept lots of lists, the most important showing who owed him money or goods such as cigarettes, which he bartered for other saleable items.

Domenico stood up. 'Well, I'm off to see Shipwreck before he closes the shop. I'll see you later.'

'Domenico,' shouted Shipwreck, as Domenico walked into

the canteen. He was sitting at a table talking to a couple of men, which was virtually his sole occupation when he wasn't playing chess with Domenico. 'How about a game tonight? Perhaps I'll let you win.'

Domenico nodded to the other Italians. 'Yes, I'll give you a game.'

'What can I do for you today? I was just about to lock up.'

'Toothpaste please.'

Shipwreck's real name was Primiano Malvolti. He had been an outstanding sportsman before the war but arrived on Lamb Holm leaning on a heavy, knotty stick and had never been without it since. He refused to discuss the injury to his leg, but due to his disability he had been given the shop and canteen to run. Domenico almost felt guilty as Shipwreck struggled to his feet and walked behind the counter.

Shipwreck rarely left the camp and was such an easy figure to spot that he had become quite well known, and liked, by the guards. He had gained his nickname due to an incident with a 'peedie' boat that had sunk, leaving him to swim ashore holding a carton of cigarettes above his head all the way. The name had stuck.

'Here,' said Shipwreck handing over the tube of toothpaste.

Domenico put a one shilling token on the counter.

'I suppose you want the balance made up in paper so you can do your drawings?'

Domenico smiled. The little shop sold an assortment of toiletries, stationery and food, and even had a few musical instruments. The POWs could purchase items with their camp tokens, which they received once a week in the mess hall. Italians had gradually taken over an increasing number of skilled jobs from the construction workers and several were now driving the steam and diesel trains, or operating the diggers and dumper trucks.

The summer rolled by and the war in Europe continued without the men in Camp 60. German planes targeted the ships moored far to the west of Lamb Holm, and were not interested in camps on small islands. For the POWs, life centred on building the barriers, or 'causeways' as they were now officially called. They worked their eight-hour shifts, six days a week, making five-ton concrete blocks in the block-making yard, putting together wire bolster nets, filling them at the quarry, working on the railway lines or the workshops and unloading supplies from the never-ending stream of barges.

The blocks and bolsters were dropped constantly into the sea from the huge cableways; two across Kirk Sound, which included the greatest depths, and one each across Skerry, Weddel and Water Sound. The huge cableways that stretched between the islands were known as 'Blondins' after a famous nineteenth-century tightrope walker. Four of the five cableways had been transported all the way from Iraq, where they had been used to build a barrier across the River Tigris. The fifth had travelled less far, having been last used to construct the Dornie Bridge in Ross-Shire.

Despite the tens of thousands of tons of rock and concrete blocks dropped into the channels along the line of the cables, nothing was visible above the water. By the autumn, many people working on the project were beginning to lose heart so it was decided that, in two of the channels, everything would be dropped in one particular spot.

'I still think they're mad,' said Aldo, who had never forgiven the British for cutting holes in his uniform.

He was part of a gang working at the Lamb Holm end of causeway number one. Domenico, Buttapasta and Micheloni were standing nearby. They had just attached a skip to the steel wire that hung down from the 'bicycle', which ran along the top of the main cable. It stretched 2,400 feet between Lamb Holm and mainland Orkney. They had repeated this task so many times they no longer watched the skip's progress as it travelled across the water to tip its heavy load with a great splash into the sea. At the beginning they had been fascinated.

'I hear most of the local people think the British are insane and the channels will never be blocked,' added Aldo.

'They say the tide runs at more than ten knots in the channels and under the water's surface everything is simply being washed out to sea,' said Micheloni.

'We're wasting our time,' said Aldo.

'They're hopeful that dropping everything in one spot will show some results soon,' offered Buttapasta. 'Apparently the British divers who go down to check what is happening on the seabed say the blocks are rising steadily.'

'I don't believe them,' said Aldo. 'They've been saying that for months.'

They turned at the sound of shouting and could see several men running towards the shoreline.

'Come on. Let's find out what's happening,' said Buttapasta.

They jumped from the wagon and headed towards the gathering crowd, where men were pointing excitedly towards mainland Orkney. When Buttapasta and the others arrived, they realised people weren't pointing at the land opposite, but at a tiny piece of bolster sticking above the water. It had worked. The tide was well out and the few rocks from the quarry, held within their steel cage, would soon be covered again. But it had worked. Bolster upon bolster had been piled all the way up from the seabed. The men, Italians and civilians alike, started clapping and cheering. Balfour Beatty engineers shook hands enthusiastically with nearby Italians. They were not the enemy but fellow workers who had helped achieve what many said was impossible.

'What's wrong with Aldo?' asked Buttapasta of Domenico.

The two were as pleased as anyone that the heavy work they were involved in was not simply a huge waste of effort. Domenico looked over at Aldo, who had moved away from the crowd and was checking the small notebook he always carried in his jacket pocket. Domenico chuckled.

'Our young friend has taken several bets on when the first bolster would appear above the water's surface and I think this is rather earlier than he hoped,' he said.

'He'll probably argue the point that it's only visible at low tide.'

'No doubt! Come on. Let's try and cheer him up.'

'Why do I find so much of my time is taken up looking after Aldo,' asked Buttapasta, as he walked after Domenico.

Few of the Italians had any idea of the enormous amount of research that had been carried out prior to any actual work starting on the causeways. This had included meticulous experiments by scientists at Manchester University with scaled down models of the islands and tiny blocks of concrete, to calculate the most effective size and weight of blocks and the pattern in which they should be laid. With the construction of the causeways expected to cost more than two million pounds, there was a huge sigh of relief in many official quarters at the success that morning. The bolsters were once more dropped along the entire length of the cable.

Men found it difficult to decide whether the experience of their first few months on the island had helped to prepare them for the forthcoming bad weather or made them more wary of it. Either way, the days grew colder and daylight shorter. The routine of the camp gave the men some structure to their lives, if not actually purpose. In the long dark evenings men stayed close to the stoves in their huts or gathered in the recreation hall, where there were now three concrete billiard tables complete with concrete balls.

The number of interest groups had mushroomed. A writing circle had been formed and the number of men who carved and etched grew constantly. Domenico and Dino started giving sketching lessons and often had a small group around their table after supper. Most huts had at least one musician and men sang and listened to music around stoves, while outside the wind tried to rip buildings from the steel wires that held them down.

There were even two theatre groups, split between those from northern and southern Italy. Art did not transcend all boundaries when it came to theatre, with the result that the two groups were highly competitive. Those from the north preferred works such as Venetian marionette productions, while the southerners stuck to playwrights from their part of the country, who they knew and understood.

The hobbies were an attempt to overcome the boredom and frustration of their lives and the numerous activities masked the despair that hung around huts like damp on a winter's night. But no matter how many games or musicals they threw themselves into, and despite pages of sketches and drawers full of carvings, that constant damp seeped into their bones and festered.

7

'Christmas will be hard,' said Carlo.

He was washing some spare clothing at one of the large stone sinks in the wash block. Dino was at the next sink, scrubbing equally furiously at a pair of trousers with a bar of hard green soap and a brush.

'It's always the worst time to be away from family and home,' answered Dino. 'You can see the men feel isolated.'

'These unnaturally short days would drive anyone to despair,' said Carlo.

'I think Doctor Rocco will be busy,' said Dino.

'There's bugger all he can do. A priest would do more good though.'

'Will you go to the mess hall later?' asked Dino.

Many Italians gathered in the mess hall on a Sunday morning to pray and read from the bible. It was the best they could do without a priest or a church, the lack of which affected them as severely as the weather. Carlo stopped what he was doing to look at his cousin. He smiled fondly. Since arriving at the camp, the two had always gone to the mess hall on a Sunday to pray. It had become a part of the weekly routine. But Dino asked anyway.

'Of course,' said Carlo. 'What else does a man do on a Sunday but clean his clothes and his soul.'

There was a flurry of parcel deliveries during the two weeks before Christmas and men shared out presents and treats with others in their hut who had not received anything. Christmas fell on a Friday that year and on the Thursday the camp had a visit by Patrick Sutherland Graeme. Accompanying him was the Catholic priest from Kirkwall, as Major Buckland had arranged for him to travel over and take a service in the mess hall that evening before supper. Permission had been given for the supper to be later than normal and for the men to remain in the mess hall for longer than usual afterwards. The cooks had juggled rations during the week to make the meal more substantial, while the men made a special effort to look smart.

Domenico had created a nativity scene, the figures and stable carved with great skill over many evenings before lights out, using scraps of wood. Before anyone arrived in the mess hall, he set it up at the front of the stage. It caught everyone's eye as they entered, helping to set the atmosphere for the evening.

The previous month Aldo and Dino had enlisted the help of half a dozen men in order to run the still continuously, which was now used to produce a spirit based on potato peelings. After supper that evening, as the small liberty boat was returning the priest and Patrick Sutherland Graeme to mainland Orkney, the group had gone around and left six bottles of pale amber liquid on the table in each hut. 'Lights out' was slightly later than normal but still before midnight. However, each hut had acquired a small stock of candles so the men gathered around their stoves, and in a semi-dark haze of cigarette smoke they wished each other 'Merry Christmas' with a brew that burned

47

throats and made eyes water. Not every tear could be blamed on the spirit.

Emotions were running high throughout the camp and only days after the men went back to work, a small riot erupted in hut three when the northerners' teasing of the two from Calabria became too much for the long-suffering men. They exploded, and had floored three of their tormentors before guards came rushing in, whistles blowing and rifle butts at the ready. Doctor Rocco had some mending to do and all those involved were given time in the punishment block, although the two men were moved to another hut upon their release.

It was a Tuesday in April 1943. Domenico crouched, hidden amongst the wood pile at the end of his hut, holding the end of a long piece of string. The idea for the prank had come to him several weeks earlier when he had spotted that the same gull often sat on the roof of the next Nissen hut while the afternoon roll call was being carried out. Since then he had been training the bird to take small crusts of bread off a line of string lying on the ground.

Today, there were several pieces of bread, each fixed carefully at about one foot intervals. On this occasion, the string went into and out of the back of a wire cage, around a stake driven into the earth then out of sight by the corner of a hut, where Carlo sat, peering anxiously. Aldo and Dino were both keeping a watch for sergeants of either army, as they didn't want to get caught halfway through their scheme.

Timing was vital. They had arrived back at the camp only a short while earlier and everything had to be completed before roll call, which was less than an hour away. Domenico was in an uncomfortable position and started to get cramp in one leg. He held the string that would collapse the cage around the gull once it entered — assuming it did — and, being so near, he didn't want to move too much in case it saw him. The men waited, checking their watches regularly, having agreed that if they reached a certain point without the gull taking the bait, they would abandon the idea until the next opportunity.

Domenico was about to call a halt when the gull dropped from the sky and ate the first piece of bread. Carlo pulled gently at his end and the morsels of food moved slowly along the ground towards the cage. The bird was used to this and hopped along, grabbing the second piece. Carlo continued. By the time the gull had eaten the third crust the fourth one had been dragged inside the cage. Carlo stopped. The bird looked but remained still. The cage was something new. Domenico's leg was throbbing. Under his breath, Carlo was cursing the bird for its cautiousness.

Suddenly, it hopped into the cage, stooped to get the bread and Domenico yanked away the two sticks. The gull appeared quite undisturbed and continued to eat the other crumbs that had been left at the rear of the trap. Carlo whistled, which brought Aldo and Dino running, while Domenico retrieved his tools from beside the woodpile.

Carlo had designed the cage so it could be unclipped in sections and undid a small flap at the top, which enabled Dino to put in his hand and grab the gull's head firmly from behind. The rest of the cage was dismantled in a moment and three of them held the now alarmed bird. Domenico didn't take long to fulfil his part and when he had finished they released their prey, whose angry screeches could be heard by the entire camp as it flew over the perimeter wire.

'I hope we haven't gone through all of this for nothing,' said Aldo.

'Yes,' admitted Domenico with a sigh. 'It would be a shame.'

They heard the trumpet and, after putting everything quickly into the hole they had created within the log pile, they threw some wood on top and ran to join the lines of POWs on the parade ground. Domenico didn't know if the bird would return that day, nor if it would ever come back after its indignant treatment. By the time the British officer had counted two thirds of the men, he was resigned to there being no further excitement. Then he saw it. The gull had landed on a different roof but was quite visible to the lines of men. It didn't take long for it to be spotted and within moments a murmur went up and down the rows.

'Stop that noise,' bawled the officer. 'Stop it!'

But the murmur was rapidly turning into a loud babble as men pointed and called out to each other. The officer turned around, searching for the cause of the disruption. The noise scared the gull, which took off and flew above their heads, one wing green and the other red. Domenico had painted them so that the wings and the body made three equal stripes of green, white and red . . . just like the Italian flag.

'It's an Italian aeroplane,' shouted a man then everyone was calling out. 'Italian aeroplane. Italian aeroplane.'

'Stop that racket! Get back in your lines!'

The officer was becoming increasingly agitated. A few guards told the men to be quiet but most were watching the bird with as much fascination as the Italians. It circled graciously and, as the officer called out 'Shoot that bloody bird,' the gull sent down a white deposit that landed on the front of his uniform, before it flew over the nearest hut and out of sight. A roar of delight rang throughout the parade ground.

As Domenico lay on the thin mattress in the detention block the next evening, he kept going over the events in his mind. In the bunk below, Aldo had been unusually philosophical about the situation and hadn't complained once about their punishment of two days of bread and water. Dino and Carlo were in the next room. The four had immediately stepped forward when the officer, livid with rage, had demanded that the culprits own up. They had been marched away and rather roughly strip-searched before being bundled off to the little concrete block.

Their short punishment was a small price to pay. Men's spirits had been lightened. It was something they would have talked about in their huts the previous night, even when the lights had gone out, and they would continue to talk about it for weeks.

8

Giuseppe Palumbi had not heard from home for many months, but stood in the queue of men lined up outside the mess hall entrance to receive mail, as he did every time there was a delivery. The arrival of mail from Italy was generally delayed and often out of sequence, depending upon the irregularities of war and weather. Handing out post was an agonisingly slow process, yet the routine never varied and, since the mail was chosen randomly, they had to remain until the sack was empty before they knew if there was anything for them. It exacerbated their feelings of frustration. That morning the process was held up briefly when a guard came over and spoke to the sergeant, who suddenly called out.

'Giuseppe Palumbi. Giuseppe Palumbi.'

'Here,' shouted Giuseppe, waving his arm in the air.

'Go with this guard.'

Giuseppe looked on in confusion but the soldier had noted his position near the back of the crowd and was already walking towards him.

'You're to come with me,' said the guard.

'Why?' asked Giuseppe, who had never before been given such an order.

'I don't know, do I,' said the soldier. 'How should I know why I'm doing something? But you've to come with me. Major Booth said so.'

Giuseppe followed the soldier, who led the way to one of the huts at the far side of the compound. Inside, Major Booth and the camp doctor stood around a bed on which an Italian lay, curled up on his side.

'Ah, you're Giuseppe Palumbi?' asked Major Booth. 'I gather you speak good English.'

'Yes, sir.'

'Excellent. You're to accompany Private Kemp, and this poor fellow here, to the Balfour Hospital. We can't spare the camp interpreter and this man speaks no English at all.'

Giuseppe looked at Doctor Rocco for further guidance. The doctor held a surgery for an hour twice a week after afternoon roll call. He had been allocated the end of one of the huts to use as a small infirmary, but was provided with little in the way of medical supplies and had virtually no equipment. Unless a POW was feverish or had been injured he was expected to carry out his work and the normal treatment for most ailments was 'aspirina'. The doctor spoke to Giuseppe in English so that the man on the bed wouldn't understand.

'I think he's got a stomach ulcer, but there's nothing I can do here. You'll have to translate for him at the hospital and then explain to him what the doctor says. He'll almost certainly have to stay there.'

'You can remain at the hospital while you're needed then return to the camp with the guard,' added Major Booth.

A short while later Giuseppe and Private Kemp helped the

man into the back of an army truck, which took them to the Lamb Holm pier where they boarded a small liberty boat that had come over from the mainland. An army ambulance was waiting for them on the other side. *Sometimes army efficiency works well,* thought Giuseppe. He didn't know the sick man but spoke to him softly throughout the journey, with what he hoped were reassuring comments. The only information he got out of him was that his name was Lorenzo.

The hospital reception was bustling. However, there was a spare wheelchair just inside the entrance and so they lowered Lorenzo in it, while Private Kemp went over to the desk. Giuseppe stood awkwardly, acutely aware of the stares from other waiting people, or those passing by. He felt ashamed of the red target discs on his uniform although he sensed that the interest was more of curiosity than animosity. Ill soldiers were normally taken to the military hospital ship, the *Dinard,* which was moored permanently in Scapa Flow, or to the recently built military hospital. However, the latter had, as yet, no X-ray facilities, and so occasionally a sick soldier arrived at the civilian Balfour Hospital in Kirkwall. Italian POWs were even more of a rare sight.

Giuseppe concentrated on a patch of floor just beyond his feet. When he had first arrived at Camp 60 he thought it might be wise to keep his knowledge of English to himself, and not to stand out from the crowd in any way. But it had been impossible to remain quiet during those first few weeks when misunderstandings between the guards and the POWs had led to increasing frustration and anger on both sides. He had defused many potentially dangerous situations and his ability to speak English had become quickly known throughout the camp. It was a double-edged sword.

Giuseppe was aware that someone was standing in front of

him and was speaking. He looked up. It was a nurse. She looked about sixteen and was extremely pretty.

'Can you follow me, please?' she said flashing a smile that made him momentarily forget about the target discs, the stares of the others, and the fact he was a POW far away from home.

Giuseppe pushed the wheelchair after the nurse who led them down a corridor and into an examination room. They got Lorenzo on to the bed only moments before the door opened. Giuseppe took in several things at once. The man in the white coat was big, in his fifties, and he walked towards the bed with a terrible limp.

'Hello, I'm Doctor McClure,' he said jovially to the Italian on the bed. Lorenzo remained silent and looked up with an expression of pain, bewilderment and fear.

'Sir, I am here to speak for the patient because he does not speak English,' said Giuseppe.

'No English eh?' said the doctor, sitting on the bed, gently laying a muscular hand on the man's chest. It was a tender gesture, almost strange from such a large man, but it was meant to reassure and Giuseppe took a liking to him. 'Well then, can you please ask the patient what his symptoms are?'

They spent the next ten minutes together. The little nurse writing down relevant details as Giuseppe translated back and forth between the doctor and Lorenzo.

'Right then,' said Doctor McClure eventually. 'Please explain that we're going to take some blood and then send him for an X-ray. Then I suggest you go to the waiting room. Into the corridor, turn left and it's the fourth door along. Someone will come to collect you when you're needed again.'

Giuseppe left the three of them in the room and started to walk along the corridor. It was an odd feeling. He hadn't seen Private Kemp since leaving the reception area and he felt a mixture of elation and loneliness: concern that someone might think he had escaped; excitement at a moment that was almost freedom. Most of the people walking past seemed too preoccupied with their own tasks or problems and although a few glanced at him no one said anything. He was relieved to find the waiting room empty.

Giuseppe was flicking through a copy of *Woman's Own* when the door opened and a large vase of flowers walked in. At least, that was all he could see of the person carrying them until the vase was laid on the table in front of him, then he found himself staring at what was perhaps not a beautiful face, in the wartime, pin-up definition of one, but a handsome face, strong and honest. One you could easily trust. One you could so easily love.

'Oh! Hello. I didn't know there was anyone in here.'

She smiled at him and Giuseppe felt something so utterly alien upon his own face that it took him a few moments to realise he had returned her smile. The strangeness of it, and the effect it had on him, took him completely by surprise.

'Hello. I'm Giuseppe,' he said, rising from the chair.

'I've never met anyone called Giuseppe before.'

'You have now.'

'I'm not supposed to speak to you. You're the enemy.'

Before Giuseppe could register the enormity of the words, she continued.

'Of course, there are some rules I don't pay any attention to. I'm Fiona.'

'I've never met a Fiona before. Your flowers are beautiful, just like you.'

Fiona laughed. It was instant, infectious. Giuseppe felt giddy. He could not remember when he had last spoken to a woman and she radiated such joy and health Giuseppe thought she must be one of the greatest tonics possible for the patients. He found her long auburn hair fascinating. He was close enough to smell the cleanness of her.

'Are all Italians like you?'

'No, I've heard some are quite forward.'

'Your English is good.'

'When I was nine, my father went to America to try to earn more money. He sent for me when I was seventeen and we lived in Philadelphia where I learnt to speak English and . . . *ferro battuto* . . . how to make wrought iron. But I only stayed there four years. I longed to go home.'

Giuseppe realised he was almost rambling in his attempt to keep the woman in front of him, revealing things about himself he had never hinted at in eighteen months at the camp. His mind raced to maintain the conversation.

'But you must tell me something about yourself, or I will know nothing except your name and your face.'

'Well, let me see . . . I live on a farm with my parents and younger sister. I've got two older brothers, both in the air force. We hear from them often enough to know they are safe. And when I'm not helping out on the farm I work in the hospital reception.'

'I didn't see you.'

'I saw you, with your friend in the wheelchair. You were trying so hard to be inconspicuous . . . not to be seen,' she added when Giuseppe looked as if he had trouble understanding the word.

'I've only come to translate because he doesn't speak English.'

'Do you think he will stay in hospital?'

'For a while I believe.'

'That means you'll have to come back.'

She was quick. Giuseppe hadn't considered he would have to make more trips to the hospital, but it made sense that Lorenzo couldn't be left for days on end without anyone to translate for him or explain what was happening.

'Yes, I suppose I might. Then perhaps . . .'

The door burst open and Private Kemp, looking flushed, took two large steps into the room before stopping at the sight before him.

'So this is where you've been hiding,' he said, a mixture of anger, accusation and relief in his voice.

Giuseppe felt like pointing out that it was actually the private who had disappeared, while he had been doing what he had been told. He guessed the soldier had gone off for a cup of tea and a smoke, probably chatting up any young nurses he could corner at the same time.

'The doctor told me to wait here.'

'Right, well, wait here then,' said the soldier, sitting near the door as if to bar his escape.

'I'll bring you a coffee,' said Fiona, ignoring their unwanted visitor.

'There's no need for that,' said Private Kemp. 'I'm sure you've better things to do than making coffee for the enemy.'

Fiona left without a word and Giuseppe sat down, his previous elation swept aside by seething anger.

However, about five minutes later Fiona returned, stepped over Kemp's outstretched legs before he could speak and held out a mug of steaming coffee to Giuseppe. He stretched out his hand to take it and in doing so his fingers rested on hers. Neither of them moved. Kemp couldn't see the touch, the look, the moment of intimacy.

'You'll burn your hand,' she whispered eventually.

'I don't care.'

She moved the mug around so he could take the handle, but for a few moments longer she let two fingers remain wrapped within his.

'Thank you,' said Giuseppe. Private Kemp thought the

comment was for the coffee, but Giuseppe and Fiona knew it was not.

She turned, took a few steps to the door and stopped, refusing to step over the soldier's legs a second time. Private Kemp looked up at her only briefly before quickly moving his legs out of the way, mumbling an apology.

The memory of Fiona filled Giuseppe's mind for the rest of the day, but when he woke the next morning he wasn't totally convinced he hadn't imagined her until he was ordered, after roll call, to return to the hospital. The guard was one of the older men. Giuseppe thought they might vary on every visit so that different men got a trip off the island, which was a greatly sought after prize. This time they walked to the pier and caught the first boat returning to the mainland, before thumbing a lift on an army lorry.

The guard chatted to anyone who would listen, but ignored Giuseppe, which suited him. He was totally preoccupied with plans on how to spend time alone with Fiona. She came out from behind the desk as soon as they approached and Giuseppe's face exploded into a smile that froze when Fiona totally ignored him, instead taking the guard's arm as if he was her favourite brother.

'How was your journey? You must be exhausted. I bet you could do with a good cup of tea. I've even brought you some home-made scones. They're waiting for you with today's newspaper in one of the quiet rooms so you can put your feet up for a while.'

She said this almost without pause for breath, giving the guard no opportunity to speak. As she talked, she led him away from Giuseppe, who stood watching the scene, his expression changing into one of astonishment.

'I can't leave the prisoner, miss,' said the guard at last, looking over his shoulder. 'I'll have to stay with him throughout.'

'Oh no, that's quite unacceptable. You're in a hospital now and so hospital rules apply.'

'But . . .'

'No buts. Patient confidentiality comes first. Anyway, the other young guard didn't stay with him.'

At that moment the young nurse appeared who Giuseppe had seen the previous day and took the guard's other arm. Giuseppe knew then that no matter what tactical manoeuvres or fighting experience the man might have, he was no match for these two women.

'Doctor's orders,' said Fiona, when the guard looked like he might make once last stand. She had let go of his arm and was actually waving at him as the nurse led him down the corridor, like a small boy whom someone had taken by the hand. Fiona turned, walked briskly back to Giuseppe, roughly grabbed his arm and frog-marched him in the other direction.

'And you're only here to do some translating so don't think you're going to get up to any of your funny foreign business.'

Giuseppe played the part of defeated prisoner, even hanging his head as he was taken away, muttering that he was 'very sorry.' This time they entered a different door, and he found himself in a small empty kitchen.

'You were marvellous,' said Giuseppe with admiration. 'I can't believe you just did that. Did you really make home-made scones?'

'Well, my mother made them and they were getting a bit stale, but it was worth it to get him out of the way. Ailsa and I have been working out a plan of action since first thing this morning.'

She looked at him and found she wanted his approval.

'We don't have long. Doctor McClure will be doing his ward

round in less than an hour. You need to be by your friend's bed before then and I can't expect the other girls on reception to cover for too long.'

'The doctor seems a good man.'

'He is. He lost a leg in the first war but you wouldn't think he was injured at all from the amount of energy he puts into this place. Here, I'll make us some coffee. This is the nurses' kitchen. No one will bother us while we're here. I've brought some scones from home . . . some that I made.'

Fiona took two scones out of a tin and put them on a plate, which she pushed towards him. She blushed, realising she was walking a path that was completely alien to her and potentially scandalous. She put the kettle on to boil and retrieved two mugs, washing one again to give her hands something to do. It suddenly seemed unbelievable to her that she had actually made scones the previous evening, or that she had spent a large part of the morning planning how to distract the guard. Ailsa thought it all a great game, but she was young and Fiona was a woman of twenty. And it was not Ailsa who was trying to spend time alone with an Italian prisoner of war. It was not her reputation at stake.

What was she thinking of? He was the enemy and a man she had met for only a few minutes the previous day. Giuseppe was as much a stranger as he could possibly be. And yet that was not quite true. There was something about him, in the way his fingers had wrapped around hers, as though he wanted to protect her.

'The kettle's boiling,' said Giuseppe, sensing the sudden turmoil within Fiona. 'You were deep in thought.'

'Yes.'

'Ailsa . . . she's the young nurse?' asked Giuseppe, moving the conversation along.

'Yes. We're conspirators together in lots of things,' said Fiona, pouring water into two mugs.

'I don't think many people would win an argument against the two of you.' He hesitated. 'Thank you. Thank you for wanting to see me again.'

They fell silent again. This time it was Giuseppe who wondered if he had been too forward and overstepped a boundary by saying the wrong thing.

Fiona studied him over the rim of her mug. Giuseppe was a neat man. Everything about him was tidy, including his carefully trimmed moustache and dark, wavy hair. He wasn't big, but years of working at the forge had given him muscle and strength that were not apparent when he wore his uniform.

He smiled, revealing neat even white teeth. She found herself automatically smiling back.

'What's it like, in the camp?'

'The camp is not so bad, but the work is hard and the weather is . . .'

'Unpredictable?' she offered.

'Challenging. But the summer has been good. Almost like Italy. Have you ever been?'

She shook her head and Giuseppe found his eyes being drawn to her hair. He had never seen a colour like it.

'Tell me about your farm.'

'It's more of a big smallholding.' She laughed at his confused expression. 'A very small farm. We have a few cattle and grow some crops. It's all we can manage, but we do other work because it doesn't earn enough to support us. Do you know about farms?'

'No. I know about forging iron.'

'Well, you would be very handy. There are plenty of barn

doors falling off their hinges and things that need repairing. Perhaps I should ring the commander at the camp and ask him to send you over.'

For a fleeting moment Giuseppe thought she meant it and even when they both smiled at the suggestion, he felt certain she was not entirely joking.

'We're too busy building barriers, to stop the Germans from entering Scapa Flow, like they did before. I heard they sank a ship. Do you know what happened?'

A flicker of fear crossed her face and the smile in her eyes was gone in an instant.

'I'm sorry,' said Giuseppe. 'I shouldn't have asked.'

She didn't answer straight away and when she did her voice wavered.

'No. It's not your fault. I haven't spoken to anyone about it, that's all.'

'Then don't now, if it causes you distress.'

Fiona's whole body seemed to sag with the weight of some past event and she looked down at the floor for several moments in silence. When she raised her head Giuseppe was shocked at the transformation. He found it hard to believe that a memory could alter someone so drastically. All the joy and sparkle had suddenly been taken away.

'It happened three years ago last October. I'd been working at the hospital for only a few months when the phone rang at home in the middle of the night. The girl at the other end was frantic. Something had happened and I had to get there as quickly as possible.

'When I arrived, men sat or lay everywhere. In the reception, down the corridors, in the waiting room. More were coming in every few minutes. I could see they were sailors so I knew a ship had been damaged. Some were suffering from hypothermia and shock, while others had swallowed oil or been injured during their escape.

'We had practised for an emergency that resulted in high numbers of people arriving at the hospital, but it was apparent immediately that we weren't going to be able to cope. For nearly an hour I rang every doctor and nurse in Orkney, including those who were retired but still active enough to help. Some turned up wearing coats on top of their pyjamas.

'By that time they had started to bring in the burnt men. They were screaming and screaming and we didn't have enough medical staff to treat them. We didn't have enough of anything. I didn't know what to do. I wandered into the ward and when I saw a figure all alone on a bed I went over. He was just a boy. His face was untouched but his arms and chest were . . . and the smell . . . I still wake up at night and have that smell in my nostrils . . . oil and seawater and burnt flesh.'

Fiona's voice was becoming more strained, her breathing rapid.

'Fiona. Don't,' said Giuseppe aghast at what he had started by his innocent question. But he had unlocked a door that had hidden a secret for over three years. Fiona was beyond stopping now.

'I had no medical training so I sat by the bed and talked to him. He didn't seem to be in pain. He told me something of what had happened, how some men had been incinerated in their bunks by flash fires. How men had cried out as they slid down the side of the hull because the barnacles ripped their flesh. How men had gone down deeper into the ship because they thought they were being attacked from the air. They couldn't believe it was from a submarine. Not inside Scapa Flow.

'He raised his arm and laid his clawed fingers on top of mine and I wanted to cry out with the horror of it . . . but I couldn't move. I just kept talking and talking, even though in the end I was saying nonsense just to make a noise. Then a man appeared by the bed and pulled a sheet over the body. He'd died and I hadn't realised.'

Giuseppe put down his mug and took a step nearer. Tears were falling freely off her chin. She dropped her mug, the remains of the coffee going over her shoes, but she carried on without noticing.

'When I pulled my hand away, bits of his burnt flesh stuck to my skin and I screamed. I ran to wash it off, but I couldn't find anywhere because there were men in the kitchens and men in the bathrooms and I couldn't get it off. I just couldn't get it off.'

She buried her head in her hands and Giuseppe took her in his arms. He had never heard anyone sob with such anguish.

He didn't say anything but held her tightly for a long while, until eventually she started to go limp in his arms.

'I'm sorry. I'm sorry,' she said.

'You needn't apologise to me or anyone else. You did what you could and I know the boy would have been grateful he didn't die alone.'

She pulled away from him slowly. His face was a blur through her tears.

'You have kept this deep inside you for too long. Perhaps . . . perhaps now the nightmares will stop.'

9

As she lay in bed that night, Fiona asked herself why she had waited all this time to unburden such a terrible secret to someone she hardly knew. Maybe it was because he had asked her a direct question about what happened that night, when no one else ever had. In her mind she went over the other part of the story; the part she hadn't told him.

The day the *Royal Oak* had been torpedoed, Fiona had remained at the hospital, talking to the men, helping them wash oil from their shivering, filthy bodies, hugging more than one young man who was shaking and crying. She couldn't remember how she got home that evening, but she assumed she must have cycled. Her sister Rebecca had screamed when she staggered into the kitchen, while her parents had jumped up from their chairs at the sight before them.

Fiona's ashen face was streaked with dirt, her dress covered in oil, blood and other stains. There was a smell they couldn't identify but which made their stomachs turn. However, the look of shock on her face had frightened them the most.

'Dear God above girl, what happened?' asked her father,

walking over to take hold of both of her arms as he thought she was about to collapse.

Fiona stared ahead in silence. Her mother, a practical no-nonsense Orkney woman, was the first to regain her wits and issued a stream of orders to both her husband and younger daughter, which set them scurrying to throw more wood on the fire, boil water and fill the tin bath. She led Fiona over to sit by the fire, poured a generous measure of brandy into a glass and gave it to her.

When the bath was full, Fiona's mother undressed her as if she was a small child and with the help of Rebecca eased her gently into the hot water. Fiona meekly did what she was told without comment or acknowledgement of their presence. Rebecca knelt on the floor and washed Fiona's hair while her mother tenderly sponged her body. It was only when Fiona was sitting in her dressing gown, Rebecca standing behind the chair drying her hair with a towel, that she spoke and then it was only to mutter two words. Her father was picking up the clothes still lying on the floor.

'Burn them,' she had whispered.

She said it with such an expression of despair her father thought his heart would break. He carried the clothes out into the yard and threw them on to a pile of rubbish. There was nothing left of them by the time Fiona woke late the next day. Her parents had decided they wouldn't ask questions, a point that had to be instilled severely into fourteen-year-old Rebecca. The sinking of the *Royal Oak* was in that day's newspapers so it was easy to piece together at least some of the events.

Fiona returned to the hospital the following day to find most of the sailors had been taken away, the injured to the *Dinard*. The uninjured had been transferred to other ships moored within the harbour. Doctor McClure looked as if he had hardly slept. A few sailors had been left in the wards because it was considered better not to move them.

Fiona had never talked about that day but the nightmares had never gone away. She hoped that telling the kind Italian might help.

Giuseppe lay in his bunk in Camp 60. He had been greatly affected by Fiona's distress but also by the fact she had chosen to unburden herself to him. Why? What was he to her?

By the time they had left the nurses' kitchen, Fiona had composed herself sufficiently and Giuseppe arrived at Lorenzo's bed just before Doctor McClure entered the ward. The doctor, who was also the hospital surgeon, was going to operate on Lorenzo's stomach ulcer the next morning. Giuseppe was told he should return the day after.

He spent the following day working in the quarry, locked within his own world; taking apart and analysing each moment spent in the kitchen with the striking island woman, and wishing away the time so he could return to the hospital. However, the next morning, as he clung to the side of the liberty boat that was making a nauseating journey between Lamb Holm and mainland Orkney, it was not Fiona who filled Giuseppe's thoughts. It was Mussolini.

A rumour that Italy's Prime Minister had been dismissed from office had spread rapidly throughout the camp earlier that morning, sparking violent arguments as tempers flared between those who believed the news and those who were adamant it was untrue. Guards had rushed in more than once to separate fighting men. There were plenty who didn't know what to think. Certainly, no one knew what it meant for Italy, or for them, if it was true.

When they arrived at the hospital it was obvious the guard had heard about the tea and scones because he went off with

Ailsa without a comment. Giuseppe walked silently with Fiona down the corridor. He thought she looked tired. As soon as the kitchen door was closed she turned to face him.

'Have you heard the news about Mussolini?' she asked.

'Yes, but many men think it's just British propaganda and isn't true.'

'It is,' said Fiona, taking a copy of that day's *Daily Mirror* out of a drawer. She had hidden it for Giuseppe to see.

The front page headline announced 'MUSSOLINI IS SACKED'. Italy's king had taken over the Italian forces and Marshal Pietro Badoglio had replaced Mussolini.

'What does it mean?' she asked when he had finished.

'I don't know. I don't think anyone knows. Mussolini took Italy into the war and if he's gone . . .' Giuseppe shrugged his shoulders. 'He had many supporters . . . perhaps civil war? It's a terrible thought. I'm not sure how it will affect us on Orkney. We're still prisoners of war, whatever happens.'

They were silent for a while. Fiona walked over to the sink.

'The other day...' she began, facing away from him.

'I'm glad you told me.'

She turned. There was a flicker of a smile on her face, the first since they had last met.

'So am I. I hadn't realised there was so much pain and hurt, waiting to surface, but I'm grateful you were here.'

This time her smile reached her eyes and he smiled back.

'I'll make us some coffee,' she said, putting on the kettle. 'We haven't much time. One of the girls on reception is off sick and I can't expect the other one to cover alone.' She saw the look of disappointment on Giuseppe's face. 'Your friend's doing well. Doctor McClure is very pleased.' She opened a tin. 'Here, two scones for your coffee.'

* * *

Three days later, Giuseppe was sitting in the camp canteen drinking coffee with Shipwreck and putting the finishing touches to a cigarette lighter he had been making. They were a valuable commodity in the camp and his skills with metal made them relatively easy to make. He traded them with other POWs for tokens and with the guards for items such as cigarettes, which he could then swap for more tokens.

The POWs were not allowed real money and had nowhere to spend it anyway, so it was accepted practice that the guards could 'purchase' trinkets as long as they didn't pay cash. Giuseppe was not trying to become rich, but on a wall in the camp shop was a banjo he had been saving towards for months. It was only a small four-string instrument. However, Giuseppe had been quite an accomplished player years earlier and he wanted this one badly.

Shipwreck had been giving his views on the situation in Italy. Over the previous few days, the events had become clearer and even the hardened fascists in the camp could no longer argue that Mussolini's dismissal was untrue. While some of the men were dismayed by the news and others secretly pleased, they were all bewildered. No one had any idea what it actually meant for Italy, their families back home or for them as POWs. That did not stop people from giving their own analysis of the situation, something which Shipwreck had been doing across the table for the last ten minutes.

Giuseppe listened with less than half an ear. His mind was full of what he was going to say and ask of Fiona. The day after the news had broken about Mussolini, Fiona had been too busy on the reception to do much more than show him to the ward and there had been no spare guard the day after that, so Giuseppe hadn't gone to the hospital at all.

For the last three days, Giuseppe had spent virtually every

waking moment working out exactly what to say. He wanted to tell her about his feelings and he needed to hear from her own lips what her feelings were towards him. He was going through the 'speech' in his head when Shipwreck leant across the table and poked his arm.

'I said, as if you were interested, your guard is late this morning.'

'Yes, he is.'

'More coffee?'

Giuseppe shook his head. Shipwreck got up and, leaning heavily on his stick, limped behind the counter. As he did so, the door opened. Giuseppe looked in disbelief at the figure walking slowly towards him. As the man drew near he smiled.

'I thought you might be here,' he said.

Giuseppe stared as if he was seeing a demon from the underworld. Lorenzo.

'Why are you here?'

Lorenzo's smile faltered at the tone in Giuseppe's voice.

'The doctor saw me yesterday. It took a lot of sign language but I understood he was pleased with my recovery and there was little more he could do so I could return to camp. As long as I don't work for a while, I should make a good recovery,' said Lorenzo, his smile beaming again but once more fading at the expression on Giuseppe's face.

Shipwreck had returned with two coffees and put one on the table near to Lorenzo.

'Here, this will soon make you better. You can sit and talk to me. Giuseppe's been no company at all.'

The door opened again and a guard strode into the canteen. He stood, hands on hips.

'There you are, Palumbi. Get your Italian backside to the quarry and be quick about it. You've had enough bloody skiving this last week to last a man a lifetime.'

Giuseppe hesitated then rose to his feet with the air of a man condemned.

'Get a bloody move on,' shouted the guard. However, he took a step back when Giuseppe drew near, his hand instinctively resting on the rifle slung over his shoulder, for the anger on the Italian's face made him look like a man who would strike out, who would do almost anything at that moment, regardless of the consequences.

Giuseppe worked in the quarry for the rest of the shift like a man possessed, breaking and heaving stones until his muscles begged for rest and his hands were bleeding. He had never known such weariness when he collapsed on his bed that afternoon, too tired to wash, too disheartened even to line up at the mess hall when he heard there was an unexpected mail delivery. He was lying there with an arm thrown across his eyes, when he felt something light fall on to his chest and heard the voice of another man in his hut.

'Giuseppe. You missed the mail and you've got three letters. You're a lucky man. I got nothing.'

The man walked over to his own bed as Giuseppe sat up slowly, placing a hand on the envelopes to stop them falling on to the floor. He knew the writing immediately. They were all from his wife Pierina. One had been posted more than five months earlier. He opened the most recent one and as he unfolded the letter a photograph fell out on to the bed and the image of a boy looked up at him.

Giuseppe gasped and lifted the picture to study it more closely. He might not have recognised his son. It had been well over two years since he had left home and Renato had not been much more than a baby. Now he was a proper little boy, smiling proudly into the camera. Giuseppe was consumed by conflicting emotions. Despair and guilt, love and desire

72

battled within him throughout the rest of the glorious summer of 1943.

It was this summer that a thin edge of rock emerged from beneath the sea; a line that could be seen in Kirk Sound, stretching all the way from Lamb Holm to mainland Orkney, and in Skerry Sound between Lamb Holm and Glimps Holm. The same success had been achieved between the other islands. The channels had been sealed. Even though there was still a huge amount of work to do, no U-boat would ever enter Scapa Flow that way again.

The men worked and the summer passed unobserved into autumn, without anyone in Camp 60 realising their lives were about to change dramatically.

10

One morning in September, as Major Buckland sat at his desk, his orderly stuck his head into the room.

'Sorry to bother you, sir, but the new Italian padre is here.'

'Excellent,' replied Major Buckland, 'please show him in.'

Major Buckland stood up and walked around his desk as the orderly showed the priest into the room. Not knowing if their newest arrival spoke English, he greeted him in Italian.

'I'm Major Buckland, camp commander. Welcome to Camp 60, Padre . . .'

'My name is Gioacchino Giacobazzi, but I'm known simply as Padre Giacomo.'

'Ah, Padre. Please, sit down. You'll join me in a cup of tea, or would you prefer coffee?'

'Tea would be fine, thank you, Major,' the priest replied in English.

Padre Giacomo sat down, putting his small satchel on the floor by his feet. Major Buckland returned to his seat opposite. It was obvious to both men from even these few words that Padre Giacomo was significantly more fluent in English than was Major Buckland in Italian and they slipped comfortably into the former.

'I believe you've most recently come from Edinburgh, Padre, although I suspect you got there by a fairly torturous route.'

'I was captured at Soddu in East Africa then moved around month after month with no apparent logic until I ended up in Edinburgh, along with thirty other chaplains, to be allocated to various camps around Britain.'

'Thirty! Goodness, that's quite a posse of padres. And so you got the little Orkney island of Lamb Holm.'

'The wisdom of God I do not question.'

'Indeed. Well, I'm both sorry you're here and glad. There are over 500 Italians in Camp 60. Most of them were in anti-aircraft regiments, tank corps or infantry. I've spoken with many individually over the last eighteen months and they're all good men. Oh, you get plenty of flare ups, with lots of arm waving and shouting, but it's generally over and forgotten about as quickly as it starts. No real trouble. Of course, they want to be at home with their loved ones, not here. But here we all are, nonetheless.'

'Building barriers I believe?'

'We prefer to call them *causeways*. Major Booth is deputy camp commander and should be on his way,' continued Major Buckland. 'He's an excellent fellow. If you ever need anything and can't find me then Major Booth is the man to seek. Now, what I was saying is I've got to know the men fairly well and what they've achieved inside the camp has been little short of a miracle.'

'I must say,' said Padre Giacomo, taking a sip of tea, 'I was surprised at the number of flower beds. Some huts seem almost to have small gardens around them.'

'Flower beds, vegetable plots, concrete paths so they don't have to walk in the mud when it's wet. They've built themselves a bowling alley with concrete bowling balls and even concrete billiard tables. I tried one once. It was devilishly difficult to pot anything.'

'What else do the men do in their spare time? I take it they have some time away from the quarry and the block . . .'

'The block-making yard,' said Major Buckland. 'Yes. We introduced a system whereby when a team had completed its allotted work for that day then they could return to camp. It didn't go down well with the Balfour Beatty men because they have to finish their ten-hour shifts no matter how much work they've done.'

'But it suits the Italian temperament.'

'Exactly. Several of the men are very gifted craftsmen and have turned their hand to making quite beautiful things out of ordinary objects. I've seen some intricately carved boxes, ashtrays adorned with Spitfires and Hurricanes, even a cigarette lighter that looks like the Eiffel Tower. There's also a good band and two theatre groups, so there is a variety of productions. Oh, which reminds me there's a performance tonight. I know the men would be delighted if you would attend. It gets a bit crowded in the mess hall but we manage. And there's even a fairly impressive football team.'

'They don't play with a concrete ball?'

'No,' said Major Buckland enjoying the conversation. 'We did manage to get a proper football from Kirkwall. In fact, the Red Cross have even helped to acquire kits for the team.'

'Major Buckland,' said Padre Giacomo putting down his cup and saucer so he could stress the point he was about to make. 'I sense you are telling me that the men can fill their spare time, which is all very admirable, but what they lack is something for the soul.'

'That's why I'm so glad you've arrived,' said Major Buckland. 'For all the music, sports and theatre, the men feel strongly about the absence of any spiritual guidance. Also, although many of them have accepted the fact they are here until the war ends, for some . . .'

'For some, perhaps the war continues . . . inside?' suggested Padre Giacomo, tapping his chest.

'Yes, they receive upsetting news from home and can do nothing about it or they have no news at all, which may be almost as bad. It makes it very hard for them. They chafe against their captivity. You see some individuals walking around the camp alone, rarely joining in with the activities.'

'In such circumstances the road to desperation is a short one.'

'And with that comes higher levels of illness. It's a vicious circle, Padre.'

There was a knock at door and the two men paused as Major Booth entered, accompanied by a small white dog of uncertain parentage.

'Ah, Major Booth. This is Padre Giacomo,' said Major Buckland, rising from his chair, as did the priest. 'I was just explaining how pleased we are he is here.'

'I know the men will be reassured,' said Major Booth, shaking hands with the new arrival. 'Although, I'm afraid we can only offer the mess hall for your services.'

'As it is Sunday tomorrow I would like to conduct mass in the morning if that's possible, Major Buckland?'

'I don't see why not.'

'We could announce it before the performance starts this evening,' added Major Booth helpfully. 'The play is not one that I know. Something about a baker in Venice I believe.'

'Well, I'm sure it will be good. They generally are. When we've finished our tea Major Booth and I would be pleased to show you around the camp.'

The camp was virtually deserted as the two British officers

took a leisurely walk with Padre Giacomo, who expressed surprise at the temperature this far north.

'It's not what I expected,' he said. 'The weather is so much pleasanter than I thought it would be.'

'Oh it has its moments in the winter, but in summer Orkney is a most delightful place. I hope at some point you'll be able to visit the mainland and some of the other islands. They're quite beautiful. As to the camp . . . well, the men have done an amazing job.'

'You like your prisoners Major Buckland,' said Padre Giacomo.

'Yes, I do. To be perfectly truthful, Padre, I love the Italian culture. I was stationed in the Dolomites during the First World War, which was where I picked up a few words.'

'You are very good,' said Padre Giacomo.

'You are very kind,' said Major Buckland with a smile. 'But yes, I have a great fondness for the people. In fact, my wife and I got married in Italy just after the last war.'

'Your concern for the prisoners is commendable, Major. I would say that . . . my goodness! What's that?'

The men had turned a corner and come upon a statue of St George slaying the dragon. Padre Giacomo walked up to the base and stood gazing in silent amazement.

'I thought that might surprise you,' said Major Buckland.

'I'm speechless. Surely not made by the prisoners?'

'By one prisoner to be precise, Domenico Chiocchetti. A man with a remarkable artistic skill,' said Major Buckland, 'using two of the things we actually have in great supply on the island . . . cement and barbed wire.'

'Barbed wire?' said Padre Giacomo, his astonishment becoming greater with every answer.

'Yes, I must admit I thought it was a bizarre request when

I heard a prisoner had asked for barbed wire. Normally they want less of it. I think Chiocchetti's gang may still be working at the block-making yard,' he said. 'If not, we'll meet them on the way back. How do you fancy stretching your legs, Padre?'

'After the amount of sitting I've done in the last few days that sounds like a fine idea.'

'Excellent. Let's go and find your parishioners.'

11

The three men walked along in comfortable silence, Buster following faithfully behind Major Booth. Guillemots, known locally as 'tysties', bobbed on the water's surface while a variety of gulls screeched noisily overhead. The British officers seemed decent and the conditions in the camp far more favourable than he had imagined, but there was a great deal Padre Giacomo didn't understand.

'Is building the barriers the only occupation of the prisoners Major Buckland?'

'The causeways,' corrected Major Buckland amiably. 'Yes, it's really what everyone is here for. It's a massive project. Three of the channels between the islands are around two thousand feet wide and the water in some places is more than fifty feet deep. However, all four channels . . . you'll hear them referred to as sounds . . . are now sealed.'

'So the work is almost complete?' asked Padre Giacomo, with a sudden fear of soon being moved on again.

'Oh no, Padre, far from it. There are several months of work yet to do. The activities you'll see over the next few days on Lamb Holm are being duplicated on other islands.'

'Let's hope the local people appreciate their new . . . causeways when they are complete,' said Padre Giacomo, unable to understand Major Buckland's reluctance to call them barriers. He had not yet learned that the term had been changed eighteen months earlier to defuse the tension with the Italians, following their complaint of being involved in 'works of a war-like nature.' The construction work had become a long-standing project to build causeways that would allow local people to travel more easily between the islands. Whether anyone believed this was debateable, but it helped to get the POWs back to work. Ever since, the British had avoided the word 'barrier'.

Padre Giacomo, Major Buckland and Major Booth stopped a short distance away from the *Lycia*, which had been rammed on to rocks as part of an earlier attempt to block the channel between Lamb Holm and Glimps Holm. More than forty vessels had been sunk between mainland Orkney and South Ronaldsay and in a line behind the *Lycia* were the blockships, *Ilsenstein* and *Emerald Wings*, each one progressively more submerged. It was possible to walk across gangplanks from the shore to the *Emerald Wings* but when the tide was in more than half of the ship was underwater.

Several Italians were fishing from vantage points on the *Lycia*, while others were splashing about in the water and many more sat on the bank watching and laughing. A few British guards sat around chatting.

'Fishing?' said Padre Giacomo, as he looked at the scene before him.

'They must have completed their work for the day and are enjoying some free time before going back to camp,' explained Major Booth. 'Fishing is quite a popular pastime. They can keep whatever they catch to supplement their food.'

'There's Chiocchetti,' said Major Buckland, pointing to a group of men. 'Come on, Padre. Let's go and meet the man who sculpted St George and the dragon from barbed wire and cement.'

The men on the ground stood up when they saw who was walking towards them. Major Buckland and Major Booth greeted the men by name and Padre Giacomo was quick to notice the friendliness of the British officers and the apparently genuine respect of the Italians.

'And may I introduce Padre Giacomo,' said Major Buckland.

Buttapasta was the first to shake hands.

'I'm Domenico Buttapasta. Welcome to the camp, Padre. The absence of a priest has been deeply felt.'

'I hope I can be of some help now that I am here,' said Padre Giacomo.

Major Buckland introduced Dino and Carlo, who greeted the priest with due reverence, then turned to face Aldo, who spoke before he could make any formal introduction.

'Aldo Tolino. If you need anything of a practical nature then I'm your man,' he said, taking the priest's offered hand and smiling. Anyone watching Aldo carefully might have been aware the smile did not reach his eyes and if Padre Giacomo felt the slight stiffness in the handshake then he made nothing of it.

'And here,' said Major Buckland, turning to the last man in the group, 'is Domenico Chiocchetti, whose work you so admired.'

'I'm very pleased to meet you, Padre. I know the men will be greatly reassured you are here.'

'I was impressed by your sculpture. It goes beyond an object of artistic skill and materialistic beauty.'

'Thank you, Padre,' said Domenico. 'I hope that we'll soon be able to attend mass?'

'Yes, Major Buckland has kindly said we may use the mess

hall tomorrow morning . . . once we've cleared away the theatrical props.'

The mess hall that night was full. Major Buckland and Major Booth sat at the front with Padre Giacomo and Sergeant Major Fornasier. Most of the camp guards stood around at the back of the hall but this was to watch the actors rather than the audience. Although none of them spoke Italian they always had the plot explained beforehand, so following the performance wasn't too difficult. Domenico had been extra busy during the previous few weeks. He ran the 'northern' acting group as well as producing the backdrops for each scene and this was one of their performances. After about half an hour everyone in the mess hall was laughing so much that the men on stage could hardly be heard. It didn't matter.

There was no difficulty the following morning in hearing the strong, clear voice of Padre Giacomo conducting mass in a mixture of Italian and Latin. The mess hall held about 400 men and they ate up the words spoken more readily than any meal that had ever been served.

'We are all many miles from home, from the people we love, the language, the food and the culture we understand, but never forget that God is everywhere. Never feel He has forgotten you. Keep Him in your heart and your thoughts. One day the war will be over. Many of our countrymen will not return home. So whatever we may eventually find, we are fortunate to be alive. Let us praise God for that and pray to Him to keep our loved ones safe and to end the war.'

Outside the mess hall Aldo leant against a hut, smoking and listening to the subdued voices of the men inside as they prayed. After a few moments he threw the cigarette down and walked away, hands thrust deep into his pockets.

When the service was over Padre Giacomo stood outside so that he could speak to as many of the congregation as possible as they filed out. Domenico was one of the last to leave and by this time there were several small groups of men, standing around the parade ground talking.

'Domenico,' said Padre Giacomo.

'Padre. The service was good. There were a lot of people.'

'Yes . . . and then . . . there were a lot of people not there.'

'Some will embrace God with joy,' offered Domenico, 'but I think there are others who have seen or done things before being captured that could make them feel . . .' Domenico's sentence trailed off partly because he did not know how to finish it, but also because he felt it was not necessary.

'It is difficult to believe in the goodness of God when you are surrounded by evil acts of men,' said Padre Giacomo. 'I know what you are saying, Domenico. There will be men here who I cannot influence, no matter how hard I try. But that will not stop me from trying.'

'Padre, I wanted to talk to you about something.'

'And I am here to listen, and be of help if I can. Wait a short while and then let us take a walk around the camp. I didn't complete my tour with Major Buckland yesterday.'

It wasn't long before the two men were walking round the inside of the perimeter fence.

'And there you have it, Padre. The British have a hut for administration purposes, but their camp is only about ten minutes away so they don't eat or sleep here.'

'However, the camp has certainly been transformed into something that is more appealing to the Italian eye. And your statue is the centrepiece, Domenico. It's truly a work of art.'

'In a way, that's what I wanted to talk to you about, Padre.

The statue shouldn't be the centrepiece . . . there should be a chapel.'

Padre Giacomo stopped walking.

'A chapel? You mean . . . build a chapel? In the camp? But how?'

'Not entirely from scratch. But I've been thinking . . . If we could have a Nissen hut, we could convert it,' said Domenico with nervous excitement at the unknown reaction he would receive.

'Convert a Nissen hut into a chapel? Well, it's an interesting idea . . . extremely interesting.'

Padre Giacomo had become instantly enthralled at the prospect, but hesitated at asking about the practicalities in case the idea turned out to be no more than a prisoner's enthusiastic pipe dream.

'Could you do it, Domenico?'

'Not alone, Padre, but there are many skilled men in the camp and I'm sure there would be a lot of willing hands. The idea has been in my mind, but without a priest . . .'

'And now you have one. How can I help?' asked Padre Giacomo.

'Will you speak to Major Buckland and ask him if we can have a Nissen hut? It may be that there is a spare one.'

'I'll ask him. I'll ask him with pleasure. And good luck to both of us,' said Padre Giacomo with a smile.

At that moment the two men turned towards the centre of the camp where a great deal of shouting could suddenly be heard.

'I wonder what's going on,' asked Padre Giacomo, half expecting Domenico to explain away the noise as if it was a regular event on a Sunday morning.

'It must be something big,' said Domenico.

With a silent agreement the two men, drawn by natural curiosity, made their way back to the parade ground. When they got there, they both stood open mouthed at the sight before them.

12

Men from virtually every hut were spilling on to the parade ground in whatever they happened to be wearing. A couple had come out of the wash block with nothing more than towels around their waists. Some were running around laughing, shouting and slapping each other on the back. A few were trying to tear off the target discs on their clothing. However, many were subdued and some looked utterly shocked. Domenico and Padre Giacomo pushed themselves into the rapidly growing throng of bodies. Domenico stopped the nearest man.

'What's going on?' he asked.

'The news is going around the camp,' said the man, almost breathless with excitement. 'Badoglio has signed an armistice with the British and their allies. We're not at war with Britain anymore. We're not prisoners. We're free.'

Major Buckland stood up from his desk and walked over to the window to see what was causing the commotion. There was a knock at the door and Sergeant Slater entered.

'Sergeant Slater. What the devil's going on?'

'It's just been on the radio, sir. Italy has capitulated.'

'Good God. Capitulated?'

'What does it mean, sir?'

'That's a bloody good question. If Italy really has capitulated then we've got more than 500 men in a POW camp who may no longer be prisoners of war.'

'Not prisoners, sir? Then what do we do with them?'

'Damned if I know. You'd better tell Anderson to get the War Office on the phone as quick as you can. Thank you, Sergeant.'

'Yes, sir.'

Major Buckland moved back to his desk as Sergeant Slater made for the door.

'And Sergeant Slater.'

'Yes, sir?'

'Spread the word to the men. We don't want any guards thinking there's some sort of mass breakout going on. It wouldn't do to shoot someone now . . . they're not the enemy anymore.'

'Capitulated. Well, who'd have thought it?' Major Buckland said to the empty room then he smiled and let out a bark of a laugh.

For the next couple of hours, there was complete confusion throughout the camp, with rumour after rumour first raising men's hopes then dashing them. Some thought they would go back to Italy as they could no longer legitimately be held as prisoners of war, while others thought this was fanciful wishing. Everyone felt unsettled and feared what might be happening back home. Countries they had originally gone to war against were now allies, whilst those that had been allies appeared to have become enemies.

Domenico and Padre Giacomo had eventually found Butta-pasta, Aldo and Micheloni. The group stood to one side of the parade ground. In the centre men had to shout to be heard by their neighbour as the noise was so great. Aldo was unpicking the large red target disc from the back of his jacket.

'You look worried, Micheloni,' said Buttapasta.

'I was wondering what the Germans might do in Italy,' he answered.

'Maybe they'll send us home and we can kick everyone out of Italy who is not Italian. That would be a good start,' said Aldo. Although everyone agreed with the sentiment they knew this was not a practical suggestion.

'I doubt we'll be going anywhere until the war is over,' said Domenico. 'The British aren't going to find spare ships to take us back to Italy while they're still fighting the Germans, and it would be too dangerous anyway.'

'But we can't be prisoners of war any longer,' stated Buttapasta with certainty. 'What do you think, padre?'

'I don't know, Domenico,' answered Padre Giacomo, who insisted on calling Buttapasta by his first name. 'But I suspect the British won't know either. In the end, there may be little change in our lives.'

'No change?' said Aldo, crestfallen at the thought.

'Well, we've got to be housed and fed somewhere, so I suppose we will stay in the camps. And there is still the task of completing the . . . causeways. I suppose Major Buckland will tell us as soon as he knows himself.'

But the days passed without news and the mood in the camp became sombre as men worried about loved ones. Italy was set to become even more of a battleground now than it had been before, and the danger to civilians in some areas of the country was greater than ever.

13

'Build a chapel?'

The question was put by Major Buckland, who sat at his desk facing Padre Giacomo.

'Here in the camp? Well, it's certainly an idea, padre. In fact, the Prisoner of War Inspector of Camps from the War Office suggested some time ago that we should provide a chapel for the men. But these things are easier said than done. Gordon Nicol . . . he's the civil engineer overseeing the entire causeway project . . . he and I have been talking recently about the lack of a facility to hold classes.'

Now it was Padre Giacomo's turn to be surprised.

'Classes, Major Buckland?'

'Yes. Several Italians have asked about the possibility of organising classes and there are many highly educated men here who would be eager to help. Perhaps we could look at finding some way of meeting both needs?'

'That sounds like an excellent proposal,' said Padre Giacomo, whose mind was already racing with new ideas.

'I'll speak to Gordon. If anyone can solve a logistical problem, it's him.'

'I am confident of leaving the solution in your and Mr Nicol's hands . . . and God's, of course.'

Anderson knocked on the door and let Domenico into the room. It was a few days after the meeting between Padre Giacomo and Major Buckland and the British officer had requested to see him.

'Ah, Domenico, come in. Stand easy,' said Major Buckland in Italian. He still wasn't fluent but could generally be understood.

'Sir,' said Domenico, waiting to hear why he had been summoned to the office, where he had never been before. He stood in the centre of the room, hands behind his back.

'You'll be pleased to hear that Mr Nicol has been able to secure two Nissen huts; one for the men to use as a classroom and the other to be transformed into a cathedral,' said Major Buckland with a smile.

Domenico smiled back. He was amused at the idea of making a cathedral, a word he guessed Major Buckland hadn't intended to use. However, as he thought about it, the idea appealed to him.

'Each hut is really too small by itself and will need to be moved from where they are currently situated, so I suggest they are placed end to end to make one larger building. I shouldn't think that will be a problem and joining them together will give you an adequate size. I'm not sure how you plan to convert them,' said Major Buckland. He paused and as Domenico didn't say anything he asked the one question that was troubling him. 'Can you really do it?'

'There are many skilled men in the camp, sir,' replied Domenico. 'I'm confident the work can be done really well, or we will not do it.'

There was a moment of uncomfortable silence in the room during which Major Buckland's face underwent a transformation of emotions. He reverted to English almost unconsciously.

'Not do the work? But we've gone to a great deal of trouble. Good God, man. I can't believe I'm hearing this.'

Domenico could speak some English but Major Buckland's words were blurted out in such a rush that he was hard pushed to understand what had just been said. He certainly had no idea why the British officer had become so agitated.

'Not unless it's done well, sir,' he said again, hoping that this would be the right thing to stress.

'I've never known such ingratitude,' said Major Buckland picking up the telephone on his desk. 'Not do the work. No, not you!' he shouted down the handset. 'Get me the interpreter at the double.'

Major Buckland slammed down the telephone and glared at Domenico, who was completely at a loss as to what he had done to cause the normally mild officer to be so upset. The meeting was beginning to feel slightly surreal.

'Not do the work,' he continued. 'I can't believe my ruddy ears.'

The following few minutes passed in agonising slowness, while Major Buckland huffed and Domenico waited with a mixture of alarm and bemusement. It wasn't long before they heard someone walking quickly through the main office. Major Buckland called out 'Enter' before there was even a knock at the door and moments later the interpreter stood in the room alongside Domenico.

'Major Buckland. You have a problem, sir?'

'We've gone to a great deal of effort to secure two Nissen huts, which this fellow is meant to convert into a chapel and a school, only now he says he's not going to do the work! It's outrageous.'

The camp's interpreter was an English civilian and he always appeared friendly enough, although generally rather harassed, partly as a result of not being able to understand many of the dialects used by the men.

'Signor Chiocchetti. Major Buckland seems to think you are not willing to do the work to convert the Nissen huts into a chapel and a school.'

'Not at all,' said Domenico both surprised and aghast. 'What I said was that we would not do the work unless we could do it really well.'

'Ah, you want to make a good job of it?' he said.

'Of course.'

'Like your beautiful statue of St George and the dragon?'

'But hopefully without the need for barbed wire,' replied Domenico. It was clear to him now what had happened but not to Major Buckland, who was as lost at the quickly-spoken Italian as Domenico had been at the rapidly-spoken English.

'A simple misunderstanding, sir,' said the interpreter in English. 'Signor Chiocchetti says he will work on the Nissen huts only if he believes he can complete the task to a high standard, which is what he aims to do.'

Major Buckland looked blank for a brief moment then his angry expression evaporated in an instant to be replaced by a huge grin. He stood up and walked around the table.

'Make a good job of it. Excellent,' he said and as he reached Domenico he slapped him heartily on the back. 'Bravo! Make a good job. That's the spirit, old chap.'

The following Sunday afternoon, Domenico and Buttapasta stood outside a group of Nissen huts situated a short distance from Camp 60. Gordon Nicol had suggested the Italians could have two of the smaller huts but as Domenico stood before one of them, the key in his hand, he hesitated. Unlocking the door and stepping inside would be the first physical act he had taken in this quest.

Until now he had talked and planned, bounced ideas off those he respected and obtained agreement from those in authority. But once he opened the door, the chapel would be underway, and much of the responsibility for its success or failure would lie with him. So he hesitated and Buttapasta waited in silence.

If either of them imagined there might be a spiritual feeling at this particular stage of their quest, any such notion was quickly dispelled when Domenico found he couldn't budge the door. It took Buttapasta's not inconsiderable strength to push the door inch by inch, until both of them could squeeze inside. They looked around in dismay. The hut was packed from floor to ceiling with old furniture, benches, planks of wood and twisted joists that might at one time have been considered building material. The two men stood in silence. They couldn't even begin to think of moving the hut until it was emptied.

'Come on,' said Buttapasta, seeing the disappointed look on Domenico's face. 'Let's see what the other hut is like. It might not be so bad.'

Moments later they stood in the identical hut, equally crammed with discarded items.

'Well, that's okay then. We'll soon get this sorted,' said Buttapasta.

Domenico looked at him in alarm. 'You're not thinking that we should move all this ourselves?'

'Don't be daft, Domenico. I'm just going to round up a few friends who think they've nothing better to do this afternoon than laze around on their backsides, while you go and find out where we can put it all.'

Less than an hour later, about 200 Italians in a huge human chain were passing the contents of the huts along to an area of waste ground just outside the camp. While this was taking place, Sergeant Slater gathered half a dozen Italians and took them to the Balfour Beatty workshops, where they collected as many saws, axes and wrecking bars as they could. Scores of men lent a hand to break up and cut any wood suitable for use in the stoves.

There was a lot of rubbish left and so the Italians made a bonfire, which attracted most of the camp. Aldo walked around selling distilled spirit. He was struggling to pour the liquid into mugs, take the payment, and move to the next batch of outstretched arms. But his pockets were bulging with cigarettes and tokens, so he was happy.

By late afternoon, there was a carnival atmosphere and an increasingly large circle of men danced around the fire to the music of the camp band, which had set itself up nearby. The British left them to it, so the fire crackled and men drank, laughed and danced. Aldo had eventually given up the idea of walking around and set himself up at a small table in front of which was a line of continuously moving men. Dino guarded the precious liquid, stored in a variety of bottles on the ground, and helped to take the tokens. Aldo maintained a constant monologue.

'That's it. That's it. Come and sample the finest spirit in Camp 60, the finest in any camp in Orkney. I guarantee you won't have tasted anything like this before.'

None of the men could argue with the latter statement as they coughed and choked on the burning fluid, but several came back for more.

'Aldo's doing a roaring trade,' said Domenico, looking on thoughtfully.

'Why does that not surprise me,' said Buttapasta. 'I gather he's got two stills going now and is producing a stronger spirit by distilling it twice. Of course, he sells that batch for more.'

'It's good to see the men enjoying themselves,' said Carlo. 'They work hard and there are no thanks for it, just another day of sweat and labour. The chapel is already benefiting people and we haven't even moved the huts yet.'

'Some men will feel the weight of loneliness upon them even more heavily because of the light and laughter here,' added Domenico quietly.

Buttapasta sensed some of Domenico's mood, a conflict of apprehension and excitement at what they had just began, of pleasure at the men's simple enjoyment and of sadness at being so far from home.

'Domenico, you cannot take on the responsibility to reach out to all these men. You're right. It can be difficult for those whose nature does not allow them to walk up to a party and join in, but that doesn't mean you shouldn't hold the party. Now a chapel . . . no one needs to hesitate before walking up to a house of God.'

Domenico smiled. He understood his friend was trying to lighten his mood. Unseen by them Aldo had approached, carrying four mugs.

'Hey, I hope my two favourite Domenicos are not talking shop again. You both look far too serious. You need to drink this,' he said, handing them a mug and passing one to Carlo.

'Well if we were talking of something serious I'm sure it will stop now,' said Buttapasta, sniffing the liquid suspiciously.

'Drink up, it will make you big and strong,' said Aldo, whose head barely reached Buttapasta's broad shoulders.

The men looked at each other, grinned and downed the liquid in one go.

'Heaven save us,' choked Carlo. 'What's in this?'

'Don't ask, but it's not too bad considering,' said Aldo, the hint of a slur to his speech. 'Perhaps not so much boot polish next time.'

Domenico was unable to speak at all and was still trying to catch his breath when their attention was taken by the loud blowing of a whistle, which eventually stopped the band and the dancing. The men fell quiet. A British sergeant moved into the centre of the Italians.

'Alright, you've got ten minutes to clear away and then we're going to hose the fire,' he shouted, generating a gaggle of protest. 'Don't you lot know there's a war on? If this blaze is still going by nightfall we'll attract every German bomber for fifty miles. Then you'll be complaining about the noise of bombs keeping you awake. You've got nine minutes.'

Aldo had sold out of spirit and left Carlo and Dino to collect the empty bottles. He walked a short distance away with Domenico and Buttapasta to watch the British privates as they ran out hoses from the camp. The fire was quickly reduced to a smouldering heap and without its heat they quickly felt the cold.

'Come on you two,' said Aldo. 'Let's go to the recreation hut and I'll stand you a free drink of Aldo's finest.' He and Dino would have to start all over again with their little stills, which they had only recently taken apart and hidden amongst the cooking equipment in the mess hall kitchen. Ingredients were often difficult to obtain, particularly at this time of year.

'Why do we want to drink more?' said Buttapasta, who wasn't altogether certain the comment about boot polish had been a joke.

Two days later, Domenico stood by the first of the Nissen huts to be moved. There were eight men along each side of the

97

building, which consisted of a double skin of corrugated iron sections, fixed either side of an iron and timber frame. The structure had already been loosened from the foundations and the end brick walls. All that was needed was to lift the building over one wall and carry it to the new site.

However, Domenico was worried that the frame would distort once raised or that the building might be dropped. When the recreation hut had been constructed, before the steel stays were added, the entire building had been tipped over by the wind and badly damaged. That was a much bigger and heavier Nissen hut than the one in front of him now. The wind was picking up as the men waited for his signal. He didn't want to stop. Everything was set for today. Buttapasta and another gang were already waiting at the new site. He took a big breath.

'Are you ready?' he shouted.

Men bent over, gripping whatever they could. They all waited.

'Lift!'

The hut rocked, men fought for better holds and then the entire building rose into the air, albeit rather unsteadily.

'Move!'

They started to walk sideways with short steps. Gradually the Nissen hut was lifted along its length over the brick wall nearest to Domenico, who shouted encouragement and words of warning when one side dropped lower than the other. Eventually they were clear and the little procession, watched by several hundred Italians, began its painstakingly slow journey.

By the halfway point the wind caught the hut one way and then another. Domenico was horrified. They were losing control. He shouted at the men to increase their efforts but the hut was such an awkward thing to carry that they couldn't go any faster. If anything, they were slowing down. Domenico considered calling on the help of those standing around watching, but he thought that suddenly having dozens of newcomers enthusiastically pushing in, without any real thought, could result in disaster.

He had hand-picked these men and they were balanced down each side for strength and height. He couldn't change anything now, and so they gasped and moved as quickly as they could. As they neared the new site it started to rain heavily. Buttapasta was frantic. He had already sent men to bring back stakes and rope so that they could tie the hut down and when Domenico arrived, the site was a hive of activity, with men hammering stakes into the frozen ground as fast as they could.

'I don't like this wind,' shouted Buttapasta, looking over Domenico's shoulder at the hut about twenty yards behind.

'It was fine less than an hour ago,' said the artist miserably. 'We'll never predict the weather in this place.'

As the exhausted men tried to manoeuvre the structure into position the wind took hold of it completely and started to flip it over. Those on one side were forced on to the ground, while the others felt the corrugated iron torn from their grasp. Suddenly men were shouting warnings and those in danger of being trapped underneath started to let go. Potential disaster was moments away. Domenico ran forward closely followed by Buttapasta and a dozen of his men, some of whom rushed inside the hut. Between them they took hold of every square inch they could reach and with huge efforts combined against the elements, eased the building as carefully as they could into position.

'Tie it down!' snarled Buttapasta. He was angry; angry like the wind that howled around them. 'Tie it down!'

Ropes were thrown, hurled back by the gale and thrown again, until one by one about half a dozen stout ropes straddled the hut and were tied firmly to the stakes.

'Damn this weather, Domenico. We should have seen this coming. We can't lift the other hut in this weather and we won't be able to do anything with this one other than fasten it down as best we can. God knows if the hut will still be here in the morning if we get a real storm during the night.'

'And we've already loosened the second hut. We'll have to tie it down or we could lose that one as well.'

'You'd better go back now. Take those spare stakes and rope,' said Buttapasta pointing to an Italian holding both items, 'and whatever men you need. We're not going to be able to do any more than that today. It's a bloody mess.'

14

Domenico lay in bed, going through the day's events in his mind. They had come so close to disaster right at the very beginning. He let out a long sigh to ease the tension in his body. The worst times for the Italians were at night. During the day they were always busy and there was constant inter-action.

In the dark, lying in bed alone and unable to sleep, men fretted about their families and friends. They worried whether ageing parents would die before the war was over and feared for the safety of wives and children. The severe food shortage in Italy was common knowledge in the camp. They tormented themselves that young children would have long ago forgotten who their father was, and would scream at sight of the 'stranger'.

Men wondered if they would even recognise themselves after so many years away. Could they simply pick up family life, a normal job and domestic routine after so long? Did such basic things even exist anymore? Had a sweetheart left behind already found someone else? For some, darkness meant despair, which ate away at their spirit.

There was a faint glow in the centre of the hut from the open stove, where Dino sat with a man whose descent into depression had concerned many. Sergeant Primavera and the camp doctor were aware of the situation, but there was little that could be done. It had become an unspoken rule that someone always kept an eye on the person concerned, without him being aware. Dino was leaning close and in the flickering glow from the flames Domenico could see him whispering earnestly, trying to make a connection. Domenico was reminded of their first day at the quarry and Buttapasta's comment about Dante's journey into Hades. In many ways, the man was standing at the gates of Hell and it was only the indomitable spirit of Dino that refused to let him enter.

Outside the wind and rain beat down on the corrugated iron roof. Domenico was certain he could see the sides of the hut twisting and distorting, fighting against the steel stays that held it down.

There was a new face in the hut, one of half a dozen Italians who had arrived on Lamb Holm that day. The men had been captured in Sicily following the Allied invasion of the island during the summer, and had immediately been grilled by those desperate for news about their own villages or towns. The men in Camp 60 learned about events in Europe from the radio in the mess hall, and for several days that October the main topic of conversation was the Badoglio government's declaration of war on Germany. But it was information on events that might directly affect their families back home that the Italians craved, rather than the larger, military picture. None of the new arrivals had any knowledge of Domenico's home town, Moena.

'What are you thinking?' questioned Aldo, who was lying in bed facing Domenico.

'I was wondering if the chapel will have a roof in the morning. What about you?'

'Nothing really.'

'The war won't go on for ever, Aldo. You never talk about your life back home. Who do you have waiting for you when all this madness is over?'

Aldo didn't answer and Domenico didn't press the question. Most of the men talked about their homes all the time, but if Aldo didn't want to that was his right. Domenico lay quietly, watching the wall above his head move inwards several inches as if a huge hand was pushing it from the other side.

'There's no one for me. My mother died when I was eleven and my father pined away. He gave up a few years later. By the time I was twelve I had to earn the money we lived on, otherwise we would have starved.'

'I'm sorry.' Domenico didn't want to pry, but it seemed ruder not to make a comment than to stay quiet. 'No brothers or sisters?'

'No.'

They lay in silence for a while listening to the rain beating down on the roof.

'Time and nature are great healers of scars,' said Domenico.

'I think, when you're young, some scars go so deep they mould your character. They set you upon a path that has no turning and you will forever wonder what journey you might otherwise have known.'

'God will always show you a new path, if you let Him.'

There was another pause in the conversation. 'Aldo,' said Domenico at long last, 'a crowded room can be the loneliest place on earth, while a man on an island can be in perfect peace with himself and humanity.'

'I know.'

'But do you appreciate how easy it is to create your own crowded room?'

For a long while Aldo didn't answer.

'I'm going to try and sleep,' he said eventually, and rolled over to face away. The door was closed once more. Domenico sighed quietly and looked at the bed next to him. Shortly after they had arrived at the camp Aldo had acquired several additional blankets because he felt the cold so much. All Domenico could see in the semi-darkness was a mound of blankets, under which his friend lay, hiding from the other men in the hut, hiding from the demons of his past.

15

The storm passed during the night and a sunrise of brilliant red spread across the camp. Domenico and Buttapasta walked around in silence as they examined the hut. It had shifted a few feet but was still there, intact.

'Well, I don't know if you intend this part to be the school or the chapel, but it's still here for whichever use,' said Buttapasta. 'But we'll need to secure this properly to the foundations and fix steel stays before we think of moving the other hut into position.'

'Yes, but perhaps we should try to get one of the locals to forecast the weather for us,' teased Domenico, wondering if such a thing might be an idea. He was tired. They all were, for few of the men had slept much. 'But we're not doing any of it now. Building a house of God has much less priority than constructing a concrete road.'

A few weeks after the first hut had been moved, Giuseppe and five other POWs, along with a guard, found themselves walking down a country track in Holm, on mainland Orkney. It was not uncommon for small groups to carry out repairs on local farms and this one sounded like another typical job of clearing ditches and replacing fencing. The men didn't mind. Many of them had been farmers before the war and the work was certainly preferable to being on the causeways. Also, the farmer's wife generally gave them a better meal and often some local treats. If they were really lucky there might even be some young women on the farm. When this happened the men would almost fall over each other trying to make conversation, even though they generally didn't know sufficient English to make much sense. They would beg Giuseppe to translate and sometimes he entertained himself and everyone else by altering what each side said.

They found the farm and the men sat down near the gate while Giuseppe walked up the path to the front door. He could hear someone playing the piano inside so he stood for a while and enjoyed the music. It was good. However, the guard finally shouted so he knocked and the music stopped. Giuseppe was glancing over his shoulder at the men when the door opened and he turned around to look into a woman's face, a handsome, honest face, surrounded by auburn hair.

'Giuseppe!' she said with delight.

'Fiona. I can't believe it. I'm . . . speechless!'

She laughed.

'You've come to help on the farm?'

'Yes. This is your home?

'Since I was born. Everyone else is away this morning. I've been left to tell you what to do.'

'I was . . . distraught when I was unable to come back to the hospital.'

'I know. There was nothing I could do. On the day your friend returned to the camp I didn't arrive until later that morning and he had already left.'

'Was that you playing the piano?'

'Yes. I didn't know anyone was listening.'

'You're good. Perhaps tomorrow I will bring my banjo.'

'You play the banjo?'

'Not for years, but I've bought one from the camp shop. It would be good to play together.'

Their attention was taken by a series of wolf whistles and calls from the Italians, who had spotted Giuseppe talking to the woman in the doorway.

'I'd better show you what needs to be done, but I'll think of a way to get together.'

Fiona and Giuseppe walked back to the gate where the wolf whistles grew louder. Fiona smiled when they reached the men, who stood up quickly, several taking off their hats and greeting her in Italian with a sudden show of respect and . . . admiration. She led them around the farm, pointing out the clogged ditches and the fence that needed to be put up. The new barbed wire and posts were stacked nearby. She took them into the barn to show them where the tools were kept and immediately two of the Italians wandered over to inspect the cattle, which were in the building whilst the fence was being repaired.

Fiona could see by the way they handled the animals that they had a great affinity for them. They were soon shouting questions so in the end Fiona and Giuseppe walked over.

It seemed to take a long while before any work was actually started, but Fiona liked the Italians. They made her laugh even when she didn't understand what they were saying. She returned to the house to make coffee and said Giuseppe should follow to help carry everything out. He gave her fifteen minutes and left. The guard made no objection.

'Leave your boots on,' she said to him at the door, when he

was about to take them off. 'This is a farmhouse. We'd get no work done at all if we took our boots off every time we came in.'

She led him to the kitchen.

'We seem destined always just to have a few snatched moments together,' she said. 'It's not enough, is it?'

She was testing the ground, searching for his feelings.

'No. It's not enough. I've thought of you constantly since we met,' he said. 'Have your nightmares stopped?'

'I haven't had one since we were in the hospital kitchen, when you were so kind.'

'I was greatly affected by what you told me, by the fact you told me, and no one else.'

'Sometimes we have no control over these things. They happen when they are meant to . . .'

They were quiet again, studying each other's face, and the kitchen was silent apart from the whistling of the kettle.

'I should make the coffee,' she said at last, but didn't move.

'Let them wait.'

He reached out and touched her hair gently. 'One day I would like a lock of your hair.'

Before she spoke they heard the front door open and someone enter. Giuseppe took a step back and Fiona moved to the stove. A few moments later her parents appeared.

'Hello,' said Fiona, pouring water into the mugs. 'I didn't know you would be back so soon. This is Mr Palumbi, who is one of the men helping to repair the fence. This is my father and mother.'

'Mr Palumbi. We are very grateful for your help,' said her father.

'I am pleased to meet you, sir,' said Giuseppe respectfully, taking the offered hand. He faced Fiona's mother and very formally said. 'I am pleased to meet you ma'am.' This sent Fiona's mother into peals of laughter.

'Goodness me, you can call me Margaret like everyone else.'

She was a small woman but when she shook Giuseppe's hand he felt the strength in her arm and he sensed a steely character; a person not to be deflected in the course she set, even by the fiercest of Orkney winds. Giuseppe was greatly touched. He had known many abuses and hardships over the last few years but the recent contact with local Orkney people had changed his mind about what he imagined people thought of him as a man and as an Italian.

'Come on, Mr Palumbi,' said Fiona, who had now filled the mugs. 'You can help carry these outside then I must leave for the hospital. I'm on a late shift today.' But before they left the kitchen she deliberately set the scene for the next day. 'When the men come back tomorrow father, Mr Palumbi is going to play his banjo for us.'

'Is he?' said her father, as thrilled as Giuseppe was surprised. 'Well, in that case you must all have tea with us in the afternoon, after you've finished your work.'

So the next day, six Italian POWs, who had spent the previous evening having their hair cut, polishing shoes and cleaning uniforms, sat around with the greatest politeness in the living room of Fiona's parents' house. They were even more delighted when joined by Rebecca, who at seventeen was quite stunning and wasn't going to miss the event for anything.

The only person who looked uncomfortable was the guard. He had recently arrived in Camp 60. A new ruling meant guards were changed every six months, but this man knew the regulations and their little afternoon break in someone's house was strictly against the rules. He told Giuseppe he would only allow it if the men agreed they would not mention the visit to anyone.

Certainly, none of the men had argued with this point. They sat and talked, Giuseppe translating back and forth, about the farm and the camp. The Italians spoke with great excitement about the chapel that was to be built.

Giuseppe later took out his banjo and one of the other men entertained them with his commanding baritone voice. It was an afternoon they never forgot. When the Italians returned to the camp they felt elated yet subdued at the same time. They had been treated as equals and friends, which affected them all deeply. Giuseppe, in particular, was quiet. It had been a marvellous experience but he had not managed to get any time alone with Fiona and they only had one more day's work on the farm before they would be working once more on the causeways.

However, the next day Fiona walked up to the men when they were clearing one of the ditches and said she needed someone to help her move some things in the barn. Only Giuseppe and the guard knew what she had said and Giuseppe was out of the ditch before the guard could respond.

'Do you really need help to move something?' asked Giuseppe when they were in the barn. It was silent. Even the cattle were back out in the field.

'I don't know what we're going to do,' she responded. 'I've never been in this situation before. I'm not a silly young girl. And yet here we are . . . two adults hiding in a barn.'

'Fiona, there is something I must tell you.'

'I know . . . you're married.'

'You know?'

'I guessed. You don't talk about certain parts of your life in Italy.'

'I'm sorry.'

'Don't be. You shouldn't be sorry for getting married and

I'm not sorry for how I feel. There can never be shame in loving someone. But what can we do about it?'

Giuseppe took her hand, led her to a bale of hay where they could sit out of sight, and then told her about his life in Italy with his wife Pierina and son Renato. He told her about why he joined the army and how he had been captured in Bardia along with thousands of other Italians, moved around various prisoner of war camps until finally ending up in Orkney.

'There you have it. And in a few hours we'll have finished our work here and I will return to the camp, with no reason to come back . . . other than my feelings, and I don't think the major will think that a good enough excuse.'

She leaned over and kissed him. It wasn't a passionate kiss but it was one to be remembered by. And Giuseppe would remember it.

'You must go back to the others,' she said. 'Fate may yet play its hand for us.'

They stood up and walked slowly towards the entrance but before they reached it Fiona spoke again.

'Giuseppe, there is one thing more I wanted to say. Yesterday, the men were talking about building a chapel.'

'The chapel? That's right.'

'Go and offer to help.'

'Help build the chapel? Why do you suggest that?'

She put her hand on his chest, above his heart.

'Because I think it will help to ease a troubled soul.'

She smiled at him. She was half joking and half serious but, as Giuseppe thought afterwards, inevitably right.

Towards the middle of December, Domenico and his men moved the second Nissen hut, this time without incident. Corrugated iron was fixed over the join of the huts and the two ends of the structure were cemented to the brick walls to make a watertight building. Each end wall had been built with a doorway because Domenico had already decided that the eastern door would be Padre Giacomo's entry into the vestry, which would have an internal door leading into the chancel. The western end of the building, which faced into the camp, would be the main entrance.

A few days before Christmas, Domenico and Buttapasta found themselves in the new, enlarged Nissen hut, along with Aldo and Micheloni. They had just returned from a day of unloading bags of cement from a barge. Their backs and shoulders ached with the effort and their hair was covered in fine grey powder. The two doors from the original huts had been fitted the previous evening by a couple of the carpenters, so the four men had gone to view the building now that the structure was essentially complete. A weak light filtered in through the two windows that were situated each side of the building. It was a cold, echoing, empty space. Buttapasta and Domenico went around checking joints and brickwork in minute detail, but Aldo stood in the centre looking rather disappointed.

'It's an empty hut,' he said at last, rather ungraciously.

Domenico and Buttapasta, who had spent so much time and hard work just to get the two huts to this one spot, were not pleased at the observation.

'What did you expect Aldo?' said Domenico. 'Did you think we had a self-erecting chapel? That all we had to do was assemble the parts and it would be ready for prayers?'

'All I can see is another bloody freezing cold hut.'

This was too much even for the placid Domenico, who suddenly grabbed Aldo by the shoulders.

'Sometimes you must see with your heart, Aldo. Making money is not what life is about.'

Aldo was quite taken aback by this uncharacteristic show of

anger and he felt a mixture of regret and resentment at his comment.

The two friends stood facing each other, both angry and sorry in equal measure. The atmosphere had become very uncomfortable. Domenico, realising he was still holding Aldo by the shoulders, let his arms drop with a sigh.

'Aldo does have a point, Domenico,' said Buttapasta. 'To convert this hut into a chapel will be a mammoth task. I'll help all I can, but my skill is really only with stone and cement.'

Domenico looked at Buttapasta in silence and the big man wished he had not spoken. In the end it was Micheloni who broke the stalemate.

'I've been speaking to De Vitto,' he said to no one in particular. 'You know we were both electricians before the war. We wondered if our skills could be used. We were thinking that if we run power from the nearest hut there would be light to work by and also light for the chapel when it is completed, so men could pray at any time of the day or night.'

It was such a simple observation. Domenico was greatly touched by the offer and by these men, who had been quietly working out ways to help without making a fuss.

'Your skills would indeed be most welcome. Thank you,' said Domenico, his anger of moments ago totally forgotten.

'There is almost every skill imaginable in the camp, including some you certainly wouldn't desire for a chapel, but the problem is not men . . . it's materials,' said Buttapasta.

Domenico didn't quite know what to think. It had taken so much planning and effort just to get where they were that part of him felt they should celebrate, even for a few minutes, what they had achieved. Aldo lacked the vision to see they could create something great from elements that were not individually great.

'I know,' said Domenico. 'It's something that has been on my mind. But now we have a building and can move forward from there.'

'I'm sure God will show us the way,' said Aldo sarcastically. Domenico turned around to face him, but before he could speak the door opened and an Italian entered. He looked around at the four men inside.

'Domenico Chiocchetti?'

'That's me,' replied Domenico.

'I'm Giuseppe Palumbi. Everyone is talking about your chapel. I wondered if I could help. Before the war I was an iron worker.'

'A blacksmith. I'm sure your talents could be put to very good use,' said Domenico, shaking Giuseppe's hand warmly.

'We were just saying the biggest problem facing us will be finding the right materials,' said Buttapasta. 'At the moment what we have is an empty hut and an endless supply of cement. With the best will in the world, not everything can be made of that.'

'You should try the blockships,' said Giuseppe.

'The blockships?' queried Domenico.

'When the British scuttled the ships to block the channels between the islands, they didn't bother stripping much out. At low tide you can get below decks, though not to the lower ones. There are all sorts of materials down there; iron, brass, glass, ceramic tiles and good quality wood. You just have to find a way to remove it and get it out before the tide returns.'

Blockships! Domenico and Buttapasta looked at each other. Why hadn't they considered them before? It suddenly felt they had been shown the way forward.

'Your gift is most welcome. Both of them,' said Domenico, his face breaking into a huge grin.

Buttapasta held out his hand to Giuseppe, who was smiling with surprise that his information had been so useful.

'Welcome to the team.'

16

The days rolled by and, one cold but clear Sunday morning in January 1944, Aldo appeared at the 'chapel' on a bicycle that looked as though it had been made before the First World War. The huge basket at the front contained three rucksacks. Domenico was working outside with Esposito and Sforza, who had been carpenters before being called up. Their carpentry days seemed as though they belonged to another life and the men were glad to have the feel of wood between their fingers once more.

'Domenico. What are you doing?' asked Aldo, stopping several yards away so he had to raise his voice. He was in 'wheeler-dealer' mode, full of chat; the whole world his friend.

'Hey, Aldo. We're building a frame to fit to the inside walls of the hut at the far end, where the chancel will be situated. The idea is to prevent any damp that may come through the corrugated iron affecting the plasterboard. Where are you off to?'

'The men have been busy and have a lot they want to sell. There are all sorts of appealing trinkets. Why don't you have a look? You might see something you want. I'll do you a good deal.'

'I'll leave that for the locals,' said Domenico smiling.

'I've even got a ship in a bottle. Do you know how they do that?'

'I've an idea.'

'Ha! I thought you might. Anyway I'm off to the mainland. You and Buttapasta say I should get more exercise . . . I just hope this monster doesn't kill me along the way. Did you know, some of the men want to donate their takings to the chapel? They're talking of creating a chapel fund to help buy the things you need.'

Domenico was taken aback. He hadn't heard this news and wanted to know more, but Aldo was already wobbling towards the gate. He would have to curb his curiosity until later.

'You be careful of those pretty girls,' he shouted after the retreating figure.

Aldo called back without turning around, 'Why do you think I suggested they make necklaces?'

Domenico stood for several moments watching man and bicycle disappear down the road. He still believed there was a different Aldo hidden behind armour-plated cynicism. The artist shook his head and turned back to the task in hand.

The exact status of the Italians was still confused but Aldo had obtained a permit that allowed him to travel a short distance from the camp on a Sunday, and he quickly reached the causeway leading to mainland Orkney. All of the causeways were now passable on foot, though there was much work to be done to make them suitable for vehicles.

Dividing the sea had resulted in a strange calmness to the water, which no longer raged through the channel. While there had still been gaps between the bolsters and concrete blocks, or sections over the top that water could pass, the tide would surge with a terrible force, trying to squeeze a huge volume of water through a few small areas whereas before it had the entire channel. It was frightening to see and hear. But once the gaps had been filled and the height of the causeway lifted sufficiently, the sea rose and fell quite calmly, trickling gently back and forth unseen beneath the surface.

Aldo looked along the causeway for a while before setting off. A narrow-gauge railway line had been laid temporarily along part of it, in order to transport ten-ton concrete blocks to an electric crane. The crane positioned the blocks to a carefully worked out pattern, and as it gradually moved along the causeway, more track was laid so the train could continue to supply it.

He reached the other side with nothing more than a wet trouser leg, and continued past the Rockworks block-yard and the entrance to the Balfour Beatty offices. He had no great plan other than to knock on doors and show the work that had been produced. The deal with the craftsmen was that he could keep fifteen per cent of anything sold, which was a big incentive. It wasn't long before Aldo pulled up at the first cottage.

When the front door opened his heart almost missed a beat, for the girl who stood before him was not much younger than himself and was as beautiful a vision as he had ever seen. Twenty minutes later the girl stood in the doorway wearing a pale blue necklace and Aldo had a shilling in his pocket. Aldo could have done the transaction in less than half the time but couldn't bring himself to rush the sale.

Aldo was not an imposing figure, but his delicate features and cheeky smile made him very appealing to women.

'You were the most beautiful girl on the island but now you're a queen,' he said. 'Anything you want, you ask for Aldo at Camp 60.'

The gradient of the path meant he was quickly opening up a gap between himself and the cottage.

'Don't forget, you are beautiful and I am Aldo Tolino,' he shouted.

He wasn't sure if she could hear. It didn't matter. He had made his first sale of the day, the weather was good, he was out of the camp and he was happy. The girl fingered the blue necklace and watched the attractive young Italian ride down the path.

Three hours later Aldo was heading up a hill towards a cottage he had spotted a while earlier. He had sold everything apart from one item but his basket was far from empty. In addition to buying his wares, many people had thrust food into his hands. He felt both elated at the successful afternoon and slightly humbled by the friendliness of the locals.

He now had quite an abundance of home-made items in his rucksacks, including a freshly made loaf, two jars of jam and something an elderly lady had called 'bannocks'. She had repeated the word, each time a little louder as if he was hard of hearing. In the end he had stood there, smiling gratefully, but with no idea what he was holding within the well wrapped paper, while she shouted 'Bannocks! Bannocks!'

As he approached the cottage on the hill he could see an old man sitting by the front door, smoking a long clay pipe, a picture of complete countryside contentment.

'Ship in the bottle,' muttered Aldo to himself. 'That's what you want my old friend, the ship in the bottle.'

The old man removed the pipe, his face breaking into a huge toothless grin. He held a hand to one ear, so Aldo spoke loudly.

'It's a beautiful day.'

The man nodded enthusiastically and started to speak, but with such a strong accent that Aldo had no idea what he was saying.

119

'You have a lovely cottage and I have only one thing left of all the skilfully-made items brought from the camp today, but it is the best of the lot.'

Aldo opened one of the rucksacks and launched into his selling mode.

'Several people have expressed great interest in this exquisite item, but I have refused to sell it until I believed it was going to the right home.'

With a flourish Aldo pulled out the ship in the bottle.

The old man stood up, walked over and took hold of the bottle, which he examined closely. He suddenly jabbered excitedly, accompanied by a big toothless smile and much nodding.

'Yes,' replied Aldo. 'I'm glad you agree. And I will do you a special price. Only four shillings.'

The man looked delighted and suddenly walked back to the house, clutching the bottle in one hand and his pipe in the other. Aldo was caught off guard and by the time he followed, his latest customer had entered the building and closed the front door. Aldo stood there, rather at a loss.

After several minutes Aldo started muttering to himself.

'How can it be taking him so long? He must have his money buried under the floorboards. I've heard old people do that sort of thing.'

Finally the door opened and the man stood in the entrance with a live chicken in his hands. He had tied the legs together and thrust the bird upside down at Aldo, who grabbed it without thinking.

'No, no. You don't understand. Not a chicken. Four shillings. Four shillings!'

The old man nodded twice, waved as if they were best friends parting, and stepped quickly back, closing the door firmly. Aldo looked down at the flapping bird with growing horror, not quite sure how things had gone so horribly wrong.

Later that evening Aldo was on his bed, his face a mask of righteous indignation. Domenico, sitting opposite, rocked back and forth, his laughter filling the hut so that men looked on bemused.

'It's no laughing matter, Domenico,' hissed Aldo, wishing his friend would not draw attention to them. He had already spotted Dino and Carlo looking over from their card game. 'I had to pay Giovannini out of my own pocket. I couldn't give him eight-five per cent of a chicken. I have my reputation to think of. It cost me nearly four shillings. But you should be happy because he donated the money to the chapel fund.'

'Aldo,' said Domenico, wiping away a tear, 'that's the best laugh I've had in a long time. I think that old man was a lot wiser than he made out. But what did you do with the chicken?'

Aldo looked suddenly sheepish and did not answer.

'Is it in the cooking pot already?'

Aldo pulled a rucksack from under his bed and carefully opened the flap. A chicken's head popped out and looked up at Domenico who, for a moment, couldn't quite believe what he was seeing. The creature and the man stared at each other and it was difficult to say which wore the most startled expression. It was all too much for Domenico and what composure he had gained was suddenly lost as he slapped his thigh in delight. Rolling peals of laughter echoed around the corrugated iron walls and made men smile.

'I knew you would react like this,' said Aldo in a forced whisper. 'You mustn't tell anyone. They'll all think I've gone soft in the head. But I couldn't bring myself to kill it. I thought perhaps I could keep it for eggs. Fresh eggs. Just think. Everyone will want fresh eggs.'

With great tenderness Aldo pushed the chicken's head back

down, closed the flap and pushed the bag under his bed. Domenico was wiping tears from both eyes.

'Oh Aldo, there's hope for you yet. However, I must admit, although I thought eventually a bird may soften your heart . . . I didn't think it would be a chicken!'

Aldo sat in silence until Domenico had finished. It took a long time.

'Well, I would like to know what you would've done,' he said petulantly. 'Anyway, what are those papers?' He attempted to change the subject, indicating with his head several large sheets spread on Domenico's bed.

'I'm working on designs for the chapel.'

Domenico had been busy and there was a series of drawings showing objects at different angles, such as the altar, tabernacle and holy water stoup, each with measurements written neatly by the side. There were various sketches of how the plasterboard could be painted to imitate stonework, with areas left blank for paintings. There were diagrams of the Nissen hut showing the position of the windows and with the floor area marked out to scale for the vestry, chancel and the school. It represented a vast amount of planning and thought.

'Well, you may have a cruel sense of humour but you certainly have a skill for drawing,' said Aldo, looking through the papers. 'Are you going to design all of it?'

'These are just roughs. I'm trying to create a master design to which other plans can be fashioned. But yes, I think you can only have one designer for a project like this or it will be a case of too many cooks. We ran out of wood before we had finished the frame, so work has stopped for now. However, the bigger problem will be sourcing plasterboard.'

'How do you plan to get that? You won't find plasterboard on any blockship.'

'I'm going to ask Padre Giacomo if he will speak to Major Buckland. See if he can help.'

'I think the war will be over before your chapel is built.'

'That may be. But men working on the chapel have already developed a bond that goes beyond that of the football team or the music groups.'

'Your higher purpose?'

'Not mine, Aldo.'

Aldo sighed and handed back the papers.

'It'll be lights out soon.'

'Yes, you're right,' replied Domenico, putting the sheets into order. 'I have a feeling it's going to be a long day tomorrow.'

17

Aldo was up the next morning even before it was properly light, making a rough chicken coop just outside the hut, using some of the wood pile as a windbreak. He had heard that, years earlier, a fierce storm had blown tens of thousands of chickens out to sea, along with many coops. He looked nervously at the sky.

When he had more time he would make a proper coop, or at least would ask one of the carpenters to help. Most likely, he would pay the man in cigarettes to do the whole job. Aldo wasn't quite sure what chickens ate but thought Dino would know. He looked down with affection at the chicken then hurried off to wash before breakfast.

That morning there was an unexpected incident in the mess hall when a large number of men refused to leave until they had been given more information about their status following Italy's capitulation. Although they had unofficially been granted more freedom, this was more to do with being on an island than a change in their position as POWs.

Their frustration boiled over in a mini revolt, catching many Italians by surprise, and it took all of Major Buckland's powers of persuasion to get everyone to start that day's work. However, Major Buckland had no answers and feelings of resentment continued.

Later that week, Aldo and Buttapasta could be found unloading bags of cement from a barge. The Lamb Holm block-making yard used the grey powder at a phenomenal rate. There were four other yards, two on Burray and two on mainland Orkney, and between them they produced around 300 five-ton blocks every day. It was a colossal output. Fortunately, the contractors had discovered that seawater could be used success-fully in the process, as fresh water had to be pumped over from mainland Orkney.

There were about thirty Italians involved in the task of unloading the barge that particular morning, carrying one bag at a time and loading it on to a truck, which would set off when full to be quickly replaced by another. Aldo stumbled along miserably beside Buttapasta, who seemed completely unaffected by the weight on his shoulder and broke into little bouts of whistling, much to Aldo's annoyance.

'I suppose you must be in your element,' said Aldo, his bag hugged tightly to his chest.

'In my element?' asked Buttapasta cheerfully.

'Being surrounded by all this cement.'

'Poor Aldo,' said Buttapasta laughing. 'You're not cut out for heavy physical effort, are you? Still, you can watch others work this afternoon, playing football.'

The two men reached the truck and Aldo leant against it to catch his breath.

'That's the one bright thing this week,' he said after a few moments.

'Why is that, my young friend? I didn't know you were such a fan of the game.'

'I'm not, but I've been organising bets on the outcome of the match. The locals and the Balfour Beatty men believe the Argyll and Sutherland Highlanders team will win but, of course, they haven't seen our boys play,' said Aldo, moving to one side because someone wanted to deposit their load. 'I've been watching them practise.'

'They're good, I'll give you that, but I hope you're not going to lose all that money you've spent so long making.' Aldo grinned but did not reply. 'Come on,' said Buttapasta, leading the way back to the pier.

The Orkney weather was kind to the footballers and the afternoon was bright with only a light breeze. The pitch, set up in a field nearby, was surrounded by hundreds of excited spectators, made up of men from the Italian and Balfour Beatty camps plus civilians and Orkney families. There was a loud-speaker system and the commentator, a British corporal, was positioned on a small stand where he could see everything clearly.

'We are delighted today to welcome a team from the Argyll and Sutherland Highlanders, who will be playing an Italian team from Camp 60,' said the commentator, his voice crackling over the speakers.

The players entered the pitch to enthusiastic applause and started to run around, kicking balls between themselves to warm up. Eventually, the two teams settled down and the respective captains joined the referee in the middle of the pitch. Hundreds of pairs of eyes watched the small coin as it travelled through the air, as if they could alter the outcome by staring at it. The referee and the two captains looked down at the ground, the men shook hands and the Argyll and Sutherland Highlanders team kicked off.

*   *   *

There could hardly have been a greater contrast between the noise and tension at the football match and the stillness of the chapel, where Domenico worked quietly. More wood had been found and the framework lining the walls had been completed. Domenico was now putting together the frame for the internal stud wall, which would separate the vestry from the chancel. The door at the end of the hut opened and Padre Giacomo entered.

'Domenico. I wondered if you might be here. Not interested in the match?'

'Oh, I don't mind it. But the chance to have a few hours of complete quiet is very appealing.'

'I understand. Not an opportunity to be missed. I'm sorry to disturb your peace. I see you've nearly finished the framework,' said Padre Giacomo.

'With help from others.'

'And I have some news . . .'

'The plasterboard?' asked Domenico hopefully.

'It should be here next week.'

'That's excellent, Padre. Thank you for your help and please thank Major Buckland for me.'

'He's certainly behind the idea. We are lucky to have him as camp commander.'

A comfortable silence ensued. Padre Giacomo studied the building with interest, though there was little to look at. He was carrying the small satchel that had seemed to be by his side ever since he had arrived at Camp 60.

'I have something I'm not quite sure what to do with and yet my heart tells me it should somehow be part of the chapel. I would appreciate your thoughts, Domenico.'

The priest opened his satchel and took out a tightly rolled-up cloth. When he untied the string and unfolded it, Domenico whistled at the sight of a large Italian flag.

'You brought that from Italy, Padre?' he asked, both astounded and impressed.

'When I was captured I was tending to sick and injured men who had been left behind in a field hospital attached to a camp in Soddu. When the British were virtually at the gates I sent a man to save the camp flag and I was able to stuff it into my satchel without anyone seeing. One of the steadfast characteristics of the British is they are always reluctant to search a priest, even one belonging to the enemy.'

'You want it in the chapel?'

'I thought I would hang it in the vestry when it's finished.'

'A little piece of Italy on foreign soil,' said Domenico.

The priest rolled up the material and put it back into the satchel, replacing his Bible on top.

'I hear the men have started a chapel fund?' said Padre Giacomo.

'Yes, I was greatly moved to learn of that, padre. A percentage of everything spent in the canteen shop is also being set aside for the chapel fund. The money will be essential to acquire the things we cannot make.'

The two men chatted contentedly about their favourite subject, bouncing ideas off each other. They both had a detailed knowledge of religious icons and knew what could be achieved ... with the right materials.

By the time the whistle blew to indicate the start of the second half of the football match, it was clear to everyone that the Argyll and Sutherland Highlanders team were outclassed. The commentator had been almost beside himself with excitement from the first kick of the ball and his chatter had been continuous.

The crowd were hoarse from screaming but as one of the

Italians dribbled his way skilfully past several defenders the noise became deafening. As he popped the ball, with apparent ease, into the back of the net the spectators could be forgiven for thinking the corporal with the microphone was Italian.

'It's a goal! It's a goal!' he screamed.

By the time the referee blew the whistle for the end of the match the Italians had won 4–1.

The following week, Domenico, Aldo and Buttapasta were travelling together on one of the railway wagons that transported cured concrete blocks from the block-making yard to the start of barrier number two.

'Don't you wish this train was going all the way to Italy?' said Aldo.

'Now there's a nice thought . . . to step off the train on to good Italian soil and drink good Italian wine,' said Buttapasta.

'Meet good Italian women,' added Aldo.

'Perhaps one day soon. What do you think, Domenico?'

Aldo spoke before Domenico could answer.

'I think he wants to stay here so that he can build his chapel.'

'Yes and no,' said Domenico, thoughtfully. 'I am only here because the war is continuing, which is a terrible reason. And I want to get home like everyone else. Yet while there is a war, and we are stuck on this island, I can think of no better use for a man's time than to work on the chapel. But you'll be a rich man when you finally return Aldo.'

'Yes,' said Buttapasta, 'just how much money did you make from gambling on the outcome of the football match?'

Aldo smiled his boyish grin.

'Don't you know it's coarse to discuss money? That's your trouble, Buttapasta, you're not refined like me. I reckon it comes from spending too many years with cement.'

'You shouldn't mock a man's vocation.' Buttapasta suddenly grabbed Aldo and started to move him towards the edge of the train. Aldo was completely powerless to stop him and hung on to Buttapasta's jacket.

'No. I like cement, honestly. Some of my closest friends are made of cement.'

As the train trundled along its journey, those standing on wagons further down the line could see a large man holding someone over the edge and hear the increasingly frantic shouts of the smaller figure.

The train slowed down as it neared the barrier and blew its whistle in three sharp bursts. Men jumped off even before it had completely stopped and quickly gathered in small groups. A Balfour Beatty man walked up to them.

'I need four men to go to the workshop and the rest of you can follow me,' he bellowed above the noise around him.

Aldo was near the back and as soon as the Balfour Beatty man turned around he quietly slipped away in the other direction. Moments later he entered a building that housed a huge diesel generator.

He stood just inside the door and looked around for the man he needed. It wasn't long before the very person he was looking for appeared from behind some of the equipment. Bill Johnstone was responsible for running the power station and although his home was on mainland Orkney he lived on Lamb Holm during the week.

'Mr Bill,' shouted Aldo.

'Hello, Aldo. How are you today?' said the man, walking over.

'I'm okay thank you. I hope you and Mrs Bill are well?'

'Oh aye, we've nothing to complain about.'

'I wondered if . . .' Aldo hesitated, but he pulled a small bottle out of his pocket nonetheless.

'Yes, I know what you're after, another bottle of switch oil. What the devil do you do with it, Aldo?'

'Well, you know Mr Bill, we Italians like to grease our hair. It's part of our culture. And your pure oil is the best thing we can get on the island.'

The man looked at Aldo with a surprised expression for a moment. He liked the young Italian, who often stuck his head in the door for a few moments to chat and sometimes to ask for oil.

'Well, it's not something I have a need for,' he said patting his own head. 'Come on, lad, give me your bottle then you had better get going or you'll be in trouble for being in here and not where you should be.'

That afternoon Buttapasta, Domenico and Aldo were walking back to camp with about a dozen other men. The weather had turned overcast and as they approached the camp entrance the rain that had threatened to fall for the last hour began to come down in large, slow drops. The men, heads down, quickened their pace for they knew this heralded a downpour. It was Buttapasta who shouted the warning.

'Domenico! The plasterboard has been delivered and it's about to get a soaking.'

Horrified, Domenico suddenly shot up the path.

'Come on everyone,' shouted Buttapasta setting off after his friend.

Then they were all running, a couple of younger men overtaking the artist in the frantic dash to reach the precious material and save it from being ruined. The rain was falling faster every second. It took two men to lift each board and so pairs of men started to carry them into the hut as quickly as they could. Suddenly it became a race against the rain and each other, so that men were slipping, laughing and calling out and all the while rushing backwards and forwards. Buttapasta and Domenico positioned themselves inside to ensure nothing was damaged by anyone not taking sufficient care. Aldo entered, carrying the end of a large board.

'How come you two get to stay in the dry?' he complained.

'That's the difference between skilled and unskilled workers,' said Buttapasta.

It took only a few minutes to get all the plasterboard stacked safely. The men stood around out of breath, grinning at each other, while the rain pounded down on the roof.

'Another five minutes and your plasterboard would have been a soggy heap,' said Dino to Domenico.

'It was a close thing,' agreed the artist, who had been considering that very possibility.

'I think this deserves a celebration and the drinks are on Aldo,' said Carlo who knew that Dino, although Aldo's partner in the business, preferred to create things rather than make money and wouldn't be upset at his suggestion.

'Why me?' asked Aldo aghast.

'Because we happen to know you've just completed distilling your latest batch of spirit,' came another voice from the increasing gloom within the hut.

'That may be true, but it's not easy getting hold of the right ingredients. I don't just find them under my bed.'

'We know what's been under your bed,' said another man, who started to imitate a chicken. The others joined in, flapping their arms by their sides. Everyone roared at the sight and Aldo had to shout his protests to be heard.

'Oh very funny. Very funny. It was only for one night. Only one night!'

'Fancy Aldo having a bird under his bed,' said the man. 'It's an odd way to keep your pecker up!'

'Aldo's distillery,' shouted another voice. The cry was quickly taken up as several men grabbed Aldo and lifted him high in the air.

'Put me down. Don't think you're getting a drink for free,' cried Aldo desperately.

Despite his protests they carried him outside into the pouring rain and, with most of them making loud clucking noises, set off as fast as they could for the kitchen where they knew Aldo hid his supply.

'Mind my oil,' was the last thing Domenico and Buttapasta, standing in the doorway, heard from the struggling figure as the group of men ran into the falling darkness. They were both laughing loudly.

'Poor Aldo. I don't think he's going to win that argument,' said Buttapasta.

'I worry about Aldo's spirit.'

'I know, Domenico. But he's young. And I think he'll be alright.'

The hut was noisy that evening, partly because it included some of the men who had carried Aldo off earlier. Domenico sat on his bed, trying to block out the babble, writing to Maria.

My dearest Maria,

I pray daily that you and all the family are well and safe from harm. I am in good health, though of course missing you and everyone at home. I pray for the day when I can return and we can have a normal life together. Work on the little chapel continues slowly but steadily. Everyone is so eager to help but we can only progress when we obtain materials.

Thank you for the socks and the cream for my hands. Can
you send more cream? I've shared it with the others and it
has all gone. Also, could you send more woollen gloves? I put
them on under my working pair but they still wear out with
the hard work. Life in the camp is otherwise the same as ever.
We are treated well.

Aldo is sulking behind a copy of Il Corriere del Prigioniero *because the men drank his entire stock of spirit without*
paying and now several of them are quite drunk. Across the
hut, on the other side of the stove, Dino is singing to a ferret!
No, I have not been drinking! He struck up a friendship with
a local farmer who delivers vegetables to the camp's kitchen
and the man keeps ferrets. He smuggled one in to show Dino,
who immediately fell in love with the little creature.

He's named it 'Churchill' and keeps it in a cage at the end
of the next hut. He can't use this one because Aldo has made
his chicken coop here. Dino has arranged with the farmer to
use the ferret to hunt rabbits as long as the farmer can have
the skins. Dino loves animals but he is not so sentimental he
would turn down the chance to improve the men's food. Carlo
is much less sure about this development. I think he is wary
of the sharp teeth and I can't blame him. One of the British
sergeants complained that the camp is turning into a zoo, but
I think he was only joking.

Domenico stopped for a moment and looked over at Dino
singing to the ferret, which he held in his arms. Carlo was
sitting well back on his bed. He had a small pile of cigarettes
on a wooden board and was slicing them lengthways with a
razorblade. Every man in the camp received a weekly ration
of thirty-five cigarettes and it was a common pastime amongst
the smokers to cut them and rearrange the tobacco to make it

go further. The scene was so amusing that he quickly sketched the image on the paper then began writing again.

There, when you receive this letter you will see what I am looking at now. As you know there are many things I cannot talk about because it will be cut out by the people who read our mail. The British tell us their letters are also opened and read. We are all in the same position. People are not even allowed to mention the weather, even though it seems to be the main topic of conversation for everyone.

Domenico looked up. Everyone had fallen silent. All except Dino, who up until that point had been trying odd snatches of different songs to see how the ferret reacted. He put the animal on top of his mattress and started to sing De Crescenzo's 'Rondine al Nido'. A few beds away Sergeant Primavera picked up a violin and the passion that emanated from them was like a physical force that filled every corner of the hut.

When the last note died away everyone remained silent. It went far beyond a performance.

Eventually, Dino picked up the little animal and walked from the hut and only when he closed the door was the spell broken. Even then, no one made a sound. When Domenico finally looked down at his letter he saw the drawing he had done was smudged, because tears had fallen down his cheeks and dropped on to the paper.

18

Domenico, Esposito and Sforza were fixing sheets of plasterboard to the wooden frame that had been constructed in the chancel, when the door opened. Padre Giacomo and Sergeant Major Fornasier entered.

Domenico stopped work to greet the new arrivals.

'Domenico,' said Sergeant Major Fornasier. 'I trust everything is going to plan?'

'Yes, thank you, sir.'

'I see your helpers are getting on well,' said Sergeant Major Fornasier.

There was a relaxed atmosphere in the camp regarding rank. Sergeant Major Fornasier was only twenty-eight, but he was both liked and respected by his men and the British officers, with whom he was in constant liaison.

'What will be the next stage, once the plasterboard is fixed?' he asked.

'Well, once we've taped the edges to create a smooth surface then we can start painting the chancel.'

'A task that falls on your shoulders,' said Padre Giacomo.

'Which means it will be slow work I'm afraid,' said Domenico.

In addition to Buttapasta and Giuseppe there was a small army of skilled men – bricklayers, carpenters, electricians – but Domenico was the one artist. Only he had the skill to paint the chancel.

'Perhaps I could speak to Major Buckland about relieving you from working on the causeways?' suggested Sergeant Major Fornasier. 'That way you could concentrate all your efforts on the chapel.'

'That would certainly make a huge difference, sir,' said Domenico, who was taken aback at the suggestion.

'Leave it with me. One less man working on the causeways is hardly going to make any difference to their completion.'

'Thank you, sir. While you're here I would value both of your opinions on the designs I have created,' said Domenico, moving the small table into the centre of the room. 'This is the overall design for the chancel,' he said, pointing at the top sheet.

The priest had been intimately involved in the chapel's design but Sergeant Major Fornasier spent several minutes studying the drawings.

'This is excellent. Are these curtains?' he asked.

'One to hide the door into the vestry and a similar curtain on the other side of the altar to create balance, although there'll be nothing behind that one except the wall. The curtains are something I know we can't make in the camp.'

'I'm going to speak to Major Booth and see if he can help us track down a firm to supply them,' said the priest.

'And these openings here?'

'Windows, sir. At least the glass shouldn't be too difficult to obtain. I've got one of the men helping. On the left, I'm going to paint St Catherine of Siena and on the right, St Francis of Assisi. Padre Giacomo and I each chose a figure. Micheloni and De Vitto are going to position lights in the vestry so that anyone standing in the chancel will see the images on the glass lit up from behind. At least, that's the plan. I've produced designs for the altar, altar rail and holy water stoup. I was hoping to make them out of clay then create a mould in plaster into which I could pour concrete, but it might be difficult getting the clay. There isn't any on Lamb Holm.'

'Let me see if I can help,' said Sergeant Major Fornasier.

'What are these drawings here?' said Padre Giacomo, who had picked up another sheet and spotted something he hadn't seen before.

'Designs for candelabra.'

'You're not making those as well?' asked Padre Giacomo.

'No, Padre.'

'Many months of work yet?' suggested Sergeant Major Fornasier.

'It's impossible to predict just how many, sir,' said Domenico. 'Of course, everything might change depending on what materials we can get hold of. We're hoping to get some of it from the blockships.'

'The blockships?' said Sergeant Major Fornasier thoughtfully. 'I don't believe we have any divers amongst the men.'

'We'll take out only what can be brought up safely at low tide, sir.'

'Make sure the men don't put themselves at risk.'

'Yes, sir.'

The following week Sergeant Primavera found himself being led along the deck of a blockship by Carlo and Dino, who were renowned for their practical jokes. They had insisted they had found something that would interest him greatly but had declined, politely, to say what it was. And so he followed the two cousins through a hatch and down a ladder, where Dino switched on a large torch.

The three men descended another ladder and Carlo lit two lanterns he had picked up on the deck of the ship. The lanterns were always kept dry in a cabin for anyone going below decks and were put back in the same place when people left. The men were now standing in a foot of freezing water and Sergeant Primavera's patience was wearing thin. However, he took the lantern offered and followed, their splashing feet echoing noisily.

'A few of the men have been down here looking around in their spare time,' said Carlo leading the way. 'It's easy to get lost so ropes have been fixed as handrails along the corridors. Every so often there's a dash of blue and red paint. If the blue paint is furthest away from you, then you are heading towards the way out. If the blue is nearest then you are walking further into the ship.'

'It's safe enough really,' added Dino. 'If water starts rising up your legs, get out fast.'

'I hope you're not planning to get me lost down here and run off.'

'Sergeant Primavera!' said Dino.

'How could you think such a thing?' asked Carlo.

'Alright, just show me what you've found,' said the sergeant.

The men set off again and after several turns and corridors Carlo suddenly stopped by a set of stairs that went, at a crazy angle, down to another deck below.

'There! What do you think of that, sergeant?' he said, shining the torch at the steps.

Sergeant Primavera was puzzled. The stairs were black with dirt and grime and he wasn't sure if they meant him to go further down.

'What am I looking at?' he asked.

Carlo moved closer to the stairs and, taking a cloth out of his pocket, started to rub a very small patch on the top step.

139

The area had obviously been cleaned recently because the metal of the steps reflected light from the lanterns. Sergeant Primavera leant down, snatched the cloth and rubbed vigorously at the same spot.

'Brass!' he exclaimed.

Dino and Carlo beamed

'Yes, and we heard that Domenico has asked you to make brass candelabra for the chapel,' said Dino.

'Is nothing secret in this place?'

'Of course not, sergeant,' answered the men together.

Sergeant Primavera stood up, pleased.

'Well done, lads. Well done. Will you take two steps out for me?'

'With pleasure, sergeant . . . but not today,' said Carlo. 'It's getting too near to the turn of the tide. We'll get them for you tomorrow.'

Carlo and Dino were removing the two brass steps the following day as Major Buckland and Padre Giacomo walked by on the shore, enjoying what had turned out to be a surprisingly calm afternoon. The two men, who were a similar age, enjoyed each other's company and were in no hurry. For a while they walked in silence looking over at men fishing from the *Lycia*.

It was the responsibility of the British Government to provide clothing for the Italians as well as accommodation, food and other services. Since Italy's capitulation the previous September the new chocolate-coloured uniforms did not incorporate target discs and so the red circles, which had caused so much offence, were no longer seen around the camp.

'Domenico asked me to thank you for helping to find suitable paints and brushes, Major Buckland, without which the chapel could not be created.'

'Oh, it was really down to the generosity of a local artist.

Word about the chapel has got around the islands and generated a great deal of interest. How are Chiocchetti and his men getting on, Padre? I hear a lot of talk about "the chapel" as if it's almost complete, when it's no more than a hut with some plasterboard walls.'

'I think his enthusiasm and belief have inspired those around him. Virtually everyone wants to be involved in something to benefit the soul, rather than the body. Men offer to do even the smallest of tasks, just so they can say they have helped.'

'You have to admire his dedication. Without his drive and skill as an artist . . .' Major Buckland stopped walking. 'What's that man doing there, Padre?' he said, pointing at a man sitting apart from the others. 'Can you make out?'

Padre Giacomo studied the man indicated.

'Ah, I believe one of the locals, the man who runs the power station, has tried to teach him how to make a lobster . . .' Padre Giacomo was stuck for the right word.

'Creel,' said Major Buckland with interest. 'A rope box designed to catch lobsters. Yes, I believe Mr Johnstone is a keen fisherman in his spare time.'

'A creel,' repeated Padre Giacomo. 'That's it. A strange word.'

'Hah, well, he'll have to watch out for his fingers. They're vicious blighters.'

The two men started to walk again.

'So in the meantime will you continue to hold mass in the mess, Padre?' said Major Buckland with a smile.

'It serves the purpose, Major. Although the smell of the previous night's meal is sometimes not so pleasant, it doesn't stop the numbers from growing.'

'We'll have to see what we can do to help Chiocchetti. It's all in his hands.'

'At the moment, it's all in his head,' said the priest.

19

Winter arrived at the end of February, with no feeling for the misery caused to men working in the quarry, trying to transport materials through snow-blocked roads, standing guard or lying in bed at night, separated from the howling wind by two pieces of corrugated iron. It was a bleak time. The news from Italy was of fierce fighting and heavy bombing by the Allies, resulting in the destruction of the sacred Monte Cassino monastery. Men fretted about loved ones more than ever.

New faces appeared, as small groups of Italians arrived on Lamb Holm. Occasionally, a man with a particular skill was sent to work in England, where his talents could be put to more effective use. At the beginning of the month, sixty men had been moved to a camp of the Royal Pioneer Corps near Stromness, where their labour was needed in the local dockyards. Camp 60 had taken on a slightly different feel. There were several empty beds and shorter queues for washing and at meal times.

One of the warmest places in the camp was the vestry, which had been created following the completion of a stud wall. The men had been eager to fit out the little room and, with help from Major Buckland, a desk, cupboard and chairs had been secured. However, the most exciting find was a small stove, which had been obtained by Gordon Nicol. If Padre Giacomo was alone while Domenico and the other men were working in the chapel, he would leave the door open into the chancel to let through some heat.

The vestry provided about the only place in the camp where two men could have a private conversation and it became a small sanctuary and confessional, where troubled men could sit and talk with the priest. It was the place where Padre Giacomo had meetings about the men's welfare with Sergeant Major Fornasier and the camp doctor, the latter having moved his twice-weekly surgery to the vestry. At other times he would read or write letters home, just like the others.

Padre Giacomo had been called up in 1938 and had been in Gondar three years later when his father died. He had been captured not long afterwards and ever since the only contact with his family had been via very infrequent letters. He wrote to his mother back home in Missano, telling her about life in the camp and how the men were building a chapel.

On the evening that Domenico and Giuseppe were alone in the chancel, the stove was cold and they shivered under the naked lightbulbs, which Micheloni and De Vitto had hung from the ceiling.

'Can you do it?' Domenico asked Giuseppe.

'Phew, that's a rood screen and a half,' said Giuseppe eventually, letting out his breath, which instantly misted in the air.

He had spent several minutes studying the various sheets of paper Domenico had handed him. The drawings had been produced in minute detail, with every different section enlarged so that each individual curve and loop could be followed clearly. There was a master design that showed how the different portions fitted together and Domenico had calculated all of the measurements down to the last half inch. The aim was to create a rood screen that separated the chancel from the main body of the hut without obscuring the view of the altar. If it could be made, the rood screen would be a thing of elegance and strength, beauty and permanence.

'What do you think?' asked Domenico.

He appreciated that Giuseppe was working out how the wrought iron could be heated, stretched, twisted and thinned into the myriad of intricate shapes to form the physical embodiment of his sketches. He could almost see the other man beating, turning and hammering the red-hot metal in his mind. He sensed the blacksmith was assessing the practicalities and difficulties, weighing up the sheer amount of work involved for one man, as he himself would have done before commencing on a sculpture or painting. But he was still eager to hear the answer.

'It could be done.'

'Are you willing to do it?' asked Domenico, who knew he could not simply assume the blacksmith would be happy to undertake such a task. Giuseppe didn't answer straight away. He looked at the chancel that Domenico had spent so much time on.

'It will take several months but, yes . . . it will be an honour.'

Sergeant Major Fornasier had spoken to Major Buckland, who had agreed immediately that Domenico could dedicate all his time to the chapel as long as his workload was covered. By the middle of March, he had painted the plasterboard to look like stone work, leaving gaps on the walls where he wanted to add pictures. The two glass windows had been made and fitted to the openings in the stud wall either side of the altar and it was one of these that Domenico was painting when Aldo entered. He had just returned after a shift of laying track, some of which ran so near to the shore it was often damaged during rough storms. Repairing track was an on-going task.

'Of all the Italians in the camp you are the only one who I always know where you will be,' said Aldo. 'And I don't understand how you can work in this temperature.'

Aldo always let everyone know how cold he felt. This day was actually bright, dry and calm. Domenico was standing in the vestry and had left open the door to the outside to provide extra light. He had known it to be far colder in the chapel than it was on that particular afternoon.

'Aldo! What scheme are you working on at the moment?'

'Hey, can't a man come to see a friend without being accused of trying to make money!'

'Sorry,' said Domenico. 'I'm very pleased to see you.'

'Well, I thought I'd see how you were getting on. Check whether you need any guidance or advice,' said Aldo, who had not been in the building for several weeks. 'What are you putting on the glass and why are you painting it from this side?'

'I'm painting St Francis of Assisi.'

'The founder of the Franciscans.'

'At least you know who he is. If I paint his image on this side of the glass and then put black lines on the chancel side, the final result will have depth and look more like leaded glass.'

'And what about these gaps on the walls where there are no stones?'

'Oh, I thought angels might be appropriate, perhaps playing a few instruments. Up here I'm going to paint the symbols of the evangelists, Matthew, Mark, Luke and John. I've got a few other ideas as well.'

'I hope you don't get any knocks to that head of yours and forget all these ideas, or there'll be an awful lot of disappointed people.'

'I'll do my best.'

'What about the materials?'

'I can't say it's not a challenge but we're trying to be inventive. Do you know Sergeant Primavera made a lantern out of a used bully-beef tin? The result was so good I've asked him to make some more. Finding suitable wood for the tabernacle has proved difficult. However, there's a lot to do before that becomes urgent. But how are you, Aldo? It seems you're so busy with your deals and I'm so busy with the chapel we don't get time to speak.'

'Since you ask, I'm cold, I'm sick of the food and I ache from head to foot. I'm tired of spending my nights in a tin hut, listening to the sounds made by forty other men. I want to lay my head on the breasts of a good woman . . . not too good you understand. And my hen has stopped laying.'

'So, the same as normal then,' said Domenico smiling. 'That's good. I wouldn't want to think you're unhappy in any way.'

'I knew I would get no sympathy coming here. I don't know why I bothered. Anyway, there's been a delivery of parcels. It looks like you've got one from Maria. I've put it on your mattress.'

Domenico opened his parcel that evening after supper. It was packed with a variety of items such as chocolate and cigarettes, hand cream, woollen gloves and socks. There were letters from Maria, his parents and two of his sisters, as well as some recent family photographs. Maria had also packed some of his brushes, which she had retrieved from his parents' house where he had lived before the war.

After three years working as a babysitter for a wealthy family in Rome, Maria had managed to get a job in the local grocer's shop so was once more living with her parents in Moena. She had returned just before Domenico had been called up. It all seemed so long ago. He would often close his eyes and try to recall the details of Moena; its people, the smell of bread from the bakery, the sound of the church bell ringing, the feeling of peace, the joy of simply sitting and watching people going about their business in a place where everyone knew each other.

As Domenico read his letters, Dino was excitedly explaining to Carlo about the gift he had created for his sons. For weeks, he had been drawing with even more fervour than normal but refused to show anyone what he was working on. Now it was complete, he sat next to Carlo on the bed and went through it in detail.

'You see,' said Dino, turning the pages, 'it's a book telling the story of how the causeway separates a baby seal from its mother. Every day the mother calls out to the little seal, but the last boulder has been put in place and no matter how much they swim up and down, they can't get back together.'

Carlo studied the images and felt sick.

'Then a group of Italians see the baby seal's plight,' said Dino, showing a drawing of some men looking down into the water.

'Hey, they look suspiciously like us,' said Carlo, forcing a smile. 'Don't tell me . . . we save the seal?'

'You guessed it,' said Dino.

Carlo's insides tightened but he sat patiently for nearly ten minutes while his cousin went through the entire story. It was superbly done and represented an enormous amount of work that would no doubt enthral Dino's children.

'Well . . . what do you think?' asked Dino when he had finished explaining the last page.

'It's brilliant. Andrea and Roberto will love it,' said Carlo then paused for a moment. 'Dino, my friend, you can't post this.'

Dino looked at his cousin and in that one instant realised what a fool he had been. He had been so absorbed in producing the book, in the delight his sons would have even though he would not be there to read the story to them, that he had totally forgotten about the censors. Not a single drawing would be passed because every one of the highly-detailed images contained the causeways, blondins, vessels in Scapa Flow or sentries on the shore.

'The book is excellent, Dino. Put it away safely and you can read it to Andrea and Roberto yourself when you return home,' said Carlo.

'Perhaps, by the time we return home, they will be too old for such a story book.'

Carlo didn't trust himself to answer but instead patted Dino's knee in silence. He was saved from making further conversation by Micheloni shouting that a card game was about to start and their places were already set at the table.

The morale in the camp had been raised significantly by the building of the chapel, which had become a focal point, even though it was far from complete. It was the prisoners' escape, a tunnel to spiritual and cultural freedom, while their bodies remained in captivity. Men often called in to see how it was progressing and Domenico and his team of skilled workers could ask for whatever help they needed.

By April the unfurnished end of the chapel was being used as a school, and Domenico became used to hearing the group of Italians who had taken on the role of tutor. Indeed, many of them had been teachers before the war and the subjects taught were wide ranging. The number of pupils varied according to the topic but there was a lot of enthusiasm for the classes. The English lessons, which had been painful to listen to at the beginning, were always well attended and the improvement had been noticeable. A row of benches were now a permanent feature, along with a blackboard, which had been donated from a primary school in Kirkwall.

Domenico had learnt to block out the sound of the other men and concentrate only on what was before him. He stood in the chancel and looked around him. Much of what he had created had been influenced by the church in his home town, whilst ideas for other parts had come from the many churches he had worked on as a painter of religious statues.

One of the carpenters had fixed wooden panelling along the lower walls of the chancel, which had created a warmer feel. The figures of St Francis of Assisi and St Catherine of Siena flickered as the sun coming through the side windows caught on the glass on which they were depicted. The ceiling had been painted blue with a white dove in the centre.

The most difficult image, the one above the altar, had been left until last. Domenico set out his brushes with infinite care, ensuring they were clean and undamaged. The poster paints donated by a local artist had been used up long ago and Domenico had bought supplies from a shop in Kirkwall, where he had become friendly with the manager, Ernest Marwick. The paints were in small glass jars and from these Domenico could create virtually any colour. He mixed them using an old dinner plate that he had acquired for use as a palette.

He had thought about this painting in great detail, drawing sketches, taking measurements of the space he had to fill, examining the surface in detail by eye and feel so that he knew where there were tiny defects in the plasterboard. As he lay in his bed at night he had painted the image many times in his head, working out the balance of the colours, the effect of the daylight changing throughout the day and how this main image would be influenced by those around it. He had painted the angels on the side walls as though they were lit by the picture he was about to create above the altar.

Now the day had come to make those first brushstrokes. From his jacket pocket Domenico took out the tin in which he kept the little religious card showing the Madonna and Child. He opened it and with tenderness bordering on reverence, kissed the card then placed it against the window, at the feet of St Francis of Assisi. In this position he could view the picture with the least movement of his head.

Domenico knew by heart the text on the other side of the card, which called for men to recognise themselves as brothers, refrain from discord and to love and help one another. With war raging all around, the text echoed his inner feelings. The symbol that inspired him was peace. He picked up his brush.

20

Alone, Giuseppe walked across causeway number one, marvelling at the sheer scale of what had been achieved. It was a work day, so he carried a special pass in case he was stopped. The Badoglio government's declaration of war on Germany the previous October had resulted in Italy being given the status of 'co-belligerent' but it had remained unclear what this meant for the POWs in Camp 60. Were they even POWs any more?

Major Buckland was waiting for instructions from higher up the chain. However, the British Government had been in a state of deadlock for months, whilst discussions had taken place between various departments, as well as with the American and Badoglio governments. It was a quagmire of complexity.

Giuseppe reached the Balfour Beatty headquarters on the south shore of mainland Orkney without being challenged and the paper remained in his pocket. Following a call from Major Buckland, the construction company had readily agreed to supply the steel for the chapel's rood screen and help build the furnace, but they wanted the blacksmith to come to the headquarters and talk to an engineer.

Giuseppe had never been into the building before, but he walked into the reception area and a few moments later he found himself swinging Fiona around the room in a moment of utter madness and joy. She had flung herself into his arms before either of them had even spoken and he hugged her tightly, lifted her off her feet and spun her around so fast that, when he finally stopped they almost fell to the floor as they were laughing and so out of breath.

'Why are you here?' he said, beaming at her.

'New job. I'm now a receptionist for Balfour Beatty. I knew you were coming because I heard that someone from Camp 60 would be arriving this morning . . . a blacksmith. So you're involved in the chapel?'

'Yes. You look lovely.'

'Thank you. So do you.'

'You were right. It has helped. Only now I have to make a rood screen that will take months of work.'

'But you will be back at the forge.'

'I have to make one first. There's nothing suitable on Lamb Holm.'

'Can you build such a thing?'

'Well, I've done it once before. I'm here to meet one of the engineers and discuss how best to go about it.'

'It's so good to see you.'

'I've missed you so much. I've thought often of coming to your farm one Sunday, but I wasn't sure if I should . . .'

'My poor Giuseppe. Still so torn. I'll not insist that you come. It must be your decision.'

'But if I did, what would your parents say?'

'There are many things you could mend around the farm. I'll tell them we met by chance in the office and you have

152

offered to come next Sunday morning to help. In return we'll give you Sunday dinner.'

Giuseppe spent the following few days in a state of nervous excitement, filling his spare time writing poetry. It was a pastime he kept a closely guarded secret. All his poems recently had been about Fiona. Sunday finally came around and, having made himself as presentable as possible, he arrived at the farm shortly after nine o'clock. Fiona was at the front door before he had even knocked and was wearing overalls, ready to work. Giuseppe had brought his with him.

'Where is everyone?' he asked as they walked towards the barn.

'Father's gone to church. Mother's in the kitchen cooking and Rebecca's working as a maid at the Kirkwall Hotel. Many of the hotels have been taken over for military people. She'll be back for dinner, full of tall stories about the handsome officers she's met.'

'She's a beautiful girl.'

Fiona punched him in the arm.

'Not as lovely as her sister, of course,' he added, rubbing the spot she had hit. 'You've got a good punch. I think I'll enter you for this afternoon's boxing match.'

'Boxing!'

'They hold them now and again. The men have gloves and there's a referee so it's all done properly.'

'Men and aggression!'

'It helps to relieve some of the tension.'

They reached the barn and stopped in the doorway.

'I hope you don't fight, Giuseppe,' she said, gently rubbing his arm where she had hit him.

'Why? Would you be worried?'

'You know I would.'

'Not as much as I would be! Some very big men enter the boxing matches. They would make cut meat of me. What . . .? What have I said?'

'I think you mean mincemeat.'

'Mincemeat?'

'Yes,' said Fiona, sill laughing. 'They would make mincemeat of you. But cut meat sounds good. I understood what you meant. Come on, we've got work to do.'

Fiona showed him the first job to be done, which was to repair the hinges on one of the barn doors.

'It hasn't closed properly for years but it's become so bad now that the cows are complaining about the draught.'

He climbed a ladder to examine the top hinge. They worked well as a team. The two of them sparred, swapping from a frivolous subject to a serious one with comfort, talking openly of their hopes and fears, of their pasts, their likes and dislikes. They didn't talk of their feelings and, by unspoken agreement, didn't talk about the future.

Giuseppe was fascinated by her, from the life she lived in Orkney to the way she moved within the too large overalls, which belonged to one of her brothers. He loved the way she laughed so freely, her big brown eyes, so full of mischief and fun.

'You're barkit,' she said. They were facing each other, both out of breath because they had been moving heavy bales of hay.

'Is that bad?' he asked, having no idea what she was talking about.

Fiona reached up and touched his cheek.

'It means you need a good wash before dinner.'

'Oh, does it. Well don't think I'm the only one around here that's . . . barkit,' he said, tweaking her nose.

They heard someone approaching the barn and so moved apart just as Mrs Merriman entered, carrying two mugs.

'There you are. I thought you might be ready for some tea,' she said, handing them each a mug.

'Good morning. Thank you very much . . .' said Giuseppe. He was about to say 'Margaret', but it felt too familiar and he couldn't get the word out.

'Giuseppe has fixed the barn door mother and says he'll make a new part for the plough, once he's got his forge made.'

'That's extremely kind of you. We haven't been able to use that old plough for years.'

'Oh Lord, we thank you for this food before us. We pray for the safe return of our two boys and an end to the war. And we thank you for bringing Mr Palumbi to us to help on the farm. Amen.'

The five of them were sitting around the kitchen table, Rebecca having returned shortly before, full of excited tales about British officers and secrets she had supposedly overheard. Giuseppe felt his eyes moisten at his name being mentioned in Mr Merriman's prayer and couldn't trust himself to speak for several moments. Fortunately, Rebecca maintained a running commentary for quite a while before turning her attention to Giuseppe, who then had to face a barrage of questions before Mrs Merriman stepped in.

'Becky, let the poor man eat his food.'

'It's the best meal I have had in years,' said Giuseppe honestly.

'You can't beat a good Sunday roast, Mr Palumbi,' said Fiona's father, handing over the bowl of potatoes. Giuseppe guessed he was several years older than his wife and had a manner about him as though he belonged to an earlier age. After lunch, Fiona's father offered to take Giuseppe around the farm. He had already seen it, but appreciated the gesture. The two men took a leisurely walk while the three women cleared up.

'There have been many newspaper articles in the British press over the months that have put the Italians in a rather bad light,' said the older man, when they stopped to look at the cattle. 'But in my brief dealings with the men in Camp 60 I have found them to be decent and hard-working. I believe you can only judge as you find, Mr Palumbi, and as to anything else, I leave that to God.'

Giuseppe was not sure how to answer or whether there was something more to the comment than appeared on the surface.

'We have all found the friendliness of the Orkney people to be so sincere, we have been deeply touched by it, Mr Merriman.'

'Ah, do unto others . . .'

Giuseppe didn't know the saying and it showed on his face. Mr Merriman smiled and laid a hand on his shoulder to indicate they should start walking again.

The two men returned to the house sometime later in amiable friendship and Giuseppe was immediately roped in to help make chutney in the kitchen as though he was part of the family.

He lay for hours in his bed that night thinking about the day's events, and was still replaying the moments in his head the following afternoon on the parade ground, hardly aware of his surroundings. However, as roll call was coming to an end, he saw Major Buckland walking towards the front of the lines. Sergeant Major Fornasier ordered them to attention.

'Stand at ease,' said Major Buckland, standing on the crate. 'Since Italy's capitulation the governments of Italy and Britain have been in extensive negotiations. It has taken a long time and I know this drawn-out uncertainty about your position and future has caused much concern and frustration. Men have asked if they will be going home. I'm afraid that will not be

156

possible until the war is over. However, agreements have been reached between the two governments that affect all of you and there are important decisions you must make.

'Italian prisoners of war are now free to co-operate with the British authorities as volunteer co-operatives, with the ultimate aim of creating Italian labour battalions. Men in these battalions will be paid in British coinage, instead of camp tokens, for work carried out, and this can be spent within the local community. If you wish, it can even be arranged for money to be sent home to your family. Rates of pay will increase. Unskilled workers will receive seven shillings a week and skilled workers nine shillings a week.

'You will continue to work as before on the causeways, but will no longer be escorted by armed soldiers. You will instead be taken to and from the camp by your own NCOs. When your work is completed for the day, you will be able to travel up to a distance of five miles from the camp. However, you must be back inside the perimeter by ten o'clock every evening. You will not be allowed to use public transport or visit public houses. It is also forbidden to form sexual relationships with local women.

'Those men who do not wish to accept these conditions will continue to be treated as prisoners of war in all respects and be moved to other, more appropriate, camps as soon as transport can be found. This agreement will be implemented in ten days time, on 1st May. You have one hour to make your decision.'

'Thank you, Sergeant Major Fornasier.'

'Sir. Attention!'

Major Buckland looked at the lines of men standing smartly to attention. He wondered what their reaction was going to be, how many familiar faces would leave Camp 60. He stepped down from the crate, returning Sergeant Major Fornasier's salute.

'Carry on, Sergeant Major.'

'Yes, sir.'

Arguments broke out on the parade ground almost as soon as the men were dismissed. Most were willing to take a pragmatic view of their situation and felt that if they were going to be working and housed in camps until the end of the war, they may as well be paid for their trouble. Also, no one knew when the war would end and the idea of greater freedom was extremely appealing. However, there was a hard core of Italians against it.

When they reassembled an hour later to give their individual verdicts, sixteen men elected to remain as POWs and move to another camp. Most huts had at least one person who would not agree to accept the new conditions and Domenico's hut was no exception. A volatile argument between the man and some of the others raged throughout the evening, particularly with Carlo.

In the darkness Carlo and his compatriot jabbed each other in the chest. They pleaded. They swore. But the chasm that had been wrenched open between them was so huge that no bridge could cross it. There was no middle ground to stand upon. The arguments continued throughout the next day and the atmosphere in the camp became a mixture of pain and guilt, sadness and anger. Men who had been friends, who had endured hardships together and looked out for each other, before even arriving at Camp 60, hurled insults and shouted until they were red in the face.

Transport could not be arranged until the following day so another night of tension had to be endured. Extra guards were brought in. As soon as breakfast was over the small group were lined up in the parade ground with their kit. The other men had assembled outside their huts. There was a sullen but quiet tension in the air and it looked as if the last of the shouting was over until the last minute when one called out.

'You've sold out to the enemy!'

'Dirty fascists!' shouted back another man.

Insults flew thickly between the two sides as the guards did their best to hurry the small group towards the gate. As they left the camp for the last time, determined to remain POWs and loyal to Mussolini, the men could be heard chanting.

'Viva il Duce! Viva il Duce!'

But for all the aggression and anger, the greatest emotion for most that day was deep hurt and sorrow. It was a feeling that would stay with Carlo and many others for decades, until the end of their lives.

21

Major Booth had received a message from the construction company agreeing to lend one of their small Nissen huts to house the proposed forge. The Sunday after Giuseppe's visit to the Merriman's he and Buttapasta walked to the Balfour Beatty workshops on Lamb Holm with four Italians, including the bricklayers, Barcaglioni and Battiato.

A few days earlier a lorry had dropped off a small quantity of carefully selected stone from the quarry and this had since been joined by several bags of cement. Both items lay on the ground by the building they had been given. Buttapasta was keen to look inside to make sure it didn't need emptying, and when they entered Giuseppe's eyes widened in surprise at the object in one corner.

He walked over and picked up a hammer; a blacksmith's hammer, the large, heavy head made silver by years of use. He tested the balance of it in his hand and it felt familiar and reassuring, like stroking an old faithful dog. Giuseppe struck the anvil that lay on the floor, hitting it from horn to heel and back again so that the hut was filled with ringing, which was more beautiful to him than a cathedral choir. When he finally stopped and turned around the others were standing in a group, grinning. Reluctantly, he gently put the hammer on the floor.

'Well, someone's a lucky boy,' said Battiato.

Giuseppe shrugged his shoulders.

'I'm not sure where it came from, but I'm not about to refuse it.'

'Come on,' said Buttapasta, 'if we're going to build a forge in one day we had better get moving.'

The bricklayers went outside to start mixing cement, while the two other men began to carry in some of the stones. Giuseppe and Buttapasta marked the outline of the forge on the concrete floor at the far end of the hut. Giuseppe had produced carefully drawn sketches, showing the thickness of the walls and how they curved at the back, the height of the bed where the fire would burn and where the hole should go for the entry of the bellows.

Giuseppe was outside, looking at the roof, when the engineer arrived.

'Mr MacDonald,' said Giuseppe, shaking his hand. 'Is it you I have to thank for the anvil?'

'Well, I simply put the word about. The person you really need to thank is Mr Mowatt, the blacksmith on South Ronaldsay. The anvil and tools have come from his smithy.'

'I'm very grateful.'

They were quiet for a while, but the small Scotsman had not missed the fact that Giuseppe had been studying the roof.

'You'll need to put a hole in that for your chimney. I guess you could do with a ladder?'

He was back ten minutes later, followed by three civilian workers carrying a couple of ladders and a large box of tools. The Balfour Beatty engineer had taken such a keen interest in what the Italians were doing that a short while later he was on the roof with one of the workers, happily cutting a suitable opening for the chimney, so Giuseppe could go back inside to supervise the building of his forge.

A strange compulsion seemed to take hold of the little group and the work took on a frantic pace. This wasn't some monstrous task, so large that its completion was only a vague event in the distant future. This was something that could be accomplished that very day, if they could only work fast enough. Even the Balfour Beatty men were keen to help, but the hut was too small for more people to be sensibly employed. Instead, they did what jobs they could outside and brought over regular refreshments from the nearby canteen.

By the end of the afternoon the forge had been built and a stone plinth erected in the middle of the hut. They all gathered inside the building to watch the stonemason and the black-smith lift the heavy anvil and when they laid it gently on the newly-made plinth the men broke into applause.

'That's a grand day's work by anyone's reckoning,' said the engineer, reaching into the rucksack at his feet and pulling out a bottle of locally-made Highland Park whisky.

'Here, get rid of your cold coffee and put some of this into your mugs. I'll bet it's a damn sight better than the stuff you make in camp.'

'To the forge,' said MacDonald.

'To the rood screen,' said Buttapasta

'To the chapel,' said Barcaglioni.

'To peace,' said one of the civilian workers.

As they drank, Giuseppe studied the forge with his eyes. But his thoughts were on what had been said, for it seemed to him that the forge and the rood screen, the chapel and peace, were all part of the same thing.

Domenico had to wait until the following Sunday afternoon

before he had the chance to walk over. He felt the heat coming out of the open door even before he entered. Giuseppe had his back to him so Domenico waited quietly, watching with fascination as the blacksmith heated the steel, ready to force his will upon it.

For the last few weeks one of the camp's carpenters had been working closely with the camp's cobbler to construct bellows to a design drawn by Giuseppe, who now raised the temperature of the fire by gently moving the long wooden handle up and down, while holding a rod of steel in a pair of long tongs. Eventually, he turned around to lay the cherry-red metal on the anvil and noticed Domenico.

'Have you been there long?' said Giuseppe, his face running with sweat.

'I didn't want to disturb you.'

'That's alright. I'm trying to make myself another pair of tongs, but it's slow work at the moment,' said Giuseppe, leaving the bar to rest on the anvil. 'The forge and I are like new lovers . . . we have to get to know each other's intimate likes and dislikes. I need to find out how to keep a good heart in the fire with these bellows, which are not as big as I wanted. When I've done that, there's the problem of the metal.'

'The metal?'

'It's the floor sweepings of the junkyard.'

Domenico walked over to the pile of bars that were lying on the floor and picked one up.

'Reinforcement bars for concrete blocks?' asked Domenico.

'The steel is a mixture of metals, everything from old farm machinery to kitchen pans, and the impurities make the rod inconsistent.'

'Is that a big problem?'

'It will be a challenge,' said Giuseppe. 'It means along its length the rod is likely to react differently to heat, so some parts may soften more quickly while other parts may be more brittle and likely to fracture. Also, each rod will vary from the one before it.'

'I'll stick to my paints,' said Domenico, putting down the rod. 'Is there anything I can do?'

'Now you ask, you can break up those lumps of coal into smaller pieces . . . about the size of a walnut,' said Giuseppe, indicating a pile of coal in one corner.

Domenico, walked over and his attention was taken by a small mound of what looked like clinker next to it.

'What's that?' he asked, gently kicking the substance. 'It looks like the leftovers from a stove.'

'It is,' said Giuseppe. 'I mix it with coal to achieve the type of fire and heat that I need. That pile is from a couple of huts during the last week, but I need much more and it has to be cleaned so I'm left with only the coke and charcoal. I was wondering if I could show one man from each hut how to gather and clean the remains of the previous night's fire then bring it over here perhaps once a week . . . what do you think?'

'I don't see why not. You know the men will do anything to help,' said Domenico, picking up a lump of coal and examining it. 'The size of a walnut you said?'

'A walnut,' confirmed Giuseppe.

Domenico looked over at his friend.

'Any particular variety?'

22

Oaths flew, if not with the same frequency as the raindrops, then at least with a similar ferocity. It had started raining four days earlier and on the third day a steam train leaving Lamb Holm quarry had come off the track, which had become unstable. Five wagons had overturned, sending their cargo of skips and rock spilling across the entrance. All quarry work was stopped immediately and since the accident men had cursed, heaved and gasped with the effort required to manhandle the rock out of the way.

A crane, larger than the diggers used in the quarry, had been brought from barrier number two to pick up the wagons and place them, one by one, further along the track. For the last hour men had been working out how best to lift the engine. Carlo sat in the crane's cabin, which would have provided him with an excellent view across to Glimps Holm and Burray beyond, if the weather had not been so foul. He had become one of the most skilful crane drivers on the construction site and sat patiently waiting for the Balfour Beatty engineers to finish their preparations.

He wasn't entirely without apprehension, for he thought the

steam engine was probably heavier than the maximum weight the crane was designed to lift. Men and machinery were all being pushed to their limit in this race to build the causeways and one of the other large cranes had toppled over the previous month. No one had been hurt, but Carlo felt good luck should not be relied upon so soon.

At least he was dry. He looked down at the quarry. The men around the train looked about as miserable as it was possible to be. Dino had found a sheltered spot under a large overhanging rock a short distance away from the activity. He had been drawing sketches of the wagons as they were lifted back on the track and was waiting to draw a picture of the train. He had jokingly asked Carlo to hold the engine in the air for as long as possible so he could get the correct perspective. Carlo smiled at the thought.

Carlo could see men signalling to him. Like most crane drivers he relied on experienced men on the ground to guide his actions with clear arm and hand movements. He grasped the long handles that controlled the workings of the crane and gently took the slack out of the steel rope. As it went taut he could feel the structure of metal beams beneath him shifting. This was going to be a close fight between gravity and mechanical strength. He moved the levers with a tenderness that would not have been out of place caressing a lover's cheek. The men around the train stepped well clear apart from one engineer, who was winding his hand quickly to indicate the train should be lifted.

'You come up here and lift the bloody thing then,' muttered Carlo under his breath.

He pushed the lever and felt the cab sway. He tried not to think of the huge strain being forced on rivets, wires and girders, but a feeling of danger hung around the edges of his mind.

The train seemed to be embedded in the waterlogged ground.

He moved the lever further and with a sudden jerk the train was free and started to swing wildly. More than forty men were holding ropes tied to strategic points and between them they struggled against the wind to steady the load. Carlo raised it slightly higher then moved the engine as gently as he could to a stable part of the track. This was the most crucial point of the operation and where he was completely dependent upon the eyes of the men on the ground. To drop the wheels on to the track required the train to be lowered precisely, with no more than a couple of inches of leeway.

Men squinted into the rain, fought with ropes that slipped through fingers and slithered in puddles, while the wind rocked the train and cab. Carlo kept his eyes on the engineer, who had one hand on a buffer as if this would let him guide several tons of metal. His other arm moved in slow motion. Down . . . down. Carlo guessed the wheels were still at least a foot off the track. He never knew whether a steel wire snapped or some connection came apart but the train fell with such force he felt the vibration through his feet.

Several men lost their balance and fell over, while the engineer threw himself backwards in fright, to land yards away in a huge puddle. He wasn't hurt and was quickly helped by a couple of Italians. Everyone crowded around the train, which was neatly standing on the track, as if it had been there all along. A great cheer echoed around the quarry and the Balfour Beatty man gave a 'thumbs up' to the cab.

But when the engineer looked he was astounded to see Carlo coming down the ladder with no apparent concern for safety, descending with a combination of sliding and jumping, as he missed rung after rung in his desperate bid for speed. The engineer slowly dropped his arm, as more men noticed the

Italian's manic flight and went silent in surprise. As soon as he was on the ground Carlo started running, screaming as he went, as though he had lost his wits. He skirted around the outside of the group without slowing, men following his journey with startled eyes. Moments later, as they realised where he was heading, they felt their hearts crushed with dread.

When they caught up with him, Carlo was kneeling on the ground. Only part of an arm was visible from beneath the over-hang of rock, which had sheared off completely from the rock face and now lay in three huge broken sections. Dino's hand still held tightly on to the little sketch pad on which the half-finished picture of the train was blurring quickly in the falling rain. Men crossed themselves and several fell to their knees to pray.

Carlo tenderly removed the fingers from around the pad and put it inside his coat then he held Dino's hand and wept. He cried for the loss of his cousin and friend, for the beautiful voice that was gone forever, for the two small boys who would never see their father again. He cried for the loss of a man who could reach out in the darkness and bring someone back from the brink of despair. As the tears falling down his cheeks mingled with the rain, he wept for the utter waste of it all.

23

Dino was buried with full military honours at St Olaf cemetery about a mile outside Kirkwall. Padre Giacomo conducted the service and a platoon of men from Camp 60 was given permission to attend. Sergeant Major Fornasier wrote to Dino's family and his few possessions were wrapped up and sent to Italy via the Protecting Power. Carlo wrote to his own family and to Dino's wife, enclosing some wildlife sketches that had been drawn for the boys. He carefully put away the other pictures Dino had produced. When the war was finally over, he would take these back to Italy himself and give them to Dino's sons.

Carlo could not bring himself to keep the picture of the train and tore it from the sketch pad. Then one afternoon, shortly after the funeral and when the hut was almost empty, he burnt it in the stove. He sat watching the paper turn black and disintegrate, disappearing into the embers of the wood and coal, then he picked up the poker. He was completely unaware of how long and how viciously he had been thrusting the poker into the stove but stopped suddenly, as if coming out of a trance, when Sergeant Primavera gently laid a hand on his shoulder and suggested they go for a walk.

*   *   *

Padre Giacomo, with the help of Major Booth, had been in touch with J. Wippell & Company, an old established firm of church furnishers in Exeter. Following some correspondence during May, the cost, dimensions, colour and design of a pair of curtains had been agreed. The firm had promised to send them on a certain date, but it was impossible to guarantee when a package sent from the south of England would arrive in Orkney. The money for the purchase had come from the chapel fund.

One day around this time Major Buckland and Major Booth arrived at the chapel. Domenico was inside. He was using part of the school floor to work on clay brought back by a group of Italians from a nearby farm. Everyone in the camp knew that Domenico Chiocchetti required clay to make the altar and it had been with pride that these men marched into camp, carrying their heavy load in sacks given to them by the farmer. When the two smartly-dressed British officers entered Domenico was on his knees, wearing an apron made out of an old blanket and fighting a substance that did not quite wish to do what he wanted. He stood up.

The officers greeted him warmly, for they liked this quiet man, always working with skill and determination to create something for his fellow men and for the glory of God.

'We've heard you've completed your painting above the altar and wanted to see it for ourselves,' said Major Buckland. 'Would that be alright with you?'

'Yes, sir. I'd be grateful for your comments,' replied Domenico.

The three men walked to the chancel and stood looking at the picture of the Madonna and Child reproduced from the little religious card. Around the image of the Blessed Virgin and the Infant Jesus, Domenico had added cherubim holding a scroll inscribed *Regina pacis ora pro nobis* (Queen of Peace pray for us).

One cherub, on the left hand side of the altar, carried a blue shield, the heraldic badge of Moena, depicting a boat sailing out of a storm and into calm waters. The cherub on the opposite side was sheathing a sword. No one spoke for several minutes.

'I'm sorry, Domenico,' said Major Buckland eventually.

'Sorry, sir?'

'I had no idea. I don't think I really understood what you intended to create. I never thought it would be this. What you've painted here is a true work of art. It's a masterpiece.'

'Thank you, sir,' said Domenico, feeling rather embarrassed. 'Many people have been involved in working on the chapel and it's not finished yet by a long way.'

'What's the next step?' asked Major Booth.

'I'm using the clay to make a mould for the altar and altar rail,' said Domenico, indicating with his head the lump on the floor, which was still pretty much as he had taken it out of the sacks earlier that day. 'Palumbi did a good job building the forge and spends all his spare time working on the rood screen, but it's painfully slow work.'

Domenico paused, hoping the hint would not be ignored.

'Well,' said Major Buckland, choosing his words carefully, 'as long as their work is covered, I think Major Booth can speak to Sergeant Major Fornasier about relieving the men you need of other duties. How does that sound?'

'Thank you for your understanding, sir, and also for arranging the materials for the rood screen with Balfour Beatty.'

'Oh, they were quick to volunteer when I explained what it was for,' said Major Buckland.

'Various things have already been made and stored away, such as the candelabra and lanterns,' said Domenico. 'Actually, as you're here, sir, there's one thing I wanted to ask. Padre Giacomo, Sergeant Major Fornasier and I have been talking with the men and everyone agrees there's such a contrast between the chancel and the remainder of the hut that they think this should also be converted, so the whole building can be used as a chapel.'

'What about the classes? I hear they're going really well,' said Major Buckland.

'The men are happy for them to be held in the mess hall or the huts, sir. No one has come up with any objections to the idea, unless you have any, Major Buckland?'

'Well, I can't see that I can object if this is what the men want. Do you see any problems, Major Booth?'

'Not at all, sir.'

'There's one thing,' said Domenico.

'Yes?'

'Once we've fixed a wooden framework to the rest of the building we'll need to purchase more plasterboard.'

'So I need to get on to my friendly Orkney supplier again,' said Major Buckland with a smile.

'My idea is to paint the plasterboard in the nave to look like bricks, with a dado running along the bottom of the walls to resemble carved stone. But the area to paint will be too much for me.'

'What do you suggest?' asked Major Buckland.

'In Camp 34 there's an artist, Sergeant Pennisi. I knew him well before we arrived on the islands. If he could be transferred to work with me then the job would be possible.'

'Now we've seen what you've created here I can't imagine how anyone could refuse,' said Major Buckland. 'Leave it with me. Let's see if we can get Sergeant Pennisi to join the team.'

'Thank you, sir.'

'Oh, by the way,' said Major Booth. 'I heard Wippell sent

your curtains yesterday, a little earlier than expected. They should be here soon . . . unless the Germans have other ideas.'

One Sunday around mid-June Domenico was putting the finishing touches to the life-sized altar he had made out of clay, while Sforza and Esposito were fixing plasterboard in the nave. The camp had been alive during the previous week with the news that Rome had been liberated by the Allies and that Badoglio had stepped down as Prime Minister. Domenico was lost in his own thoughts about home when he heard his name being spoken.

'Sergeant Pennisi!' he said, putting down his tools and walking over to shake his friend's hand.

'Domenico,' said Pennisi, a big smile on his face. 'How are you?'

'Very well,' said Domenico beaming. 'And you?'

'I'm well and interested to know about your chapel. I hear people talking about it everywhere I go. When I heard I was being moved to Camp 60 I was instantly intrigued.'

'You're now in the Sixtieth Italian Labour Battalion,' said Domenico. 'Also, you're going to work on the chapel full-time.'

'Full-time . . . not on the barriers at all?'

'Major Buckland agreed it readily. As well as me, Palumbi the blacksmith and Buttapasta the stonemason dedicate all their time to the building. The jobs we should do are covered by the others.'

'Excellent!'

Pennisi walked over to look at the paintings in the chancel.

'This is a wonder, Domenico. The story of what you've been doing here doesn't do justice to what you've created. I stand in awe.'

'Coming from you that is a great compliment.'

'You know we have a chapel in Camp 34?'

'I've heard. I'm sure you were instrumental in helping to build it.'

'I worked on it, but it's not on the scale of what you've done here. I understand the difficulties you must have had in obtaining suitable materials.'

'I can't say it's been easy.'

Pennisi walked around in silence, studying the paintings, looking at the ceiling then going back to the image of the Madonna and Child. Their conversation was interrupted by the arrival of Buttapasta who seemed, even before he spoke, particularly pleased about something. The big Italian had not met Pennisi before, but had heard about him so often he felt he was already a friend. Domenico did not miss the fact that Buttapasta was carrying a black square tile and he waited until the other two men had finished their brief conversation about their respective homes before mentioning it.

'I see you've found a tile.'

'Oh this,' said Buttapasta, as if he had forgotten the thing was there. 'Yes, I thought you might like it for the floor of the chancel.'

'It's very nice,' said Domenico, taking the tile to study it more closely. 'But I might need a few more.'

'Will you? I thought that one might do . . . sort of in the centre. Though I suppose I could bring in more. There's a pile of them outside the door along with some white tiles of the same size.'

Domenico knew that Buttapasta was enjoying the moment.

'Don't you want to know where they're from?'

'I'm hoping you'll eventually get around to telling me,' said Domenico.

'They're from the floor of a bathroom in the *Ilsenstein*. I've been removing them for the last couple of weeks.'

'I wondered where you'd been disappearing to.'

Now Buttapasta was grinning widely and so was Pennisi.

'I didn't want to leave it to someone who wouldn't take care removing them. They were well stuck on but I got the last one off yesterday. Micheloni and De Vitto have just helped me to get them up here.'

The three men walked outside. Pennisi picked up a tile.

'They'll look good,' he said. 'I'm sure you could lay them to a design, Domenico.'

'We'd be lost without Domenico's designs,' said Buttapasta.

At first glance the tiles were actually in a pretty poor state, but the three artists could see beyond the dirt and stains.

'I'll clean them up in the workshop and if you draw a design I'll lay them to it,' offered Buttapasta.

'It's a deal,' said Domenico.

24

For three months men had talked about it, trained for it and planned for it. There had not been as much excitement in the camp since Italy's capitulation. Sports day was an event that would bring together the Italians, most of the British army and civilians on Lamb Holm, not to mention a large number of local Orkney families. The sky was cloudless, the sun was hot and the wind had gone to blow elsewhere. There was to be no work this day and, for a short while, people could put the fact that half the world was at war to the back of their mind.

Later that morning, the inhabitants of Camp 60 began to filter out of the gate and make their way to the fields. Everyone was leaving, except Aldo. As Buttapasta and Domenico walked past they saw a diminutive figure sitting on the steps of a hut, smoking a cigarette.

'Aldo,' said Buttapasta as he and Domenico walked over. 'Aren't you coming?'

'You know me and exercise. Even watching it tires me out and all those men running around a field! The idea alone makes me want to lie down.'

'Think of all the pretty girls you could meet,' said Buttapasta.

'Hey, I know all the local girls already. Anyway, I might have a little surprise for you two when you return.'

'What are you up to, Aldo?' asked Domenico.

'You'll have to wait, won't you?' said Aldo smiling.

'Be careful, whatever you're planning,' said Domenico.

'Careful is my middle name. Go on the two of you.'

'We'll see you later,' said Buttapasta.

Aldo waved as his two friends walked away.

The camp was emptying quickly. Buttapasta and Domenico joined the stream of men. Aldo sat contentedly watching them leave, occasionally shouting a comment or simply waving at those who spotted him. When he had first arrived at the camp, the older men had called youngsters like Aldo 'I Balilla del Duce' meaning they were Mussolini's boys, the Italian version of the Hitler Youth, but they were all older now and the term had long since lost its entertainment value.

Most thought Aldo would follow once he had finished his cigarette but he was still sitting when the last man hurried out the gate to catch up with the others. He felt strangely calm. He shook himself, not sure if he had actually fallen asleep, stood up and went to retrieve his rucksack.

It didn't take Aldo long to reach the *Lycia*. He was surprised to find Micheloni and De Vitto fishing from the other side, where he had not seen them.

'Aldo,' they said together, equally taken aback.

'You're not at the sports day?' asked De Vitto.

'No, it's not for me. All that running about! But why aren't you there? I didn't expect to meet anyone up here today.'

'This is the sport we like and when can we ever get such peace?' said De Vitto. 'There are normally so many noisy people they frighten everything away.'

'What are you up to?' asked Micheloni.

'I'm off to do my own fishing. I've discovered some first class teak in the *Emerald Wings*, so thought I'd get it for Domenico's tabernacle. He's had trouble finding the quality of wood he wants and, well, this is a surprise.'

'I didn't know you had become involved in the chapel,' said De Vitto.

'I'm doing it for a friend,' said Aldo. 'Enjoy your fishing.'

'Don't stay down long,' called Micheloni. 'It's too nice to be below decks.'

Aldo walked to the stern and wobbled across the gangplank between the *Lycia* and the *Ilsenstein*, trying not to look at the sea far beneath his feet. The *Ilsenstein* was the vessel that had provided the tiles for the chancel floor, which had been cleaned and laid by Buttapasta and his helpers to Domenico's design. Aldo reckoned that at any one point in time there was at least one group talking about the chapel somewhere in the camp. And here he was, about to get involved.

He wasn't quite sure why he was so reluctant to let the chapel become part of his life. Perhaps it was all tied up with his past, with feelings buried deep within. He knew Domenico and Buttapasta meant well when they tried to show him aspects of life other than the ones he followed, but making deals and money was his means of escape; what made him feel safe.

He reached the stern of the *Ilsenstein*. Lamb Holm appeared quite different from this vantage point. Domenico and Buttapasta didn't understand him because they had chosen alternative paths in their lives from those he had walked.

Unless it was to do with a sale, Aldo didn't analyse a situation too much. But as he looked back at Lamb Holm he acknowledged his fear of being poor again; a horror of being the way he was after his mother had died, when his father had fallen apart. It had been a terrible time until Aldo had taken control of the situation. He sighed. Examining the past was not the purpose of today. The teak would please Domenico and that was enough reason to sacrifice a few hours.

Turning his back on Lamb Holm, he started across the gangplank to the *Emerald Wings*, a steamer from the 1920s. The ship had been purposely sunk in 1940 along with the two others in order to block the channel between Lamb Holm and Glimps Holm. Aldo picked up three paraffin lamps stored under cover on the top deck and went down one level. He didn't like going below and it was only the possibility of finding something to sell that had encouraged him to explore the sunken ships in the first place.

He lit one of the lamps and walked to the ladder leading to the deck below. He landed in about two feet of water. He had never known such blackness before entering the ship for the first time and the completeness of it had astonished him. A few yards further on Aldo hung the first lamp from a hook in the ceiling, lit the second lamp and set off again.

He had a mental plan of how to get to the room that contained the teak cabinet and walked upwards, back towards the bow, which remained dry even at high tide. Stopping at a cross-section of corridors, he hung the second lamp from a peg on the wall before lighting the third. He quickly found the room he wanted. It may have been an officer's cabin, perhaps even the captain's. He didn't really care. What mattered was that it had a beautiful teak cabinet that would provide the perfect material for the tabernacle.

Aldo took off his rucksack from which he produced a torch and tools. He knew he would have to be methodical or would end up damaging the wood, as he had no aptitude for this sort of work. He shivered. The ship groaned as a gentle movement of the water caused it to rock where it lay on the seabed, reminding him of that fateful journey across the Pentland Firth. He stopped.

When was that? He thought about it. He had been on the island for two and a half years. In a few weeks it would be his twenty-second birthday. Perhaps he would celebrate with Domenico and Buttapasta. His latest batch of spirit was the best yet. This was not the place to daydream. He picked up a screwdriver.

On the field where the competitions were about to take place, close to 2,000 people were determined to have a good time. Even before events began there was a huge amount of activity. One Italian from Camp 34 had gone to great effort to make a suitable clown's costume and paint his face.

Both children and adults stood open-mouthed as a group of Italians performed mid-air somersaults and other acrobatics. The bands from both camps had set up at opposite ends of the field and took it in turns to play. Men from each camp looked out for old friends and the reunions taking place around the field added to the carnival feel.

It wasn't long before the four Italian teams marched on to the centre of the field. The applause almost drowned out the loud speaker system.

'And here we have Sergeant Rizzato, the sports instructor, leading the four teams on to the field. Here they are: Sparvieri, Ardente, Limatori and Disperata.' The corporal who had provided commentary for the football match was once more behind the microphone.

The teams lined up in front of the highly decorated podium and Major Buckland returned Sergeant Rizzato's salute, then they dispersed, running to various points around the field. In addition to their training, Sergeant Rizzato had ensured men knew the sequence of races and how they fitted into other competitor events. British and Italian sergeants acted as stewards.

Domenico and Buttapasta found a good position near the starting line and waited patiently for the runners, who were currently gathered around one of the stewards a short distance away. Their 'pre-race' lecture over, the eight men walked to the start line and began a series of stretches and exercises. One man in particular stood out because of his vigorous and obviously well-practised routine.

'Look!' said Buttapasta, pointing.

'I don't believe my eyes,' said Domenico.

'Is it a joke?'

Other men from Camp 60 who had seen the same individual started to cheer. The Orkney families standing nearby and the men from Camp 34 couldn't understand why people were laughing at the athletic-looking man, limbering up with such precision. They didn't know him, didn't know that he was called . . . Shipwreck.

'If it's a joke, it's on the British,' said Domenico.

Then they both started laughing and cheering and clapping. The runners lined up and the sergeant called for quiet before he fired the starting pistol.

'And they're off, with Meozzi and Marinucci taking an early lead, and Malvolti a close third,' said the corporal at the microphone. 'It's quickly developing into a race between the two team mates from Ardente. And it's Marinucci at the line, Meozzi second, ensuring Ardente gets off to a huge lead. Malvolti coming in an impressive third.'

It did not take long for the other events to get underway, accompanied by constant bursts of applause from around the field.

'Well, the excellent weather is certainly being matched by some brilliant performances in the javelin, including some good throws from Malvolti, who I have just been informed has entered virtually every discipline,' said the voice from the speakers.

The only sound on the *Emerald Wings* was from a black-headed gull, sitting by the hatch that Aldo had descended earlier, and of water lapping against the deck. Each time the sea covered a few more inches before retreating. Below decks, Aldo found his mind wandering, going over events earlier in his life. Memories that hadn't surfaced for years invaded his thoughts.

Back at the field the crowd hardly had a moment when they were not being entertained.

'There's certainly some good skill on the field,' said Buttapasta. 'And what about Shipwreck? I bet he's in for some trouble after today. He looks as though he could have been a successful sportsman if there hadn't been a war.'

'All our lives would have been different if there hadn't been a war,' answered Domenico. 'We wouldn't be on this tiny island so far from home.'

'And we wouldn't be here had the German U-boat not sunk the British battleship in Scapa Flow.'

'I wonder where we would have ended up,' said Domenico. 'I should have been transferred from an Egyptian camp to India, along with the others, but I got to know a Scottish corporal and, at the last minute, he included me in the group being sent to Britain. I never saw him again but here I am.'

'Maybe if you'd gone to India, you'd have helped to build a chapel there. You'd at least have been a bit warmer.'

* * *

On the *Emerald Wings* the gull had taken off, its warnings replaced by the sound of water pouring into the open hatch.

Domenico was enjoying the day, but something kept tugging at the back of his mind, putting him in a reflective mood.

'When we eventually leave the island, there'll be no one who will know . . . There'll be nobody to tell our story. What will we leave behind?'

'A chapel in which people can pray? Causeways for the locals to drive over?' offered Buttapasta.

'Helping to create the chapel has been the noblest thing I've ever done. But it's still a Nissen hut and will one day collapse and be lost.'

'But at least while it survives it will touch people here,' said Buttapasta tapping Domenico on the chest.

A voice boomed over the loud speaker system, effectively interrupting normal speech.

'And now we have one of the highlights of the whole day, the four by four hundred yards relay.'

Buttapasta put his arm around Domenico's shoulders.

'Come on, my friend. Let's go and watch the runners and leave the cares of the world behind us for a few minutes. I wonder how Shipwreck will do in this event.'

As the third group of athletes began running around the track, Aldo tied together the bundle of teak he had so carefully removed. He replaced his tools and torch in the rucksack, tucked the wood under his arm and picked up the lantern, wanting to get into daylight and fresh air once more. The rusty metal walls were beginning to press in on him and the ship was groaning and moving more than it had earlier. But he had no doubt that the sight of Domenico's face, when he presented him with the quality teak, would be worth any discomfort he had put up with.

By the time the athletes were running the end of the third leg the crowd were screaming wildly.

The commentator, almost hysterical by this point, could hardly be heard.

'And here we have Meozzi about to hand over the baton for the final leg to his team mate Marinucci.'

Marinucci took the baton in a text book changeover and set off at a blistering pace, the ground seeming to disappear before him. When he was fifty yards from the finishing line nobody could make out anything coming over the loud speaker system, but the corporal screamed into his microphone nonetheless.

'What a performance. It's going to be Marinucci. No one can touch him now. What a race. It's Marinucci! It's Marinucci!'

Aldo sensed something was wrong. The ship felt different. He took the second lamp off its peg and carried on at a faster pace with both lamps in one hand. At the next corner he stopped. The bundle of wood fell to the floor with a sickening thud.

25

The edge of the water was only yards away from him and as he stared, it crept even nearer, little icy fingers of death reaching out for his toes. To get out of the ship Aldo had to head towards the stern, but this now appeared to be totally submerged. The ship had become a giant, rusty coffin.

Aldo had not shirked from the fighting in North Africa but he had faced those dangers along with his friends. But to die alone . . . One lamp slipped and went out as it crashed to the floor. It catapulted him from immobility to action and he began to splash wildly through the water, distorted echoes and shadows following his flight.

When he reached the last corridor the water was up to his chest, but the first lamp, hanging from the ceiling, was still lit, like a beacon. He threw away the one he was carrying so he could use both hands to pull himself along. The seawater was pouring down the steps from the deck above. This was the way out.

Aldo felt his body going numb. His chest seemed to be encased in iron straps. Aldo knew he was going to die. He wouldn't be handing over the wood for his tabernacle or see the chapel completed. He would never again lie in the heat of an Italian sun and drink wine with Domenico and Buttapasta, as they had talked about so often. Instead, he would be left behind, buried in the cemetery like Dino.

By the time Aldo reached the steps, the water was almost at the base of the lamp. He would only get one attempt at climbing the steps. Stretching out, he took hold of the handrail, his arm instantly pummelled by the force of the water, but there was no going back. He launched himself and grabbed the second rail, but his feet were swept off the steps and he remained purely by the strength in his arms.

He fought desperately to get a foot hold. It was now a race in slow motion to climb the steps with speed and caution. He managed four steps when everything went dark and in that one instant of surprise he slipped. His leg seemed to explode as it hit something then Aldo was swept back, down into the blackness below.

Domenico and Buttapasta met Major Buckland, who had left the podium to stretch his legs and talk to the men.

'I see our Shipwreck isn't as wrecked as we thought,' said Major Buckland amicably.

They looked at him in silence, feeling rather embarrassed, as if they had been in on the deception. However, the British officer continued without any hint of accusation.

'I've never known such a day. It makes me feel old watching them sprinting around like that.'

'Sometimes it feels as though we'll all be old before we return home and our lives will have been spent on this little island,' said Domenico. 'I was just explaining earlier, sir, how a chance meeting with a Scottish corporal in Egypt resulted in me being sent to Lamb Holm and not to India.'

'Perhaps it was your fate,' offered Buttapasta.

'Ah yes . . . fate,' said Major Buckland. 'We all like to believe we control our lives and destiny, particularly when we're young and full of energy and certainty. But we often have no more control than a leaf blown by the wind.'

The three fell silent. Domenico and Buttapasta weren't quite sure if the officer had more to add, or had said what he intended. Major Buckland seemed to be considering something else. Eventually he spoke.

'When I was a young man I worked as a steward on board the great ocean liners, which ran between England and America.'

'That must have been quite an experience, sir,' said Domenico.

'Indeed, I met people from all walks of life. A new world was opening up and with it previously unheard of opportunities. By 1912, I was working on the SS *Cedric* doing regular trips between Liverpool and New York, when I was offered the chance to sail on a much grander ship, about to make its maiden voyage across the Atlantic. I was beside myself with excitement, then at the last minute another steward was sick and I had to remain where I was.'

Major Buckland paused for a while, so lost in the memory of what he was recalling that he was almost talking to himself.

'Yes, and on the night of 14th April, I was so very disappointed that fate decided I should be stuck on the *Cedric*. I could have been part of history and felt cheated.'

He looked at the two Italians and saw their slightly confused expressions. It seemed to bring him back to the present.

'Oh, I'm sorry. I'm rambling. The other ship . . . the one I should have been on . . . it was the *Titanic*.'

'Mamma mia!' said Buttapasta.

'My poor mother was frantic because she thought I'd

transferred ships and it was several days before I was able to contact her. All because someone else was sick and I had to take his place.'

On the *Lycia*, Micheloni and De Vitto were packing away their fishing rods and their best-ever catches, both in excellent spirits.

'Time to go,' said Micheloni. 'I don't think I want to carry much more than this back to camp.'

'I wonder how the sports event is going. I bet there'll be a few tales to tell over tonight's meal.'

They made their way to the ladder that led down to the ground. Micheloni climbed over the side and put out his hand for the catch. But De Vitto was staring at him, the fish held limply by this side.

'What's wrong?' asked Micheloni.

'We've not seen Aldo,' he said.

'Aldo?'

'He could only get off by passing us,' pointed out De Vitto.

'Well he can't still be on the *Emerald Wings*,' said Micheloni. 'Most of it's underwater.'

The two men looked down the length of the *Lycia* beyond the *Ilsenstein* to the *Emerald Wings*. De Vitto dropped the fish and started to sprint.

'Shit!' exclaimed Micheloni.

The two men raced from the bow to the stern of the *Ilsenstein*, across the gangplank and on to the *Emerald Wings*. The hatch was completely submerged.

'What can we do?' asked Micheloni.

'British divers,' screamed De Vitto over his shoulder, running recklessly back on to the *Ilsenstein*. 'They're always training somewhere nearby. Find British divers.'

* * *

Buttapasta was just about to say something to Domenico when an army truck came wildly across the ground, horn blaring continuously. The truck screeched to a halt and the door flung open. The driver stood on the step looking out over the crowd.

'Something's up. Come on,' said Buttapasta, who started jogging towards the truck.

Micheloni saw them move away from the gaping crowd and waved at them to run faster. When they were within hearing distance he shouted.

'Aldo is trapped by the tide inside the *Emerald Wings*.'

Domenico and Buttapasta didn't wait for further details but raced around to clamber in the other side of the cab. The truck squealed in protest at being turned around in such a tight circle and shot off back down the field.

A group of people crowded around something lying on the ground under the shadow of the *Lycia*. Two British divers sat nearby, trying to get their breath back. Buttapasta pushed through the crowd and stared down at the crumpled body. Aldo looked like a child.

'I'm sorry,' said De Vitto. 'He's shown no signs of life since he was brought up.'

Buttapasta was suddenly a frenzy of activity, pushing De Vitto out of the way.

'Aldo! Aldo! You're not dying on me, you little bastard. You hear me.'

Domenico was frantically searching for a pulse in Aldo's neck.

'I'm not sure, but I think there's something,' he said.

The two men looked at each other across the body of their friend.

'The Balfour Hospital is the nearest,' said Buttapasta.

Men darted forward, lifted Aldo and ran to the back of the

truck. Speed was everything. Buttapasta and Domenico jumped into the back and the others handed up Aldo's limp body.

'The Balfour Hospital,' shouted Domenico.

Micheloni had remained in the cab with the engine running, and on hearing Domenico he slammed the truck into gear and once more had it screaming in protest.

He drove like a man possessed and kept his hand on the horn virtually for the entire journey, so when they slithered to a halt at the hospital entrance a doctor and nurse were already running out before Buttapasta had jumped down.

'His name's Aldo Tolino and he's been trapped inside a block-ship by the tide,' blurted Buttapasta who, with Domenico, was helping to lift Aldo's body. Micheloni ran from the cab just as a sister came charging out of the hospital doors pushing a trolley.

Aldo was transferred quickly and the sister and doctor shot back inside the building, pushing the trolley between them with practised efficiency, despite the doctor's terrible limp.

They were about to follow but the little nurse got in front of them as they reached the hospital doors.

'You can do no more now,' she said putting a hand on Butta-pasta's arm 'Leave him with us. We'll let you know as soon as there's any news.'

26

The next day, Domenico and Pennisi were transforming the plasterboard that had been put up in the nave, skilfully making them look like walls of brick and carved stone. The deception was cleverly carried out and it was already apparent that the effect would be very realistic, with the added illusion of making the ceiling seem higher.

Giuseppe was busy fitting a section of the rood screen. He had made virtually all of it and over half had been erected. The bottom section stretched across the full width of the hut and when fully assembled the rood screen would rise to the ceiling in four columns to create three Gothic arches, providing the congregation with an uninterrupted view into the chancel.

Within the central arch were two gates, the left one incorporating the word 'Maria' and the other the letters 'IHS'. The previous week, it had quickly become clear that Giuseppe had created a work of art that equalled anything else in the chapel. Now so much of it was assembled a steady stream of admirers drifted in and out.

However, no one called that afternoon and the mood in the building was sombre. The three men worked in silence, alone with their thoughts. Buttapasta entered, carrying a bundle of teak, which he laid gently on the small table. Domenico and Pennisi walked over but Giuseppe carried on as he needed to finish securing his section to the wall.

'I went down into the *Emerald Wings* to see what Aldo had been doing and found this,' said Buttapasta. 'It's first-class teak. I think he meant it for the tabernacle.'

Domenico fingered the wood but didn't speak. They had all been hit hard by the accident and waiting for news from the hospital was wearing down their nerves.

'I didn't think he was interested in the chapel,' said Pennisi.

'Perhaps it touched Aldo without him realising it,' said Buttapasta. 'He certainly went to a lot of effort to obtain this and he was so keen to do it himself he kept it a secret from everyone else.'

'I wish he'd told us,' said Domenico. 'We wouldn't have let him get caught by the tide.'

None of them could think of anything to say and were standing around in awkward silence when Major Buckland arrived.

'Is there any news, sir?' asked Domenico.

'I've just had the hospital sister on the phone,' said Major Buckland. 'Aldo is awake. I thought I would let you know straight away.'

The three men broke into a bout of shouts, handshakes and back slapping. Buttapasta stopped himself only at the last instant from giving Major Buckland a huge pat that would probably have sent the slightly built man flying into the chancel.

'He's not out of the woods entirely. He's broken his leg so is going to be in hospital for a while. I wouldn't be surprised if he's already got his eye on some pretty young nurse,' said Major Buckland with a smile.

'That would be Aldo,' said Buttapasta. 'We probably won't see him for weeks, even after he's recovered. He'll be spinning it out until the war ends.'

'Well, the sister has promised to keep us up to date.'

Major Buckland walked over to look at the painting of the Madonna and Child as he always did when in the chapel.

He turned to face them. 'I can see that when you've finished the nave this could be a church anywhere in the world. It's just a pity the outside looks like an extremely unattractive Nissen hut. But the inside is incredible.'

The men respectfully said goodbye to the major as he left and then stood around in silence for a moment.

'I'll give Aldo such a bloody thump when I see him,' said Buttapasta. Leaving Giuseppe to continue with his rood screen the others walked outside. They stopped several yards away from the front door so they could look back at the building.

'Major Buckland has a point,' said Pennisi. 'From the outside it looks uninviting. It's not what you want from a house of God.'

They fell silent once more, staring at the Nissen hut as if they had never seen one before.

'We could make a new entrance,' said Domenico eventually. 'Build a façade to hide what's really there.'

'That would be a big job but I'd be happy to lend a hand,' said Pennisi.

'All we have is time,' said Buttapasta.

'Time and cement. I think this is a job for an artist in cement,' said Domenico innocently, looking up at his friend. Pennisi smiled but said nothing. The big man held out for only a little while.

'Alright. I suppose I'm not really doing much else at the

moment. If one of you draws a design I'll make up the parts, but I'll need a team to help construct it.'

'The latter is hardly a problem, you can pick virtually any man in the camp,' said Domenico. 'As for the other, perhaps you'd consider designing the chapel's façade Sergeant Pennisi?'

'I'd be delighted,' replied Pennisi. 'Come on, let's get a coffee and plan this in more detail.'

Shipwreck had just handed over their mugs when a British corporal opened the door to the canteen and bellowed.

'Shipwreck to the commandant's office, at the double!'

Shipwreck set off, looking rather crestfallen and certainly odd without his large stick. His 'offence' had been made worse at the end of the previous day's events when he had been awarded the cup for the best athlete on the field. Major Buckland had been forced to congratulate him and shake his hand in front of nearly 2,000 spectators. When they reached Major Buckland's office the corporal knocked, opened the door and announced.

'Malvolti's here, sir.'

Shipwreck marched into the room, saluted and stood to attention. The door was shut firmly behind him. The men in his hut had spent most of the previous evening trying to decide what punishment he would be given. He had spent a sleepless night. And now he stood in front of Major Buckland, who ignored him as he read through various papers. After a considerable time and without looking up or speaking, the British officer held out a small card. Shipwreck stepped forward, took the card and stepped back to stand at attention, glancing quickly down as he did so. The card had one word written on it. 'Quarry'.

Shipwreck stood a few moments more but Major Buckland, apparently totally preoccupied with papers, did not say or do anything else.

'Thank you, sir,' said Shipwreck loudly, then saluted smartly, turned about and left the room. Everyone thought he had got off very lightly. He later fixed his walking stick to the wall above his bed and hung the trophy from one end.

The next afternoon Buttapasta was up a ladder above the doorway to the chapel, holding a tape measure and calculating various distances and angles based on a design that Pennisi had produced the previous evening. The drawings still needed to be worked on but Buttapasta had been impressed by the sergeant's quick grasp at what was required and his ability to convert ideas into sketches and workable plans. He had asked for some measurements to be taken, which was why Buttapasta found himself up a ladder when Major Buckland appeared.

The normally easy-going officer was tense.

'Is everything alright, sir?'

'Is Domenico inside?' said Major Buckland, ignoring the question.

'Yes, sir.'

'Perhaps you'd better come in and hear what I have to say.'

Domenico looked up when the two men entered. He had been mixing more paint to create a colour as near to that of brick as possible. He even had a brick on the table as a permanent guide.

'Ah Domenico,' said Major Buckland. He paused and looked at the artist, 'I'm afraid I have some bad news. I wanted to let you know myself.'

'Bad news, sir?' said Domenico, perplexed at what could be so wrong.

'It's your friend, Aldo.'

'Aldo? But you said yesterday sir that he was alright apart from his leg,' said Domenico.

'So I did. However, I've just had the sister on the phone and I'm sorry to inform you that Aldo has developed pneumonia.'

'Pneumonia!' said Buttapasta who had stayed quiet until now.

'According to the sister I'm afraid it's very serious. Apparently it's come on rapidly and Aldo is extremely ill.' Major Buckland paused once more. 'I'm very sorry. The message I got was that . . . that they weren't very hopeful.'

Pennisi and Giuseppe stopped what they were doing and stood quietly to one side. They were all devastated.

'Aldo,' said Domenico.

'You can be sure they will do everything possible at the hospital.'

Domenico seemed not to have heard what Major Buckland had just said.

'If he dies because of a pile of wood, I'll never forgive myself,' he said.

'No,' said Major Buckland forcibly. 'Not for a pile of wood. His actions were fuelled by a desire to be a part of what is being created here. There is always a risk going below on the blockships. He was willing to take that risk.'

They were all silent for a while.

'Thank you, sir,' said Domenico. 'I appreciate you coming to tell us yourself.'

'I promise I'll get word to you as soon as I hear anything from the hospital.'

There was nothing more Major Buckland could say, so he left the men to cope as best they could.

'He's right you know,' said Buttapasta to Domenico. 'It's not your fault. You can't take responsibility for another man's actions.'

After a few moments the door opened and an Italian that

Domenico only vaguely recognised came in. He walked over without speaking and knelt in front of the nearly completed rood screen. They instinctively turned their backs to give the man some privacy, but immediately two more people came in, then Carlo entered and a few moments later two more men arrived. They all knelt to pray in silence.

'I suppose word has got around the camp about Aldo,' said Buttapasta.

The four friends looked at each other. Without speaking they knelt. Outside, little groups of men made their way across the parade ground.

The weather continued to be fine and the Italians enjoyed the long hot days, when it was light from early morning until late in the evening. Camp 60 had its own monthly newspaper called *Sole d'Italia*, which was produced on a small duplicating machine in the administration hut. Some of the Italians showed great talent for creating crosswords, puzzles and stories. Pennisi drew illustrations for the front cover. His artistic skills were often called upon by the local amateur theatre group in Kirkwall and he was given permission to travel to the town on several occasions to create scenery for their productions.

The classes flourished in the mess hall and accommodation huts, and the gardens became more impressive, helped by visits to Graemeshall to obtain bulbs and flowers. There were always several games of one sort or another taking place, with football matches held regularly between the Italians and British army personnel who were manning the nearby batteries. The band had grown in number and included a range of instruments from accordion and banjo to trumpet and guitar. Domenico played the mandolin. Music filtered through the camp most evenings.

The number and sophistication of the plays had increased

considerably since the arrival of Padre Giacomo, who had quickly revealed a passion for amateur dramatics and had taken over Domenico's role in running the northerners' acting group. As soon as the priest realised he had such a large and willing cast he had contacted a friend in Italy, who sent the first of many playscripts.

It was one of these weekend shows that gave Giuseppe the opportunity to return the invitation to the Merriman family, whom he had visited regularly for the previous two months. Several men in Camp 60 had made friends with Orkney families and an extra performance was being held on the Saturday evening, to which local people could be invited. Giuseppe had insisted he escort the family to the camp. He managed to get away early that afternoon and when he arrived at the farm Fiona was waiting for him in the kitchen.

'The others are shopping in Kirkwall,' she said, before he had even said hello. 'They won't be back for at least an hour. That means you can give me a hug without fear of interruption.'

He walked over to her and took her in his arms.

'You know, of course, this is against regulations,' he said after a few moments.

'Regulations?'

'Part of the agreement between the British and Italian Governments is that Italians held in captivity should not visit public houses or form relationships with local women.' He held her tightly so that she couldn't move. 'I think not being able to have a drink is the worst restriction.'

He laughed as Fiona struggled against him.

'It'll be very strange for me to be inside the camp and actually see where you live,' said Fiona.

'Well you'll see some of it, but I can't take you into the accommodation hut.'

'No, it wouldn't be proper.'

'You sound like your mother!'

Mr and Mrs Merriman and Rebecca returned just as Fiona and Giuseppe were putting the finishing touches to the meal. They swapped news as they ate, Giuseppe giving them an update on the chapel. When they had finished, Mr Merriman sank into his favourite chair near the stove, while Giuseppe sat at the kitchen table, reading the front page of the *Daily Telegraph*, which told how Soviet troops were capturing an increasing number of German strongholds.

When the three women had tidied up they began what seemed to be a knitting frenzy. Giuseppe studied them, trying to follow the patterns woven in the air by the needles.

'We're making woollen squares for a patchwork bedspread,' said Mrs Merriman.

She spoke without slowing down or looking up, knowing Giuseppe was watching intently. Mrs Merriman felt he was almost part of the family. It worried her. What would happen in the future? She didn't want to see her daughter get hurt, but this relationship couldn't have a happy ending.

The evening began with Major Buckland informing everyone that Aldo was recovering well in hospital, which resulted in a huge cheer. Coriolano, with his fine baritone voice, was amongst the men who sang, while the band outdid itself. Padre Giacomo was delighted with the performance. Giuseppe, sitting between Fiona and Rebecca, received many envious stares from the other men.

By the summer of 1944 the work on the causeways was virtually complete, resulting in a huge exodus of Balfour Beatty workers, mainly to the south of England. Since the first men had arrived in May 1940, there had been regular changes within the workforce, but some had been working side by side with the Italians since they had arrived two and a half years earlier. Many friendships had flourished and several people swapped addresses with offers to visit when the war was over. There were unofficial farewell parties and more than one man with a strong accent tried to teach the Italians how to say goodbye in his local dialect.

The near completion of the causeways meant the Italians were increasingly sent to help on farms or with other tasks. They became a familiar sight in the streets and shops in Kirkwall. One Italian from Camp 60 was a frequent visitor to J. M. Stevenson, which sold a variety of items. He rarely bought anything but often stayed after his friends had gone, hanging around near the door. One day he went in by himself and handed over a sheet of paper to the girl who worked at the counter, before rushing out again without speaking. The girl was so taken aback that she gave it to the shop manager, Ernest Marwick. He laid the letter on the counter.

Dear Miss, I am obliged to write you for telling you my feelings towards you. Since first time I saw you; I feel something in myself that is very difficult explain it tell you but it is not possible because I do not know it. You understand the reason for these few word that I write to you. You do not know how great my love for you. Our eyes understand how much deep our love. My heart would never be tired to sing this loving hymmm but, I must close because I can't write long how you know – I am waiting a your reply, and if you please I beg you a your writing clear easy. With all my love.

Tony.

'Tony' never came back to the shop again.

When the altar was complete Padre Giacomo held the first mass in the chapel. Men squeezed into every possible space. Major Booth had managed to borrow a gramophone and this had been set up in the vestry to provide the music, which included a Gregorian chant. Mass had been held every Sunday since then and each time more men managed to squash themselves inside. However, the Reverend John Davies, who had arrived in May as the local army chaplain, held a service in the chapel once a fortnight for British soldiers, the few non-Roman Catholic Italians in the camp and anyone else who wanted to attend.

Giuseppe had completed the rood screen in four months, working full-time at his forge. Domenico had finished the altar and altar rail. Candles, purchased out of the chapel fund, stood in four brass candlesticks made by Sergeant Primavera, and two made in wrought iron by Giuseppe. The lanterns made from used bully-beef tins did not look out of place, where men had used the materials at hand to create a place of worship.

James Sinclair was Orkney's best known photographer and the only civilian with a permit from the military to take photographs on the islands. He had already recorded occasions such as the football match and the sports event. When the altar was finished Major Buckland called him back with an idea to create a postcard using a picture of the altar on the front. James Sinclair took the photograph and Major Buckland arranged for a local printer to produce the postcards, which the men were later able to buy in the camp shop.

With strict censorship regulations, all that could be written was a man's signature and the date. But the postcards at least allowed loved ones back home to see a picture of the chapel altar where the men worshipped. The postcards were stamped

'POW *Mail Post Free*', along with the camp number and the official censor '*Passed*' mark.

Domenico and Pennisi were still painting the walls and ceiling in the nave, while Buttapasta and his small team of helpers were working on the façade, which was being built in concrete sections and had reached roughly chest height. Barcaglioni and Battiato altered the brickwork of the end wall to create two openings either side of the door to match the shape of the lancet windows that were to be incorporated into the façade. Buttapasta's team had erected a rough wooden scaffold, allowing the men to position the concrete sections at a higher level and Buttapasta was on top of the scaffold one afternoon in August as Domenico emerged from the door beneath him.

'Hey, Domenico. I've got an idea.'

Buttapasta jumped down and led Domenico a few yards away so they could look back at the chapel's roof. Like all the Nissen huts, the chapel's corrugated iron roof made the building cold in winter, hot in summer and noisy when it rained.

'I've been thinking about the roof,' said Buttapasta with his usual eagerness.

'The roof?'

'Well, we've virtually completed the chancel and now we're working on the nave and the entrance, but we still have a corrugated iron roof. You've got to admit, it's ugly.'

'So what's your idea?' asked Domenico with a smile, knowing that his friend would have thought in great detail about whatever he had in mind.

'Cement and sand.'

'Cement and sand?'

'Yes, applied by hand a small amount at a time to cover the whole roof. If we laid down steel bolster netting first, the final result would be even stronger. It'd be painfully slow and messy work but we could have several men working on each side at the same time and they don't need to be skilled, I just have to show them how to do it.'

Domenico studied the roof. In his mind's eye he was trying to work out what the corrugated iron would look like covered. But he liked the idea of strengthening the whole building and making it watertight for years to come.

'Well, we've got a concrete floor, altar and altar rail . . . why not a cement roof as well?' he said eventually. 'Let's go and find Sergeant Pennisi, then I suppose we should tell Padre Giacomo that he's about to be surrounded by the stuff. I hope he'll be pleased!'

28

By the end of August, the city of Paris had been liberated and the chapel's façade had risen to a height of eight feet. The next layers would start to taper as they rose, until eventually they would form a bell tower. Everyone thought the idea of covering the corrugated iron roof was excellent and one day the entire camp made a special effort to finish their quota of blocks and tasks quickly so they could return early.

Buttapasta stood on the scaffolding like a conductor. His 'musicians' consisted of around forty Italians, half of them standing on scaffolding erected along each side of the building, from where they could reach the higher parts of the roof. The remainder stood on the ground to apply cement to the lower sections, down to the top of the concrete walls that had been built shortly after the Nissen huts had been joined.

There were men assigned to mixing cement and others with the job of taking full buckets to those applying it and collecting their empty ones to be refilled. It was a hive of activity and people not involved watched from the sidelines, shouting out encouragement and insults in equal good humour.

Before long, their natural competitiveness had them racing

with each other. Each man put a hand into his bucket and scooped out the cold, wet material. The task might not have required skill but it was fiddly nonetheless and needed care to get an even finish over the top of the ribbed metal. It also had to be equal to the thickness of the man doing the next section.

'Hey, you,' shouted Buttapasta, to someone about half-way down the left-hand side. Several men looked up but the stone-mason was staring at one in particular. 'Don't put so much on.'

The man acknowledged the advice and carried on. Butta-pasta had spent hours with Domenico and one of the Italians who had been a structural engineer before the war, discussing the load-bearing properties of the building. When the cement set it would be significantly lighter and carry its own weight. But until then it was a soggy, heavy mess and they fretted over how much could be applied safely at one time.

Domenico was standing by himself when Major Buckland, Sergeant Major Fornasier and Padre Giacomo appeared beside him.

'Domenico,' said Major Buckland. 'It looks as though you've attracted the entire camp.'

'Not me, sir. I'm just a bystander today.'

'The chapel has been the best thing possible for the men,' said Major Buckland. 'Ever since the Nissen huts were moved, it has given the whole camp a focus.'

'I think you could say it has been a team effort,' said Padre Giacomo.

'I imagine that Buttapasta is enjoying this immensely Domenico,' said Major Buckland.

'He has been in an even more jovial mood than normal sir,' said the artist. 'Of course, the news that Aldo is making a good recovery has cheered up the camp most.'

'He has caused a great deal of concern to a lot of people,'

said Major Buckland. 'But yes, the news of his recovery has been a tonic to everyone.'

'Aldo has been the subject of many prayers,' said Padre Giacomo. 'I gather he has been moved to the military hospital but his leg will keep him there for a while yet.'

'So it would seem from the sister, who has been most diligent at informing us about his condition,' said Major Buckland. 'We just need the war to be over then we can all go home. How does that sound, Padre?'

'I pray daily there will soon be an end to the violence in the world,' answered the priest.

'Amen to that,' said Major Buckland. 'I wonder if the chapel will be completed before we leave the island. I don't expect we will be here long now the causeways are almost finished. Then we'll probably all be off down to England. They're desperate for workers. What do you think, Domenico? How much is left to do?'

'Many jobs can only be carried out at a certain speed, sir. Much of the inside is complete although there are still a lot of small tasks to do and I haven't even started to make the holy water stoup. Buttapasta and his team have much to do on the façade, and then there's the roof.'

The four men fall silent for a while, watching the interaction of the different groups. Just at that moment an Italian picked up a hose and turned it on to some of those standing nearby. This caused a huge cheer and the men who had been drenched chased after the culprit, who ran off behind the chapel.

'This process will have to be repeated several times,' said Domenico, continuing his explanation. 'We have to let the cement set in small amounts to support its own weight before adding more. And we need good weather.'

'I believe the forecast is for sun,' said Padre Giacomo.

'It has been a glorious summer,' said Major Buckland. 'Before the war Orkney was a delightful place to visit.'

Their attention was taken by a roar from the crowd as the man who had turned the hose on the others appeared from behind the chapel.

'It looks as if the jester has had an unfortunate experience with a couple of buckets of wet cement,' said Major Buckland, chuckling loudly. 'If he's not careful he'll be turning into a permanent statue. Perhaps you could put him next to yours, Domenico.'

Domenico turned his head slightly to look at the statue of St George and the dragon behind them.

'It seems so very long ago since I made that. It sometimes feels that so much has happened and yet so little. We're still here, carrying out the same work we were doing nearly three years ago.'

'The causeways represent a huge achievement, particularly in wartime,' said Major Buckland.

'Perhaps the greatest change to the men has been to the part that is not visible to the eye,' said Padre Giacomo.

They fell silent.

'The realisation that we may be leaving the island soon has sent everyone into a fever of activity,' said Domenico. 'No one can bear to leave the chapel unfinished when so much has been done.'

'You must feel that more than anyone,' said Major Buckland.

'It seems to have been my sole purpose in life for quite some time,' said Domenico. 'I was extremely grateful for your permission to let some of the men work full-time on the chapel sir. It's made a huge difference to what we have been able to achieve.'

'Well, I have tried to do my part, but it's been the men

themselves who've done the work,' said Major Buckland modestly. 'Yes, all things considered, we've been very lucky on our little Orkney island.'

Later that afternoon, Giuseppe went to the farm. He had fallen into the habit of going there a couple of evenings each week and for most of the day on a Sunday. The visits were golden moments of joy that had changed his life completely. With the rood screen finished he had more free time and his days were spent thinking about the visit he had just had, or the one he was about to make.

Since he had fixed it, the farm gate opened silently. He closed it, walked up to the front door and knocked. Immediately, he could hear the sound of angry shouting and a woman screaming. He thought it was Rebecca. Giuseppe's hand went to the handle but the door was wrenched open before he reached it. He stepped back instinctively at the sight before him. A large part of the face of the man in front of him seemed to have melted. The ear was missing from one side of his head, as was the hair, while the skin was horribly red and puckered. The eyes that stared at Giuseppe looked as though they belonged to someone who was completely demented.

The man tried to take a step forward but Mr Merriman and Fiona fiercely held on to an arm each and the three of them crammed into the doorway, a mass of squirming misery. Giuseppe could see Fiona's mother and sister just behind him and all of the family were shouting and crying; everyone except the young man, who was livid with a rage that seemed to be directed at him.

'Not nice, is it?' he shouted, still trying to get free. 'Have a good bloody look. This is what I got for trying to free your country, fighting the Germans while you were here safe and sound, eating at my table.'

209

Giuseppe was struck dumb by the unexpected horror, unable to understand what was taking place. Even with his terrible disfigurement there was something familiar about the man. Giuseppe had seen him before and his mind groped for a memory, anything that would make sense of the nightmare in front of him. Then it came. It was a picture he had once seen of two handsome young men in uniform ... a picture Fiona had shown him of her two brothers.

'Why weren't you there?' shouted the man. 'Why weren't you there instead of me? Why was I fighting your war?'

In an instant, the anger went out of him and he crumpled, sobbing against his father who was holding him tightly in his arms. The old man's face was ashen and wet with tears. Mrs Merriman pushed Fiona out of the front door so she could get to the other side of her son.

'Take Giuseppe away, Fiona,' she said.

'But Mother ...'

'It's for the best, love. Go now.' Mrs Merriman gently took her son's arm. 'Come back inside.'

She led him back down the corridor. Mr Merriman didn't look at Giuseppe, but quietly closed the door, leaving the two of them standing outside, shaken.

'Fiona, what's happened?'

Fiona was crying so much she couldn't talk, but instead took his hand and led him into the barn, where she sat on a bale and he knelt at her feet. It took a long time before she was calm enough to speak.

'It's Bill. We received a letter two days ago saying he had been injured and was returning home, but we had no idea he was so badly hurt or would arrive so quickly. He turned up this morning. Everyone was so upset but he seemed alright until Rebecca mentioned you. Then he went berserk. We could hardly control him, he was in such a rage. I was on my way to stop you from reaching the farm, but you were early.'

'I'm sorry . . . sorry for all of you.'

'Bill was so beautiful. Now, I don't know what will happen to him. None of our lives will ever be the same again. You know he doesn't hate you personally, Giuseppe. How can he? He doesn't even know you. But because you're Italian and are here, it's easy to blame you.'

'I've read it often enough in the newspapers. Why are British people paying to feed and keep Italians safe in this country when they could be armed and sent back to free Italy? I have no answers to these questions. Such decisions are made by the British government, not by Italians in the camps. We'd be willing to go back and fight for our homes.'

'I know. You mustn't think badly of Bill.'

'He's right to be hurt and angry. And I don't blame him for hating me. I would do the same in his position.'

'I must go back soon, or he'll feel I am betraying him by staying out here with you.'

'Yes,' said Giuseppe. There was a truth in what Fiona said that could not be denied. 'You should go and I'll return to camp. Is there anything I can do?'

'I'm sorry . . . but you'll have to stay away from the farm.'

Giuseppe was crestfallen at the suggestion but he knew she was right.

'We could meet elsewhere,' he said, hopefully.

'Give me a few days, until I've worked out what to do for the best. I need to spend some time with Bill. He needs me. I promise I'll get a message to you, even if I have to write a letter to you at the camp. Trust me.'

He looked up at her.

'Always,' he said.

29

The face of Christ, a crown of thorns upon his head, stared at Domenico and Buttapasta. The circular bas-relief had been moulded in red clay by Pennisi, who laid it gently on the table in the chapel for his friends to see. It was another skilled creation, amongst so many works of art adorning a building only seventy-five by sixteen feet in size.

'It's beautiful,' said Domenico, gently running his fingers over the clay, enjoying the feel of the fine detail. 'It'll be striking when it's added above the door.'

Pennisi had succeeded in capturing an expression that could be interpreted in many different ways depending upon the person viewing it.

'I would be honoured if you would let me fix it. It'll be the centrepiece,' said Buttapasta.

The façade had been a combination of angles and measurements, mixing concrete and hard physical labour. No one could dispute the effectiveness of what Buttapasta and his team had achieved for it did far more than hide the ugly end of the Nissen hut; it invited the observer to enter, but the impact of the bas-relief of Christ was breathtaking.

The façade had been completed with a small bell tower, although there was no bell, and on top they fixed a small iron cross. The porch, supported by two columns resting on steps that led up to the entrance, complemented the bell tower and both these, and the main gable, were decorated with cusps. Buttapasta had fitted the floor of the porch with inlaid stone, carefully cut and polished, to read 1944 in Roman numerals. He had carved two pinnacles out of concrete, which required many hours of work to chisel the solid blocks into the shapes drawn by Pennisi. The pinnacles had been added to the top of the square columns that formed the edges of the façade.

There was very little remaining to be done. Pennisi had already painted the arching the colour of terracotta. The contrast with the rest of the façade, which had been painted white, was extremely effective. A group of men had taken only a few hours to dig a border around the chapel and a small delegation from every hut had planted flowers.

The chapel was alive both outside and inside its walls. It was rare for there to be no one praying or thinking in the silence. It was as Major Buckland had said; once inside you could be anywhere in the world.

A few days after Buttapasta fixed the bas-relief, Major Buckland arrived with James Sinclair just as Domenico and Giuseppe were making adjustments to one of the gates in the rood screen.

'Ah, I'm glad I've found you here,' said Major Buckland, walking up to the chancel. 'Mr Sinclair has been kind enough to come to the camp to take some photographs of the chapel. Would you mind if he took your photograph outside the entrance? It's such a lovely day and, well, we won't be here much longer.'

'Of course, sir,' said Domenico.

The four men stepped out into the sunshine.

'Where would you like us, sir?' asked Giuseppe.

'How about one either side of the entrance?' said Major Buckland.

Domenico and Giuseppe each stood beside a column at the front of the porch, while the Orkney photographer set up his tripod.

'That's excellent,' said James Sinclair, his finger poised on the button ready to take the shot. 'It's a pity about the bell tower. It looks rather bare.'

'The bell!' cried Domenico. 'We've no bell. Can you give us ten minutes, sir?'

'Yes, of course,' said Major Buckland. 'But why?'

'We're just going to find a bell,' said Domenico. 'Come on.' This was directed at the equally puzzled Giuseppe. Both men ran off towards Domenico's hut, leaving the rather bemused officer and James Sinclair to take photographs of the chapel.

The two Italians soon returned, Giuseppe carrying a ladder and Domenico a piece of cardboard that he had cut to the shape and size of a suitable bell. Between them they quickly fixed the cardboard in the bell tower and then stood by the tripod. It looked surprisingly convincing.

'Well, that's quite amazing,' said Major Buckland delightedly. 'Your makeshift bell looks real from here and in a photograph you'll never tell.'

'Let's hope there isn't any wind for the next few minutes, sir,' said Domenico. 'The slightest gust will have our bell on its way to Scotland in an instant.'

However, Domenico wasn't happy that there was only a photograph of the two of them and asked if James Sinclair would come back. He knew it would be impossible to gather everyone who had lent a hand, but they managed to get the main craftsmen together and, later that day, James Sinclair took a photograph of twenty-four men outside the chapel.

As fate would have it, shortly after the photographs were taken, a bell was retrieved from a sunken blockship. It took Buttapasta, Domenico and Pennisi several hours to hang it in the bell tower, attaching a rope that could be pulled from inside the front door. When the job was complete they each took turns, to the joy of everyone around.

Since the summer, rumours had been circulating as to what was going to happen to the Italians once the main reason for them being on the islands had been removed. There were plenty of small jobs to be completed on the causeways, but even laying tarmac on the surface was to be carried out by Orkney Council employees. One day in September, when they were assembled on the parade ground, Major Buckland addressed them about their future. His Italian had improved greatly since he had arrived at the camp.

'As you all know the huge task you set out to do nearly three years ago has been completed. It has been a colossal project that could not have been achieved without your enormous efforts and sacrifices. Connecting the islands of South Ronaldsay and Burray to mainland Orkney will be a great benefit to the people of these islands for generations to come. I know many of you have made good friends of local people and I am certain you will be made welcome if you return in future years.

'At the end of next week, you will be transferred to Overdale Camp near Skipton, which is in Yorkshire. Farms in England are very short of labour. I think you will find the work less cement-based. Although I'm sure you will be pleased to avoid another Orkney winter, I think many may be sorry to leave these islands.'

The service Padre Giacomo held that Sunday was attended not only by the Italians and British of Camp 60 but also by a large number of Orkney families and civilians. Row upon row of seats and benches had been laid out facing the chapel entrance for the hundreds of people who could not fit inside, and even then many men stood. Micheloni set up a speaker system so that everyone could hear what was said. Major Booth had been able to borrow a harmonium, which was brought over from mainland Orkney in an army truck and positioned to the right of the porch. Fortunately, it was a warm, dry morning.

Inside the chapel people could hardly have been more squashed. Soldiers, officers, engineers and workers were all mixed up with local people. Some of the smaller children sat on the knees of Italians, much to the delight of both. People sat, dressed in their Sunday best, and exchanged excited whispers.

The atmosphere in the little vestry was very different. Padre Giacomo had been there for several hours, praying, reflecting quietly on his life and thinking of those back home. Every now and again he re-read the letter that had arrived a few days earlier from his brother, telling him that their mother had died. Over the months, he had consoled many men who had received sad news but his letter shocked him greatly. The priest had not told anyone in the camp.

He could hear the murmur of voices from the congregation. They were waiting for him. Everyone went instantly quiet when Padre Giacomo emerged from the vestry through one of the curtains that had reached their destination undamaged. He walked to the microphone and paused for a few moments.

'When you arrived on this little island that cold, wet January night, I know your hearts must have been gripped with dread, both for your future in this strange, apparently hostile land and for your loved ones left behind. Who could have foreseen the journey you were about to undertake; the hardships, the

216

dangers, the loneliness and the despair? At times it must have seemed like a journey without end. And yet here we are, on the brink of leaving.

'But what wonders we have also found along that journey together: friendships with our fellow prisoners, selfless acts of help; great understanding and compassion from the commandant, Major Buckland. Many of us will leave behind friends amongst the British and the local Orkney people, who have demonstrated huge kindness and embraced us with an open heart. I know that a piece of my heart will be left behind on this little Orkney island.'

The congregation sat in mesmerised silence. This wasn't a normal Sunday service but a reflection on where many of them had come from and what they had become.

'Long after we have left, and Camp 60 has been erased and the land returned to the owner, this little chapel will remain. It will stand after our bodies have returned to the earth and our souls to the Lord. Here will remain a monument to the ability of the human spirit to lift itself above the greatest adversity, to touch others regardless of race or religion, to join together and create, out of the scraps of another war, a place that transcends physical beauty.

'The chapel will reach out across generations to those not yet born. For as long as these walls stand, those who enter will never forget what has happened here. The war still rages in Europe and many of our countrymen alive today will tragically not return to their families. Let us pray for them and let us thank God . . .'

Padre Giacomo stopped. People inside the chapel initially thought that he had finished his sentence and was simply pausing before the next. But an increasing number became aware that the priest was staring down the aisle to the door, which had been left open for the service. When he spoke again his voice had taken on a different timbre.

'Let us thank God for the safe return of a lost son. For what greater joy is there in Heaven? Welcome back, Aldo.'

Everyone turned. There, standing in the doorway, was Aldo. He looked thinner than ever and had a walking stick in one hand. His other arm was looped tightly through that of a young woman, the nurse who had met them at the hospital entrance the day of his accident. All of this could be taken in at a glance. But what captured people's attention was the expression of pure joy that beamed on Aldo's face. Many thought afterwards they had rarely seen anyone radiate such elation.

'Come, my son. Your friends will make space for you at the front.'

It was a morning of so many mixed emotions; remembrance and regret, rejoicing and hope. Padre Giacomo was equally bombarded by conflicting emotions and heard his own voice waver when he spoke again.

'Let us continue with a hymn. Thanks to the generosity of one of the Kirkwall churches we have books for our service this morning, so let us turn to hymn number eighty-two.'

There was a general commotion as everyone stood up and tried to find the relevant page in their books, most of which were shared between two or three people. Sforza, who played the accordion in the camp band, was at the harmonium and had the music ready. He started to pump the pedals and play the first few bars. He had pulled out all the stops and pushed out the swell pedals with his knees to get as much volume as possible. Sforza stopped for a moment to ensure that everyone had found the right place and when he began once more hundreds of voices joined in praise and friendship.

'Immortal, invisible, God only wise . . .'

The sound of singing drifted across Lamb Holm and over the water. To the south, on Glimps Holm, a pair of seals lazing in the sun lifted their heads and twitched their noses, while to the north a lone soldier walking on the shore of mainland Orkney stopped to listen. He looked over at Lamb Holm and could see the chapel. A little girl sat on top of a man's shoulders, her long hair golden in the sunlight. The soldier couldn't remember when he had last sung a hymn, but the whispered words were pulled from his body as if they feared what might be released with them.

'Unresting, unhasting, and silent as light . . .'

He had been involved in almost continuous fighting for longer than he could remember, until he had been wounded and eventually returned to Britain. He had been posted to Orkney only a few weeks earlier.

'Thy clouds which are fountains of goodness and love . . .'

During the last fourteen months, he had lost every friend he had had in the battalion, and in all that time he had never shown emotion at their deaths. He had not cried in Sicily, when he had buried his first friend with his own shovel. There was nothing to bury of the second, who had disappeared before his eyes, hit by an artillery shell. He had left the third by the side of the road in Salerno, patting his helmet and saying he would see him later, both of them knowing he would not. It had continued until there was no one.

'Great Father of glory, pure Father of light . . .'

And in all that time he had never cried. They began calling him 'Hard Jock'; a big, tough man who would barely acknowledge anyone. But his fighting days were over.

'All laud we would render: O help us to see . . .'

And he couldn't see for the tears flowing down his cheeks.

'Tis only the splendour of light hideth Thee.'

The congregation stopped and the harmonium fell silent. The stillness was physical. Everyone's attention was captured by the chapel, the head of Christ on the façade and what was happening inside. Only the little girl from her vantage point looked across the water and saw a tiny figure on the opposite shore, saluting. The smartest salute he had ever given. People put down their hymn-books and knelt to pray. The soldier on the opposite shore couldn't make out the words but he could tell what was happening and hear the murmur of voices. He knelt in the sand.

30

Domenico and Buttapasta were mesmerised by the expression of wonder on the face of a small boy, who was being shown by an Italian how to peel an orange. A couple of men had collected fruit that had arrived in parcels from Italy and had brought it out to share once the service was over. They had gathered quite a crowd of inquisitive children, but the men in the hut were generous and there was plenty for everyone. The scene was causing much amusement amongst the adults, for many children were completely baffled by some of the objects. The two men, both fathers themselves, were in their element, explaining and helping small hands to peel skins.

The congregation inside the chapel had quickly emerged into the sunlight to join those outside and there were now more than a hundred different conversations taking place around the building. A few elderly ladies from South Ronaldsay had remained seated and several Italians had moved chairs around so they could speak to the women about their lives on the island. Many people were swapping addresses and there was a great deal of handshaking and hugging.

Beside the harmonium, Aldo and the nurse were in deep

conversation with Padre Giacomo. Giuseppe stood on the other side of the crowd, talking to Mr and Mrs Merriman, having arranged to meet Fiona later so they could say their goodbyes in private. Giuseppe wished he was already at the farm. He hadn't been back since that terrible afternoon two weeks earlier, but no one mentioned it that morning. Mr and Mrs Merriman wished him all the best in his life back in Italy. It was a sad parting.

A short distance away Domenico and Buttapasta stood watching the various scenes around them.

'It's a shame the chapel has been in use for such a short time before we leave,' said Buttapasta.

'Yes, but as Padre Giacomo pointed out it'll be here for generations to come. At least, I pray to God it will,' said Domenico, who was concerned about the chapel's future. There was nothing they could do once they left the island, which was scheduled for the end of the week.

'It'll be strange leaving Lamb Holm after all this time,' said Buttapasta. 'It's an odd place. It seeps into your bones until you feel yourself becoming part of the land.'

'Remember when we first arrived? Dino said . . . Dino said we had arrived in Hades and discovered it wasn't hot but freezing cold,' said Domenico.

'I don't think I thawed out until the August,' said Buttapasta.

Domenico was about to speak when Aldo walked over. They hadn't seen him since that fateful day on the *Emerald Wings* and each now embraced him.

'Aldo. How are you?' said Domenico.

'We've kept up to date with your recovery but it's not the same as seeing you and hearing about it from yourself,' said Buttapasta.

'You look thin,' commented Domenico.

222

'Do you want to sit down?' added Buttapasta

All this was hurled at him almost in one breath, so Aldo had no chance to answer.

'I'm fine. I'm fine,' he said laughing. 'I've had a good rest and having my leg in traction made a nice change from you two pulling it. They say I won't need the stick for much longer and everything will be back to normal. To be honest, I've never felt better.'

Domenico studied his young friend. Something about him had altered, which had nothing to do with the loss of weight or his slightly pale colour.

'You look . . . changed,' said Domenico.

'A near-death experience can do that to a man,' said Buttapasta.

'No, it's not that,' said Aldo happily.

'What then?' asked Buttapasta.

'The service was good,' replied Aldo, ignoring the question. 'Well attended.'

'You know how to make an entrance, I'll say that for you,' said the stonemason.

'I couldn't miss the service after all the work and sacrifices made by so many people to build the chapel.'

'You seemed engrossed in conversation with Padre Giacomo,' said Buttapasta. 'That must be a first.'

'Yes. He's actually a good man.'

'Haven't we been saying that to you for months?' said Buttapasta.

'You're hiding something,' said Domenico.

'Oh?' said Aldo.

Domenico didn't answer, but stood looking at him.

'Alright, I was about to tell you. It's one of the reasons I'm here. Ailsa and I are getting married.'

223

'Married!' said Buttapasta.

'To the young nurse?' asked Domenico.

'That's the idea,' said Aldo. 'It won't be until I'm out of hospital, which means you'll all have left, including Padre Giacomo. Ailsa insisted we speak to him about it.'

'Married,' said Buttapasta again. 'I had no idea. I don't know what to say.'

'Well that's another first then.'

'But what will you do, Aldo?' asked Domenico.

'Marry. Have children. For the first time perhaps, be happy and content. If we have a boy we'll name him Domenico and please you both in one go.'

'But where will you go?' asked Domenico. 'How will you live?'

'We're hoping to stay here.'

'Stay in Britain?' asked Buttapasta.

'In Orkney,' said Aldo. 'I suppose when I'm fit enough I'll have to work for the British until we're all released after the war, but Orkney is Ailsa's home. It's where we want to be. She has a house near Kirkwall, so it's a start. Perhaps I'll be allowed to work on the islands and not be repatriated. I suppose . . . it's in God's hands.'

Domenico slowly held out his hand.

'I think I see a different Aldo before me. The boy has become a man.'

'Thank you,' he said shaking his friend's hand. 'I have never thanked you both for helping to save my life.'

Aldo let go of Domenico and held out his hand to Buttapasta but the big man grabbed him in a bear hug and lifted him off the ground.

'Oh my leg. Mind my leg.'

'Little Aldo getting married. That's the best news I've heard in years. Well done, lad. Well done.'

'Put me down or I won't be doing anything but going back in traction,' said Aldo, but he was laughing . . . laughing and crying and hugging Buttapasta.

It struck Domenico it was the first time he had ever seen Aldo with tears in his eyes. The commotion attracted the attention of several people nearby, who watched with smiles and nods. Ailsa and Padre Giacomo walked over just as Buttapasta put Aldo back down.

'I believe congratulations are in order,' said Domenico to Ailsa, kissing her on both cheeks.

'Thank you. And thank you both for looking after Aldo while he's been in the camp.'

'We now officially hand that responsibility over to you, Ailsa,' said Buttapasta stumbling over the name, which seemed so strange to him. 'We've done our best to train him, but it's been an uphill job at the best of times.'

'Hey, do you mind,' said Aldo. 'I demand more respect in front of my future wife, not to mention Padre Giacomo.'

'I can think of no better way to end our enforced stay on the island than learning of Aldo and Ailsa's plans,' said Padre Giacomo.

Giuseppe slipped away unnoticed as soon as he had said his farewells to Fiona's parents and set off for the farm, carrying a parcel under his arm. Fiona had written and told him to arrive late that morning. It was the worst journey he had ever made and he ran much of the way, despair eating away at him. When he arrived, the front door was open. Fiona was standing in the kitchen. Giuseppe put down his parcel and they looked at each other for a long time without speaking. When he finally broke the silence, his voice cracked with emotion.

'I'll never see you again.'

225

They both knew it was true. Their paths were to part from that day onwards. Giuseppe's love had brought him great joy, but no peace. He felt as though he had been broken into a thousand tiny parts and no matter how they were put back together he would never be the same again.

'No,' said Fiona gently. 'Your future doesn't lie here, so far from the life you know. You must go home to your family. You have a wife who deserves to have you back, and a son who needs his father.'

'I have missed them so much,' said Giuseppe. 'Lying in bed at night, I try so very hard to remember what it was like to hold Renato and I'm frightened he'll not even like me. I'll be a total stranger.'

'He'll like you. Just be yourself and I know he'll be proud of his father and that you'll be proud of him. Be happy in each other's company.'

A single tear fell down his face. Fiona reached up and tenderly brushed it away. She left her hand cupped around his cheek.

'There will always be a place in my heart that loves you, no matter what happens in the future,' she said. 'Never forget that.'

He could not speak and she pulled him to her and held him tightly. He buried his head on her shoulder. It was a long time before she let go of him and when she did it felt that this was their goodbye, even though they had several hours left together before he returned to the camp. This moment, standing in the kitchen, was their parting.

'You've brought a parcel,' she said at last, wiping away her tears.

'I made something for you.'

'What is it?'

'You must open it.'

She went over to the table and untied the newspaper to reveal two wrought iron candlesticks.

'They're beautiful.'

'I wanted to give you something. I had thought about making a ring, but perhaps one day . . .' He stopped, unable for a moment to finish the sentence. 'One day you will meet someone else and a ring might be difficult to explain. But no one will question where two candlesticks came from and when you light the candles you might think of me.'

'It's a lovely thought. Thank you. I will treasure them always. And what are these?' she asked, picking up a bundle of papers that had been underneath the candlesticks.

'They are poems I've written while in Camp 60.'

'I have something for you,' she said.

Fiona took an envelope off the dresser and pulled out a photograph of her that had been taken a few weeks earlier at the Kirkwall studio of James Sinclair. He studied the image for several minutes in silence.

'I don't need a photograph to remember your beauty but it is the best present you could have given me. Thank you.' He hesitated for a moment. 'But there is one other thing I would like.'

'Name it,' she said.

He put a hand in his pocket and removed what appeared to be a small lighter. He had made many over the months and had even given one to Mr Merriman as a present. This one appeared to be old and was certainly battered. Fiona looked puzzled until Giuseppe pressed a secret catch that allowed the 'lighter' to open into two empty halves, like a large locket.

'I made this to hide a lock of your hair, which I will keep with me always.'

Without speaking, Fiona walked over to a drawer by the

sink. She rummaged around inside to gain some time then brought over a pair of scissors.

'You do it,' she said handing them over.

He carefully cut a small piece of hair so that no one would notice and put it into the 'lighter'. She took it out of his hands to study more closely.

'Such items tend to disappear easily and occasionally they are taken by guards during the searches carried out when changing camps,' said Giuseppe. 'I've made this one to look worthless and it obviously doesn't work, so no one will want it.'

She gave it back and he put it away inside his jacket.

'Everyone has gone for the day,' she said.

'I saw your parents at the service. I was glad I could say goodbye to them. They looked very tired. What about Rebecca . . . and Bill?'

'I had to bribe Rebecca to go to a friend's after work. But she sends her love and said to pass on her wishes.' She hesitated. 'Bill has gone out walking. He can't bear to be shut in, but visits places where he doesn't think he will meet anyone. Sometime he goes out at night, in the dark. It's very difficult for him.'

'It is difficult for all of you.'

'Bill is a good man. He will come around eventually, but he has had no time to adjust. Tell me about the service,' she said, trying to lighten their conversation.

'It was very moving. Padre Giacomo's sermon was good, but the highlight was when Aldo walked in. I don't think there was a dry eye in the entire chapel. The rumour is that he is remaining on Orkney while his leg mends and that he is going to . . .'

'Marry a local girl,' said Fiona finishing his sentence.

'Yes, but how did you know?'

'Because he's marrying Ailsa.'

'Ailsa? From where I sat I couldn't see the girl Aldo was with and then I was keen to get away. It seems so long ago when she helped you get rid of the guards at the hospital.'

They were quiet for a while. Giuseppe took her hand and kissed it.

'There is something else,' he said. 'In the chapel, I have left something for you.'

'In the chapel?' What is it?'

'You must find it.'

'But how will I know what it is?'

'You will know because you are looking for it, but I don't think anyone else will ever notice it, even though it is there for everyone to see. It is in the very heart of the building.'

Fiona knew he was not going to tell her any more so accepted she would have to go to the chapel to find out.

'Come on,' she said. 'We can't stay indoors all day. Bill isn't the only one to know secret paths and places where you are unlikely to meet anyone. I've made us a picnic. I don't want our last day together to be full of sadness.'

Fiona and Giuseppe walked hand in hand down empty country tracks and talked about their futures and their hopes. Every moment was filled with a memory to be treasured, but their time together was over quickly. They had both agreed he should leave before any of her family returned and by mid-afternoon they were once more standing in the kitchen, facing the final goodbye.

'I have one more thing to ask,' said Fiona.

'What is it?'

'When you eventually return home, tell your wife about me.'

'Tell her? Why?'

'Because, Giuseppe, you will not be able to hide it. You are too open and she will guess. And if she asks and you deny it, then it will always be a barrier between you both. It would be better to confess what has happened and suffer the consequences.'

'She might not forgive me.'

'I think she will. You have been away a long time. It may take a while but I believe she will. Trust my woman's instinct in this.'

Giuseppe's walk back to the camp was the loneliest he had ever made. But it was over. Upon reaching the gates he went straight to the chapel and was still kneeling in front of the altar when the trumpeter announced supper. Giuseppe had said his goodbyes and his prayers, what the future held in store only time would tell. He got up and went to join the others in the mess hall.

Giuseppe's was not the only farewell taking place that week. Carlo obtained permission to visit Dino's grave and a few days after the service he caught a lift into Kirkwall on an army truck then walked the mile or so out to St Olaf cemetery. No one else was about and as he had plenty of time he started to read the headstones. Some were very old and he saw the same surname repeated often, where generations of an Orkney family were buried near to each other. Carlo tried to work out the various connections but sometimes the writing had worn away too much or he simply couldn't fathom the links.

He moved on and came across the graves of servicemen killed in action during the First World War and the war still taking place. He was struck by how death had brought people together on that one spot who were perhaps so different during life. A 'Boy, 1st Class', aged only sixteen was buried next to a Petty Officer of forty-eight. Deckhands, airmen and mechanics lay in the ground yards from each other.

There was a headstone for a leading photographer from HMS Tern, a reference that appeared on many graves. Carlo had heard of HMS Tern, which was an airfield north of Stromness. It was the custom of the Royal Navy Fleet Air Arm squadrons to name land bases from which they operated after ships. He knew of another, north of Kirkwall, called HMS Sparrowhawk and he soon came upon several graves of men from this squadron.

Carlo walked on, reading the inscriptions at the bottom of the headstones. Two unnamed sailors were 'Known Unto God'. A leading airman of nineteen had 'made the supreme sacrifice', while an airman of twenty had 'answered the last call'. Carlo had shed many tears for Dino and had been determined this day should not be a morbid parting, but the waste of so much young life weighed heavily.

He stopped suddenly in surprise when he came across the headstones of two Germans. He couldn't tell if they were airmen or sailors, only that they had been in their twenties. Carlo supposed in death men could no longer be enemies. They had followed orders and fought for their country.

He left the German graves behind and walked over to stand by the place where Dino was buried. It was in a corner of the cemetery by a tree. Carlo thought Dino would have liked this because there were lots of birds in the branches and they were singing away for all they were worth. At the bottom of Dino's headstone, underneath the name and date, it simply said 'A good man'.

There was so much he had wanted to say but now that Carlo stood in front of Dino's grave he felt it unnecessary. Dino would know what was in his heart.

He turned suddenly and walked away, out of the cemetery gates and headed towards Kirkwall. He didn't look back.

31

The few remaining days passed quickly and the morning of departure arrived. Although a cold wind blew steadily, it was a dry and bright morning as the Italians gathered on the parade ground. They were to walk to St Mary's where a fleet of buses was waiting to transport them to Stromness, from where the old steamer *St Ola* would take them across the Pentland Firth to Scrabster. Then they would make their way to Thurso and catch a train all the way to York.

Domenico and Major Buckland stood outside the chapel, near the gate. Domenico had been granted permission to remain with the small detachment of British soldiers who were to clean up the camp, dismantling and packing equipment that could be used elsewhere.

'It was good of you to allow me to stay behind and make the holy water stoup, sir,' said Domenico. 'When that's done, the chapel will be complete.'

'It would have been a pity not to have finished something so important. Major Booth and his party should be here for about ten days while they load everything worthwhile into trucks. You can't leave equipment like the kitchen ranges or beds to simply rot, not in times of war. They'll be put to good use in other camps.'

For a while they stood in amiable silence and watched the men lining up on the parade ground.

'It will be strange when it's empty,' said Major Buckland. 'In one morning the camp will have changed from a noisy, vibrant place full of Italians shouting and waving their arms to . . . well, I think it will be a desolate place. Best to pull it down as quickly as possible. Let it return to nature.'

'And the chapel, sir?'

'I truly wish I could make you a promise, Domenico, or that I had Padre Giacomo's conviction that the chapel will be here for generations to come. When the rest of the men leave next week, I'll have no authority or influence at all over what happens here. The land will be given back to Mr Sutherland Graeme and technically it's meant to be in the same condition in which we took it on.'

'The Orkney people said they would look after the chapel and so did Mr Sutherland Graeme.'

'Yes, I'm sure you can rely on them but, between us, I fear bureaucratic orders from London and also the Orkney winters that will beat the chapel mercilessly.'

There were shouts from the parade ground and the first lines of Italians began to march towards the gate. During the previous few days the entire camp had been busy washing, mending and ironing uniforms. Buttons and belts had been polished and boots cleaned, while the camp barber had been working late every evening.

Someone had even gone to Aldo's friend at the power station to obtain extra oil so the men could grease their hair. Bill Johnstone had been presented with a lemonade bottle, which contained a beautifully carved crucifix, in thanks for all the oil he had supplied. Several Orkney families had also received gifts over the previous few weeks. They ranged from an engraved rolling-pin to a scaled down model of Milan cathedral, which had been painstakingly made out of matchsticks.

The men marched towards the gate with pride and precision. It could not have been a greater contrast to the night when they arrived, shivering and sick from their journey, full of dread and resentment. As the NCO at the front of the first platoon reached the chapel he saluted Major Buckland and called out.

'Eyes right.'

The men turned their heads smartly to face the British officer, who returned the salute. Domenico had tactfully moved several steps away. He would join the men in a couple of weeks, but he still felt a pang of sorrow at seeing them leave. A few caught his eye, especially the imposing figure of Buttapasta. He winked as he drew level and Domenico broke into a big grin. Major Buckland had to hold back a smile when he saw Shipwreck, his walking stick pointing to the sky from his rucksack and the trophy he had won on the athletics day fixed to the top.

Unfortunately, Padre Giacomo had taken ill suddenly the day after the service and was expected to be in the military hospital for quite some time, so he wasn't amongst those leaving that day. The men in Camp 34 were to remain on Burray for a few months longer, whilst the sixty Italians who were billeted near Stromness were staying in Orkney for the foreseeable future. Sergeant Major Fornasier was near the middle of the column. He marched up to Major Buckland and saluted smartly.

'I would like to thank you, sir, for all the help and kindness you've shown the men during their stay here.'

'I appreciate your comments, Sergeant Major Fornasier. I hope you and your men return to Italy as safely and as quickly as possible, though only God knows when this war will be over.'

The two men looked at each other. They had met as enemies and were parting as friends. Major Buckland shook the Italian's hand with great warmth.

Sergeant Major Fornasier stepped back, saluted and marched away to join the rear of the column that was just passing by. Domenico and Major Buckland watched as the last of them marched out of the camp and down the road. They walked to the gate, where they stood for a long time, following the column with their eyes as the men left Lamb Holm and headed towards mainland Orkney across barrier number one.

They were Churchill's Barriers, the greatest engineering feat of the Second World War, defying the predictions of many who said the job could not be done. They had held back the tide. The project had consumed over 900,000 tons of rock and concrete and taken more than four years. Men had been injured and had died during their construction, but they had been built. The sea had been tamed and no vessel would ever again enter Scapa Flow between those eastern islands.

At St Mary's, Major Booth was waiting by the buses along with a couple of Balfour Beatty men and a small delegation of Orkney people, including Patrick Sutherland Graeme, his daughter Alison and granddaughter Sheena. There were thank you and farewell speeches from every quarter. Their lives had been thrown together and now were to be separated. No one knew if they would ever meet again.

Gifts were also exchanged. Sergeant Major Fornasier presented the seven-year old Sheena with a cleverly made wooden toy, which consisted of a series of ducks on top of a board. When this was moved, a weight hanging underneath made the ducks bob up and down. She was delighted. So was he. Their brief contacts with local Orkney children meant a great deal to the Italians during their captivity.

Although Giuseppe and Fiona had agreed they would not see each other again, he still looked for her at the farewell ceremony, and then again as the men lined up to board the *St Ola*. He searched frantically, but saw no one. She was there, hidden, observing the scene on the quayside through her father's old monocular. It had been difficult to pick out Giuseppe at first amongst so many men dressed in similar clothing. However, when Fiona finally spotted him, she followed his every movement and knew he was looking for her.

Fiona stood watching the men as they filed on board the ship. She could no longer identify Giuseppe amongst the crowded men on the decks. Eventually, the steamer cast off and began its journey across the Pentland Firth. She remained long after the *St Ola* was out of sight.

Fiona caught a bus to Kirkwall, picked up her bicycle and cycled to Holm, but instead of going to the farm she ended up at barrier number one. A couple of workmen from Orkney Council were examining the new tarmac surface, but apart from them there was no one around. She went across the causeway and cycled to the gates of Camp 60. Fiona propped her bicycle against the fence and thought she might have to pretend there was something wrong with it, while she waited for a chance to enter the camp. However, there was nobody around so she simply walked in.

She had been in the chapel only once, on the evening they had attended the concert in the mess hall, but on that occasion it had been full of local people having a tour before the performance. This time it was empty, and she wasn't prepared for the stillness and quiet that enveloped her. Fiona knew exactly where to go. Giuseppe said what he had left for her was in the very heart of the building. The vestry and chancel together were the same length as the nave, which meant the centre of the building was the point at which the two gates in the rood screen met.

She pushed them open and gasped. Giuseppe had made a heart out of wrought iron and embedded it into the concrete floor, to form the stop for the two gates. Only when the gates were opened was the heart revealed. Anyone entering the chancel would be looking at the altar and the images, not at their feet. Fiona understood why Giuseppe thought very few people would ever spot what was so obvious and, of course, those who did would have no idea of its true meaning.

She curled up on the floor and ran her finger around the outline. Fiona thought of him at the forge, secretly making the one thing not in Domenico Chiocchetti's design. She imagined him heating and shaping the metal until he felt it was perfect then afterwards carrying it around in his pocket, ready to fit when the last part of the rood screen was complete. To Giuseppe and Fiona, it meant more than anything else in the building. She leant over and kissed the heart, but the metal was cold and hard. He was gone.

32

Apart from the work party of a dozen British soldiers, Domenico was now the only resident in the camp. As he lay in bed that first night, he thought of all the times he had wished for quiet in order to get some uninterrupted sleep. Now he lay for hours, unable to settle, used to being surrounded by others.

Domenico found the morning even more unnerving. There was no one to tell him when to get up, so he dressed when he felt like it, stoked the stove and walked over to the wash block. It had never been so empty.

After a surprisingly good breakfast, Domenico wandered around the camp to stretch his legs. The temperature had dropped significantly over the last few days. Autumn was in the air and the clouds threatened a downpour. He stopped by the statue of St George and the dragon.

A friend of Domenico's, Bruno Volpi, one of the many workers on the chapel, had typed the names of every single Italian who had been held captive in Camp 60. The two men had put the sheets of paper into a milk bottle along with a handful of Italian coins then closed the top. Before Domenico had cemented the last part of the base of the statue, sealing it forever, they placed the bottle directly under the dragon. It was a record of them all, which would remain on that distant piece of land for as long as the statue survived.

Domenico ended up at the chapel, the only place where he didn't feel lonely. He had decided not to work in the chapel making the holy water stoup as every single inch of it had been swept, cleaned and polished in preparation for the service the previous Sunday. Eventually, he went back to his hut, collecting en route the clay he kept in a storeroom.

He felt like a naughty schoolboy. Even as POWs they had kept their army discipline and there had been regular hut inspections. Everything had always been spotless. Now, Domenico was about to make an unbelievable mess in the middle of the floor and he smiled at the thought. He had already drawn the design for the holy water stoup and made sure all the materials were to hand. He worked quickly and precisely, moulding the clay to the right shape and size, following his own drawing carefully.

He joined the British soldiers for meals and they often brought a mug of steaming coffee to the hut, checking if he needed anything else so he did not have to interrupt his work. He appreciated their kindness. One day Major Booth entered with two mugs. The two of them sat either side of the stove, surrounded by bags of cement, lumps of clay and half-made plaster moulds, talking about their lives and families.

Domenico was drawn more and more to the chapel as the days went by and if he wasn't working on the holy water stoup or eating in the canteen, he could be found praying or simply sitting and thinking about the things that had happened since he had arrived all that time ago.

Before Aldo had left to return to the hospital, he had asked Domenico to do something for him. The two men shared a small cupboard between their beds and it still contained Aldo's belongings. Following Aldo's instructions, Domenico burnt the notebook that listed who owed him money, spent the significant pile of tokens at the camp shop then distributed the cigarettes and other treats between the men in the hut. The British money was sent to Aldo.

Domenico had wanted to see Padre Giacomo, but the priest was too ill for visitors. The artist remembered all the excited conversations they had enjoyed together in the little vestry, planning the minute details of the chapel and its contents. Domenico had carefully taken down the Italian flag hanging in the vestry and Major Booth had arranged for it to be delivered to the hospital.

He thought of the triumphs the men had achieved in creating it, all the enormous obstacles and limitations they had overcome. In its own way it had been just as much of a challenge as building the barriers. He hoped the chapel would be as permanent. Men had put so much effort into it, so much of themselves into it.

On the morning they were to leave, Domenico rose early and went to the chapel as soon as it was daylight. He polished the inside then went outside and cleaned the windows, checking they were all tightly shut. None of it needed doing, but it was the last act he could perform for the building that had come to mean so much to him. The flowers left over from the service were thrown out and new candles placed in the holders.

He was kneeling before the altar when the truck's horn sounded just outside the camp gates. He stood and took a last look around, but there was nothing more to be done. He picked up his rucksack near the entrance and walked out into the sunshine, quietly closing the door behind him.

Domenico took a big breath, let it out slowly and took his

hand off the handle. That was it. He walked away briskly. Two soldiers were standing at the gates, one half of which was already closed. They were waiting for him so the artist hurried over and climbed into the back of the truck, a couple of the men helping to pull him inside. The gates were closed and locked with a heavy chain and padlock. One of the soldiers followed Domenico into the back of the truck and the second man lifted and secured the tailboard then ran around to join the driver.

The truck pulled away with a lurch. Domenico could only see the chapel through the barbed-wire gates. It suddenly looked so forlorn and vulnerable alongside the much larger accommodation huts. The truck gathered speed. Domenico couldn't tear his eyes away and sat staring back at the camp as they travelled across the barrier. He still watched the chapel as they started along the coast road on mainland Orkney, but suddenly they turned a corner and he couldn't see it any more. It was over.

33

The D-Day landings in June 1944 heralded a change in the war, and with dramatic events unfolding almost daily on mainland Europe the eyes of the world were focused on lands far away from the little Orkney island of Lamb Holm. The south of England needed men and equipment, and throughout much of that year the defences around Scapa Flow were reduced significantly. The departure of large numbers of people resulted in pockets of normality returning to the islands.

Several of the gun emplacements around Scapa Flow were now empty concrete structures, visited only by gulls, while the balloon barrage was moved to London to provide greater protection for the capital. The transfer of most of the Balfour Beatty construction workers led to the disbandment of the 2nd Orkney Battalion of the Home Guard, known locally as 'Orkney's Foreign Legion' because it contained so many civilians from the south. By November, the threat of any form of invasion of Orkney was considered to be so slight that Orkney's Home Guard was stood down.

People who lived on Burray and South Ronaldsay were now able to visit Kirkwall by simply driving across the barriers and those on mainland Orkney could visit the islands with ease. The causeways represented a significant change in lifestyle for many.

On 12th May 1945, a few days after VE Day, the Churchill Barriers were officially opened by the First Lord of the Admiralty. Strict wartime censorship and travel regulations meant many people living in the northern islands were totally unaware the barriers had been built and were surprised by news of their official opening. Several of the admiralty and invited guests stared at the little chapel as the convoy of cars swept along the causeways. But once they reached mainland Orkney they had other matters to attend to and the building went out of their mind.

The years rolled by and, gradually, the war faded into memory while the chapel's presence endured and its fame grew. People were enjoying holidays again and Orkney became a popular destination. The easy access to Lamb Holm and the uniqueness of the chapel made it an obvious tourist attraction for visitors to the islands, while the Orcadians themselves often visited the little gem on their doorstep. However, the winter winds and rain beat the building fiercely, making the old ship's bell ring out as if a signal of distress. But no one took heed of the warning, and the state of the building deteriorated with every season.

Eventually, the force of the winds rocked the hut sufficiently to crack the concrete roof and the constant dampness in the air during the winter rusted the rood screen. The main door had rotted at the bottom, allowing access to mice looking for shelter. They ran around the nave, occasionally nibbling the surface of the plasterboard. The once-white façade was dirty and the plaster chipped. Pennisi's beautiful bas-relief of the face of

Christ was wearing away and the fine detail was disappearing. On top of the bell tower the tiny cross had rusted so badly that part of it had snapped off, whilst the dragon nearby looked up with scorn at the noble knight and his growing white crown provided by the local seabirds.

One day in June 1958, an elderly woman entered the chapel with Father Joseph Ryland-Whitaker, the Catholic priest for Shetland and Orkney along with Father Frank Cairns.

'Every time I come here I am amazed by the beauty of it,' said Father Whitaker.

'As you know, Father, the local women have a rota to come and clean the chapel. Between us it's tidied on a regular basis.'

'And an excellent job you do of it.'

'But the condition of the building gets worse every year. Now, there's water coming in. You can see the damp patches on the plasterboard. I thought I should let you know how badly it's deteriorating.'

'You were quite right to have brought it to my attention. The question is what to do about it.' He was standing looking up at the Madonna and Child and carried on talking whilst looking at the picture. 'I suppose the first step is to contact Mr Sutherland Graeme. After all, he owns Lamb Holm so any restoration to the chapel has to be sanctioned by him. I know he's had concerns about the building and will be eager to help. I'll call on him this afternoon.'

A few weeks later the Italian Chapel Preservation Committee held its first ever meeting. The committee consisted of Father Whitaker, Patrick Sutherland Graeme, Beatrice Linton, Cecil Walls and Ernest Marwick, the same man who had been manager of J. M. Stevenson and had supplied Domenico with poster paints. He had put his shopkeeping days behind him and was now working for the *Orkney Herald* newspaper.

Father Whitaker, who had taken on the role of chairman, began the meeting.

'If I may, I would like to formally start the first meeting of the Italian Chapel Preservation Committee by thanking Mr Sutherland Graeme for his instant agreement to be involved and, indeed, for his willingness to be the committee's president.'

'As you know,' replied Sutherland Graeme, who was now Lord Lieutenant of Orkney. 'I've voiced concerns for years about the condition of the chapel but I've always been advised that, due to the materials it is made of, nothing can be done to preserve it. However, I would be delighted if this is proved to be incorrect and there is some way that the deterioration can be halted and the building saved.'

The five people fell silent. No one had any instant answers to the problem but they shared a determination to do something to save a monument they all felt strongly about.

'I understand the number of visitors going into the building is greater every summer,' says Miss Linton, who taught classics at the local school.

'You know,' said Marwick, 'the best person to help us would be the original artist, Domenico Chiocchetti, but as far as I know nobody has had any contact with him since the Italians left in 1944. I don't think anyone here even knows where in Italy he lives. If, in fact, he is in Italy.'

'Or if he's still alive,' said Walls.

Several of them nodded at this depressing possibility.

'I think Ernest is right. If there's a chance we could get Mr Chiocchetti to help, we should do everything possible to find him,' said Father Whitaker. 'Certainly the paintwork is one of the most urgent things to be restored.'

'The most pressing need is to stop the water getting in,' said Walls. 'There's a gap between the façade and the hut that is particularly worrying, and there are several broken windows. I propose the first task is to organise the relevant local tradesmen to make the building watertight and ensure the façade is safe.'

'We'll need funding,' pointed out Marwick.

'There is some money,' said Sutherland Graeme. 'Visitors often leave coins in the holy water stoup. Every so often my daughter Alison collects this and gives it to Father Whitaker when he is over from Shetland.'

'Yes, I've been storing it in the church's safe, but with no particular plan as to what to use it for,' confirmed the priest.

'Why don't we leave a donation box for visitors to put money into?' suggested Miss Linton. 'We could advertise that it's for the chapel's restoration.'

They looked at each other around the table. It was a good, sensible start, but they all felt the need for something more, a grander action.

'As ever, it's the first step that's the most difficult, but to stop any more water getting into the chapel is a good beginning. I'm just not sure what we do next,' admitted Father Whitaker.

'Perhaps,' said Marwick, 'we should start making a noise about the chapel, contact some national newspapers? Stir up some interest in the building and its plight.'

'That's a good idea,' agreed Father Whitaker. 'We could get in touch with some of the radio stations, or even some relevant Italian organisations. They might be able to help us track down Domenico Chiocchetti.'

'Excellent,' said Sutherland Graeme. 'Let's start creating some waves and see what washes up.'

34

A cold mist wrapped itself around the black Morris Minor on the morning in March 1960 when Ernest Marwick drove his guests away from Kirkwall airport. In the back seat were two men. One was Charles Ricono from the BBC. The other, who peered intently, trying to see beyond the mist to the country-side beyond, was Domenico Chiocchetti.

'I can't imagine the thoughts going through your head at this moment, Signor Chiocchetti,' said Ricono, who had already inter-viewed Domenico over the telephone for a radio programme on the chapel, broadcast on the BBC Home Service the previous year.

'I feel such a mixture of emotions I'm not sure what my thoughts are,' said Domenico. 'But one of them is certainly grat-itude to you and to Signor Finoglio at the BBC. Without the huge efforts you both went to in order to track me down in Moena, and without the BBC's generosity in paying for this return trip to Orkney, I wouldn't be here today about to see the chapel once more.'

'The chapel,' said Ricono, 'has created a huge amount of interest. When word reached us there was a small group of Orcadians, desperately fighting against time to save a beautiful chapel made by Italian prisoners of war and trying to trace the man behind its creation . . . well, we knew there was a story to be told. And it's incredible just how many want to hear that story. People have been deeply moved by the plight of the little chapel and by what you and the other Italians achieved during a period of great hardship.'

The car emerged from the fog just in time for Domenico to see the causeway across Kirk Sound and a few moments later they were surrounded by water. It all looked so different. The coils of barbed wire had gone, as had all the machinery and equipment . . . all the mess of construction . . . all the mess of war. The barriers were proper roads. However, Domenico took this in at a glance because he could see the chapel in the distance and leant forward in his seat as if willing the car to get there faster.

A small welcoming committee was waiting and as the Morris Minor slowed down Domenico thought he recognised a couple of faces. He was overcome by the strangeness of seeing the chapel without the camp. He had known it had been completely taken away, but that was not the same as seeing the place without it. The chapel had never been visible from this position without looking through barbed-wire fencing. He was glad the statue had survived, with the names of all the POWs from Camp 60 sealed inside the base.

They got out of the car and Domenico was pleased to meet Alison Sutherland Graeme again. Her father had died soon after the formation of the chapel preservation committee and she had taken over as president. The Graemeshall home farm, including the island of Lamb Holm, had been sold to the Sinclair family who had been tenant farmers on the land for decades.

'Signor Chiocchetti. It is a great pleasure to see you again,' she said.

'It is I who must thank you. I know without your help and

that of the preservation committee I would not have this opportunity to see the little chapel again.'

Ernest Marwick made introductions where needed. Father Cairns was now based in Orkney and had taken over as chairman of the committee. The conversations were kept brief.

'There will be plenty of time to speak to people over the coming days, Signor Chiocchetti. I know you must be eager to see inside,' said Marwick, expressing verbally what was clearly shown on the artist's face. 'Please do not feel you have to hurry. We'll wait for you here.'

'Thank you,' said Domenico gratefully.

His trained eye took in the general state of the façade as he walked to the door. However, as he stretched out his hand to the handle, he hesitated. Domenico had lost count of the times he had wished for this moment, but now he feared what might be awaiting him. There had been varying descriptions about the severity of deterioration and damage inside.

The serenity of the chapel enveloped him immediately and it felt as though he had stepped back sixteen years in time. He walked along the nave. The rust on the rood screen could be seen from yards away and the gate creaked alarmingly when opened. But then he was standing before his painting of the Madonna and Child. Domenico looked at it closely, from further back, then closely again. He had been more concerned about this painting than about anything else but it did not appear to be damaged, only faded. He set about inspecting the rest of the interior.

The committee had acted quickly after its formation to organise urgent repairs and these had stopped any further water entering the building, but not before damp had affected the paintings to the right of the altar, in particular the icons of St Matthew and St Mark. The images on the other side seemed untouched as did the ceiling with its white dove. Domenico quickly looked around the rest of the inside to obtain a general idea of what needed repairing.

When he weighed everything up, his heart sank. The BBC had paid for him to travel to Lamb Holm and work on the chapel's restoration for three weeks, but he would make little impression in such a short time. He was back in front of the Madonna and Child, wondering what to say to the people waiting patiently outside, when Father Cairns appeared quietly by his side.

'Still a wonder after all these years, Signor Chiocchetti,' said the priest, looking at the image above the altar.

'I am very relieved that, of everything, this picture has survived so well. Although I feel it has faded slightly. But I'm afraid a great deal of the inside needs major restoration as well as the façade. I don't think the condition of the building is good. In the three weeks that I'll be working on the chapel, Father Cairns, I think only a fraction of the work needed can be carried out. I'm worried I'll disappoint everyone, when so many people have gone to a great deal of trouble to get me here.'

Father Cairns appeared not to be bothered at all by this and gave a reassuring smile.

'Signor Chiocchetti, we appreciated the short time available and the enormity of the task, but you can be sure of as many willing hands as you need. You've only to ask and people will be delighted to help. We've already had several offers of support from local Orkney tradesmen. Also, there's an artist in Kirkwall, a man called Stanley Hall, who would be willing to work under your guidance to retouch the paintwork.'

Domenico was quiet for a while, looking up at the painting inspired by the image on the little prayer card, that he had carried throughout the war. When he finally returned to Moena this had been put in a glass frame and placed next to his bed. Before leaving for Orkney, he had removed the card and brought it with him. Domenico was both touched by Father Cairns's comment and slightly daunted. There was to be a team of workers again, only this time they would all be strangers.

'Perhaps not exactly like the old days of Buttapasta, Pennisi and the others,' he said, almost to himself.

'No, I suppose not, but maybe . . . new friends instead.'

Everyone else had tactfully remained outside. Domenico looked at the kindly priest. He held out his hand.

'New friends indeed, Father.'

The chapel preservation committee organised a special supper. Although Domenico had been delighted to have been met at the airport by Ernest Marwick, it was not until the evening that the two friends had an opportunity to catch up on news. They enjoyed reminiscing about the days when Domenico had travelled to J. M. Stevenson in Kirkwall to buy poster paints with money from the chapel fund. Ernest Marwick recounted the story of the love letter handed over to the shop assistant, but Domenico could shed no light on who 'Tony' had been.

Domenico met Stanley Hall and the two artists immediately began an intense conversation about paints, colours and how best to tackle the restoration. Domenico was surprised at how much English came back to him as he had had little reason to use it in his home town. Only occasionally did Charles Ricono or Beatrice Linton have to step in. Domenico would have been happy to talk of paints all night, but there were several guests around the table who wanted to hear about his life. Bill Johnstone, who had started his own business after the war, was keen to know what the artist had done since leaving Lamb Holm.

'Some of you may know that I stayed in the camp in order

to complete the holy water stoup after everyone else had gone, apart from a small work party,' said Domenico. 'I caught up with my friends in Yorkshire only a week or so later and we worked for a while on local farms. My last ten months in England were spent with a group of Italians in Kew. We had to clear away derelict buildings but I was able to see something of London. We used to give cigarettes to the English driver to take a different route every day from our lodgings, so we could see more of the city.

'Eventually, I boarded a ship in Southampton that took me to Naples and in February 1946 I was reunited with my parents, brothers and sisters, after being away for six years and eight months.'

There was much nodding in appreciation of the loss and waste of so many years. But people were eager for more and Domenico was not allowed to stop.

'But what happened when you were home?' asked someone further down the table.

'I married two years later and Maria and I now have two girls and a boy,' said Domenico proudly, taking out a picture and handing it around. 'It would have been impossible to make a living as an artist in a small town, so I started a business as a house decorator. However, I paint landscapes and portraits when I can and sometimes I get the opportunity to work on religious statues for local churches and monasteries. Life is good. I am content.'

If Domenico thought this explanation would satisfy his audience he was wrong. They wanted to know how the Italians had arrived at Lamb Holm, what life was like in the camp and how he had found the work on the barriers. They wanted to hear about what he did before the war. And, of course, they wanted to know about the chapel.

It felt strange talking again about Buttapasta, Pennisi, Giuseppe and the others. When the Italians had returned to their homes in Italy they had been spread throughout the country. Keeping in contact had not been easy. People separated from families and loved ones were keen to catch up on lost years and wanted to get on with their own lives again. It was at this point that Ernest Marwick produced a large envelope from which he took out several black and white photographs.

'Perhaps you might like to see these, Signor Chiocchetti, as we're talking about the men who built the chapel,' he said, handing the pictures across the table.

Domenico looked at the top image with an expression of astonishment. It was James Sinclair's photograph of Giuseppe and him standing outside the chapel. He had never seen the result. The next photograph showed two dozen of the craftsmen outside the entrance. Domenico took great pleasure in pointing at figures and adding their names. There were other pictures showing various signs of camp life . . . prisoners gathered around the statue, athletes being given their prizes on sports day. It brought to mind the story of Shipwreck and how he had deceived everyone, even the doctors, for more than two years.

'These are copies, so they are for you to keep,' said Marwick, much to Domenico's great pleasure.

'I am very grateful,' he said, going back through them again.

Domenico was not without his own questions and he fired a stream of them when he felt it was time for someone else to do some talking. The evening wore on. By the time they departed for their homes Domenico was sure of one thing that was very important to him; the Orcadians had genuinely taken the little chapel to their hearts and there was a determination in the community to do whatever was necessary to save it.

253

The next morning Charles Ricono picked up Domenico from the home of Beatrice Linton, who was his host on Orkney, and drove him to the chapel. Father Cairns was already standing outside the entrance and when the three entered Domenico was surprised to see two men taking the gates off the rood screen.

'Mr Mowatt, the blacksmith, was keen to get started,' said Father Cairns in response to the expression on Domenico's face. 'As we were discussing last night, the screen needs to be thoroughly cleaned. We appreciated that you won't want a lot of dust in the air when you're trying to restore the paintwork, so as much of the screen as possible will be taken to the forge to clean.'

Father Cairns introduced the men.

'Some of the screen will have to be cleaned where it is, but we'll fit in with you, Signor Chiocchetti, so as not to interrupt your painting,' said the blacksmith. 'When the screen has been cleaned and refitted, one of the local decorators is going to paint it with something that will prevent it from rusting again.'

Domenico nodded his approval and smiled. It appeared that a lot of planning had already been done before his arrival and it helped put his mind at rest.

'You'll find a stream of workers turning up today, Signor Chiocchetti,' said Father Cairns. 'I'll stay here this morning to make introductions and ensure there is nothing I can't get for you.'

Just as Domenico was thanking the priest, Stanley Hall entered and the two artists immediately began a detailed inspection of the interior. The blacksmith and his helper went back to dismantling the rood screen, while Father Whitaker and Charles Ricono took a walk around outside.

By mid-morning the chapel was buzzing with workers and Domenico had difficulty remembering the names of all the people he had been introduced to. As a joiner and his mate examined the doors and windows, two other men started sanding and cleaning the façade so that cracks could be filled and the whole thing subsequently painted white. Domenico spotted two people walking around outside whom he hadn't yet met, but each time he saw them through one of the windows they seemed to be examining the roof. At eleven o'clock two local women arrived. Through the doorway Domenico could see that they were taking down the curtains.

'Are they removing the curtains to protect them from the paint?' he asked Father Cairns who was standing next to him and could see what Domenico was looking at.

'No,' he said with a laugh. 'They're taking the curtains away to give them a good wash.'

Domenico smiled. It did indeed appear that the Orkney people had organised themselves into a highly effective work-force. By lunchtime the blacksmith and his helper had taken away all of the rood screen that could be safely removed and the joiner and his mate had left, saying they would be back in a couple of days with a new door. Before they left a decorator arrived, examined the windows with the joiner, and agreed to come back the next morning to start preparing the frames to be repainted.

By the afternoon, everyone had gone except Domenico and the Kirkwall artist. The two men were glad they could work in peace and agreed to start by retouching the brick and stone effect that covered the walls of the nave. This was the largest area but only sections of it required retouching and was the easiest to repaint. The light was good and the weather warm so they left both east and west doors open. Domenico was happy. He had been reunited with the small part of him that he left behind all those years ago.

*   *   *

255

Later that evening, Domenico stood outside a house, checking once more the address he had written on a scrap of paper before leaving Moena. He knocked. Almost instantly the door was flung open and before he had uttered a word of greeting he was embraced by Aldo.

He wasn't quite prepared for so many strong emotions to come flooding back but both stood with tears in their eyes, slapping each other on the back and then pulling apart to look at one another before embracing again. Eventually, Aldo moved away so that Ailsa, who was standing not far behind, could say hello. She gave Domenico a huge hug, which made the artist grin widely. Over her shoulder he saw a boy and girl. The boy was only about five and looked up at the stranger with wide eyes. The girl was perhaps ten and she moved towards Domenico with grace and dignity. The girl had Aldo's finely chiselled features and Ailsa's flashing eyes.

'This is Beth,' said Ailsa.

'Hello, Beth,' said Domenico.

Beth had rehearsed a welcome speech in Italian but when she looked at the kindly artist it suddenly seemed unnecessary, so she simply rushed forward and hugged him as though he were a favourite uncle, grace and dignity forgotten.

'I think that, in the entire world, a hug is the best welcome that anyone can give or receive,' he said laughing.

The little boy had taken hold of Aldo's hand. Domenico knelt down.

'And what is your name?'

'Domenico,' said the boy, half hidden behind Aldo's leg.

'No, that can't be right. That's my name.'

'It is. It's Domenico.'

'Well, that's amazing. We both have the same name. Do you think we look alike as well?'

'No. You're old,' said little Domenico.

Everyone laughed at this, which made the boy smile and come out from behind Aldo's leg.

'Yes, you're right there. Perhaps you'll have to help me to get up.'

Domenico pretended the little boy's aid was essential to getting back on his feet and so, with such an introduction, little Domenico took the artist's hand and lead him through to the dining room because, as he explained on the way in confidence, he was actually quite hungry.

The two old friends talked late into the night, swapping news and recalling memories. Aldo had started a small café, which had been quite successful over the years. People enjoyed listening to the entertaining Italian, who sometimes had an entire room full of customers crying with laughter over a certain tale about a chicken. Ailsa had continued nursing, along with bringing up the children. Domenico could see they were happy and it pleased him greatly.

The next few days continued peacefully, with the two artists getting on quietly with their work. Various tradesmen came and went, each discussing with Domenico what needed to be done. He appreciated that they asked his opinion, but could see they were skilled men in their own fields and so was content that they carried on.

Domenico left the Kirkwall artist to continue working on the nave while he concentrated on retouching the paintwork in the chancel. He began working on the evangelists to the right of the altar, which took several days of meticulous restoration. He wanted to avoid making the retouched images look too new, as then they would clash with the other paintings that had simply faded slightly. It was a careful balancing act and couldn't be rushed.

The telephone call from the BBC the previous year had completely shocked him, because until then he had not realised that the chapel had survived. When he knew he was coming back to Orkney Domenico asked the committee to obtain the address of the camp commander. Thomas Buckland, as he was now known, had replied to Domenico's letter immediately, saying his doctor would not allow him to make the journey to Orkney but that Domenico was welcome to stay with him and his wife in Shropshire before returning to Italy. The details had been agreed.

By the end of the second week Stanley Hall was also working in the chancel. The weather stayed warm and dry and it was difficult to compare this Lamb Holm with the one he had landed on during a winter storm so long ago.

Father Cairns called every day to check that Orkney's honoured guest did not require anything he could help to arrange. Domenico received many invitations, including one from the Kirkwall art club and so one evening he found himself in a church hall, helping the delighted members draw a still life. He autographed his own drawing and left it with the club as a souvenir.

One morning at the beginning of the third week, Domenico and Father Cairns stood together outside looking back at the chapel. Two men were giving the façade a second coat of paint. It looked brilliant in the strong sunshine. All of the woodwork in the building had been mended or replaced and painted, hinges oiled and polished. Even the bell was shining, having been thoroughly cleaned whilst work was carried out to strengthen the bell tower. The words *S D Accord 1918 Aberdeen* could once more be seen clearly. The badly-rusted iron cross was replaced with an identical bronze one made by a local craftsman. Giuseppe's beautiful rood screen, now completely free of rust and dirt, was refitted and painted in red oxide before being given a final black coat. The effect was stunning.

'You are pleased with your helpers, Signor Chiocchetti?' asked Father Cairns.

'Everyone has been so extremely helpful and kind, giving up so much of their time. I can't thank you enough for your efforts Father Cairns.'

'And the painting inside?'

'That's also going well. Mr Hall has been an invaluable help and I am confident the restoration of the paintwork will be completed by the end of this week. But you wanted to tell me something of the roof, Father?'

'Indeed. We've had lots of advice on this, and as you know it's the biggest problem with the building. However, the experts seem to agree that the best way to make it watertight is to apply a layer of bitumen on top of the concrete.'

'That must be expensive to do?'

'Well, like everything else, if an item or service has to be paid for the money has come from visitor donations. We've not had to make one single appeal. And I believe the generosity of people in years to come will continue to provide the funds needed to keep the little chapel in good repair.'

'I am greatly moved, Father.'

'So is everyone who steps inside, which is why they want to preserve it. As you know, Father Whitaker, who was so involved in helping to save the chapel in the early days of the committee, will arrive here from Lerwick on Saturday to take the service on the following morning. I think you may be surprised at how many people will attend.'

Domenico was about to speak when his attention was taken by the arrival of a van and a small bus, a group of excited school children emerging from the latter. Each of them had a garden trowel or something similar, while many emerged carrying potted plants. Father Cairns, who never seemed to be surprised at anything that happened locally, provided an explanation.

'So much has been done to the building, the committee thought it would be a shame not to tidy up the surrounding area,' he said. 'The van is from a nearby plant supplier, who is going to take charge, but we thought it would be nice for local children to be involved in helping to restore the borders. Many of them have brought flowers from their own gardens.'

It was obvious the children had already been allocated individual jobs as they all knew what to get from the van, where to go and what to start doing.

'They're certainly not here to play,' said Domenico who had been chuckling at the number of children who had said 'Buongiorno, Signor Chiocchetti,' in their soft Orkney accent.

The next morning Domenico was at the chapel early. He was alone. The restoration of all the paintwork was virtually complete. There was only one thing left to do. He quietly laid out his brushes and paints then took out from his pocket the tin holding the little prayer card. He opened it and removed the card, which he looked at for a long while before placing it at the feet of St Francis of Assisi, as he had done once before, in another life.

On 10th April 1960, the day before Domenico was to leave Orkney, a service of rededication was held in the chapel. The service, some of which was subsequently broadcast on Italian radio, was attended by more than 200 Orcadians, who represented a wide cross-section of denominations. Domenico was the first person to receive Holy Communion.

Father Whitaker commented on the strong ties that now

existed between the communities of Orkney and Moena. He conveyed his great admiration for Domenico and the other men, who had fought so hard against the elements and hardships of a prisoner of war camp to create this monument to God in which they were gathered.

'Of the buildings clustering on Lamb Holm in wartime only two remain: this chapel and the statue of St George. All the things which catered for material needs have disappeared, but the two things which catered for spiritual needs still stand. In the heart of human beings, the truest and most lasting hunger is for God.'

During his three weeks working on the chapel Domenico had written a letter to the people of Orkney and he presented this to the preservation committee the next day.

Dear Orcadians – My work at the chapel is finished. In these three weeks I have done my best to give again to the little church that freshness which it had sixteen years ago. The chapel is yours – for you to love and preserve. I take with me to Italy the remembrance of your kindness and wonderful hospitality. I shall remember always, and my children shall learn from me to love you. I thank the authorities of Kirkwall, the courteous preservation committee and all those who directly or indirectly have collaborated for the success of this work and for having given me the joy of seeing again the little chapel of Lamb Holm where I, in leaving, leave a part of my heart. Thanks also in the name of all my companions of Camp 60 who worked with me. Good-bye dear friends of Orkney – or perhaps I should say just 'au revoir.'

Domenico Chiocchetti

Epilogue

Shortly after Domenico Chiocchetti's visit to Orkney in 1960, a group of artists in Moena opened a workshop to produce sacred carvings. Domenico gave up house painting and joined the business as a decorator of statues. He dedicated all his spare time to painting.

He returned to Orkney in 1964, this time with his wife Maria, who was at last able to see the chapel her husband had been so instrumental in creating. As a personal gift they brought with them the fourteen Stations of the Cross, which can be seen on the walls to this day. He returned once more in 1970 with his son Fabio and daughter Letizia. On each occasion he carried out some minor repairs.

Domenico's fame spread far beyond his home town of Moena in the Dolomites, where he was a well respected man. In 1996, at the age of eighty-six, he was granted the freedom of Moena. He was also president of the ex-POW association for Camp 60 and Camp 34, which had been formed during the late 1960s.

Domenico Chiocchetti died on 7th May 1999, only one week from his eighty-ninth birthday. Such was his standing at the time that several national UK newspapers carried his obituary.

The following month a memorial requiem mass was held in the Lamb Holm chapel, conducted by The Right Reverend Mario Conti, Bishop of Aberdeen (now Archbishop of Glasgow), and amongst the congregation were Domenico's wife Maria and their three children, Fabio, Letizia and Angela. Maria Chiocchetti died in 2007 at the age of eighty-nine.

Giuseppe Palumbi returned to Italy at the end of 1945, and was reunited with his wife Pierina and young son Renato. Giuseppe confessed everything and even showed Pierina the photograph of Fiona, which she promptly burnt. However, they stayed together and, in 1950, had their second child. When this daughter later had her own baby girl, she named her after the woman her father had met and fallen in love with during the war and so, twenty-six years after leaving Orkney, Giuseppe achieved a little part of this dream.

When he left Camp 60, he brought away a photograph of the rood screen. Many times over the following years he could be found staring at the picture, hanging on a wall at home. Giuseppe continued to work as a blacksmith and was very close to his granddaughter. He died in 1980 at the age of sixty-nine. Giuseppe never achieved his wish of returning to Orkney, but the beautiful rood screen remains one of the wonders of the chapel. The heart is still there, where the two gates meet.

A few weeks after he left Lamb Holm, Major Buckland was promoted to Lt Colonel, but by the end of 1946 his services in the army were no longer required. He set up a small commercial stationery business, which he ran from his home in Shropshire where he continued to enjoy music, singing and practical jokes. Following the visit by Domenico Chiocchetti in 1960 the two men kept in regular contact until the death of Thomas Buckland in 1969 at the age of eighty-two.

Padre Giacomo spent three months in the military hospital

in Orkney and when he came out the men from Camp 60 had long gone to the camp in Yorkshire. He spent some time based at St Margaret's Hope on South Ronaldsay, then was based near Sheffield, before being repatriated in 1945. Apart from a brief period as a military chaplain, Padre Giacomo spent the remainder of his life in various Italian monasteries. He was involved in helping to extend a small chapel in Milano Marittima where he spent many years. Padre Giacomo died in 1971 at the age of seventy-six and was buried in Missano, west of Bologna. In 1985, the nearby town of Pavullo nel Frignano honoured his memory by naming a street 'Padre Giacomo Giacobazzi'.

Like most of the Italians who had been prisoners of war in Britain during the Second World War, Sergeant Major Guerrino Fornasier was repatriated to Italy. However, while 'Rino' was based at the camp near Skipton he met a local girl whose parents were Italian, and he later returned to England to marry her. They had one daughter. Rino worked for the family's ice cream business, which they expanded, eventually moving the factory to Keighley in West Yorkshire. He continued to work in the business until his death in 1975 of cancer. He was only fifty-nine.

Sergeant Giovanni Pennisi set up a business as a decorator upon his return to Italy. He married and had a son. Giovanni Pennisi died in 1989.

James Sinclair continued to take photographs until his late seventies and when he died in 1984 at the age of eighty-three, he left a unique record of Orkney life that spanned some sixty years. His photograph of Domenico and Giuseppe is one of the most famous ever taken of the Italian chapel.

Ernest Marwick became a well known Orkney author and a writer for both the *Orcadian* and the *Orkney Herald* newspapers.

Following Domenico's visit in 1960 he remained in regular contact with the artist until his death in 1977.

Father Joseph Ryland-Whitaker was based in Lerwick on Shetland from 1953 to 1961, at which point he was transferred to Stornoway on the Isle of Lewis. He died suddenly in 1963 while working in Edinburgh.

Father Frank Cairns was based in Shetland from 1955 to 1958, when he was moved to Orkney. He took over the role of chairman of the Italian Chapel Preservation Committee, a position that has been held by successive Roman Catholic priests on Orkney for many years.

The fate of Fiona, like Buttapasta, Major Booth, Micheloni and others in the story, has been lost over time.

In 1992, eight ex POWs from Camp 60 and Camp 34 made an historic return journey to Orkney, fifty years after they had first arrived on the islands. None of the men had been back since they had left and they were treated as honoured guests, with Italian flags flying from many vantage points during their stay. This, of course, included a service held in the chapel.

By this time Domenico Chiocchetti was too frail to join them. However, amongst them was Primiano Malvolti, better known during his captivity on Orkney as 'Shipwreck'. He returned to Italy after the war, worked on the railways, married, had four children and lived to be eighty . . . without the use of a walking stick.

Another of the men who returned to Orkney in 1992 was Coriolano 'Gino' Caprara, the star of many performances in the mess hall. At the time of writing, Gino is a sprightly ninety year old, full of stories about his time in the camp and the friends he made of local people.

The small girl who was so delighted with the wooden toy made by Sergeant Major Fornasier moved years later to live in Orkney and Sheena Wenham now helps to train tour guides on the islands. Her aunt, Alison Sutherland Graeme, remained honorary president of the preservation committee until her death on 30 November 2009 at the age of 102.

Following the completion of the barriers, Bill Johnstone was called up, joined the Royal Navy and sent to the naval dockyards in Freetown, Sierra Leone . . . where he was put in charge of a power station! He died in 1981, having run a successful concrete manufacturing business in Orkney for many years after the war.

The island of Lamb Holm is still owned by the Sinclair family. The quarry where so many of the Italian POWs worked was flooded years ago and is now used by a local shell fish merchant and also as a hatchery for lobsters, which are released back into the sea.

Many Orkney families treasure gifts given to their parents or grandparents by the Italians when they left the islands. The Mathieson family in Burray have the beautiful model of Milan cathedral, made out of matchsticks, while Bill Johnstone's daughter still has the lemonade bottle containing a carved crucifix, with which he was presented in return for the oil he gave the Italians for their hair. Many other items can be seen in Orkney museums.

Today, the ties between Orkney and Moena are stronger than ever. The regular exchange trips of school children have often included one of Domenico and Maria Chiocchetti's four grandchildren, while representatives of the preservation committee have visited Moena on several occasions. The wayside shrine situated next to the chapel was a present from the Moena community.

The chapel has needed some tender loving care over the years and the unsung heroes of this story are the preservation committee and men like local artist Gary Gibson, who has overseen restoration work and on-going repairs for more than thirty years.

The committee's secretary, John Muir, has been a contact point since the 1960s for people around the world with an interest in the chapel.

The chapel has become a popular venue in which to be married or hold concerts and is one of Orkney's most famous tourist attractions. Around 10,000 visitors a month gaze upon Domenico's Madonna and Child in the summer, when services are held once a month. A special service is held every year in October, on the Sunday nearest to the anniversary of the sinking of the *Royal Oak*.

The chapel remains, fragile and immortal, a symbol of peace and hope from people long gone for those yet to come.

Author's Note

The manuscript was nearing completion (or so I thought) when I heard the story of Giuseppe and Fiona from the blacksmith's grandson, Giuseppe 'Pino' Palumbi. I had asked the Palumbi family a number of questions about Giuseppe and his time on Orkney and the story then came out about Fiona. When Giuseppe's son Renato told Pino what had happened, I think he was even more surprised than I was when I found out. I never tracked down the woman that Giuseppe loved in Orkney. Fiona Merriman is not her real name and the 'life' I have given her is entirely fictitious . . . almost.

Characters such as Aldo, Dino, Carlo and Ailsa came from my own imagination. However, while they are not meant to represent anyone alive or dead, I have attributed to them many events that are reported to have happened. At least one POW was killed in an accident during the building of the Churchill Barriers and another died of pneumonia. They were buried with full military honours in St Olaf cemetery. After the war their bodies were exhumed and returned to Italy.

The earliest article I can find about the chapel was published in 1959 by the *Orkney Herald*, following an interview with the

Camp 60 priest. In this, he refers to the blacksmith as 'Palumbi'. A few weeks later, the newspaper carried an article following an interview with Domenico Chiocchetti, and in this the spelling is given as Palumbo. Most articles have since used the latter. It was only in 2001, when Renato Palumbi contacted the chapel preservation committee to arrange a family visit to Orkney, that the correct name could be confirmed.

In the *Orkney Herald*'s article about Padre Giacomo, the spelling of the stonemason is given as Buttapasta. Many subsequent articles spell this as Bruttapasta but, according to Domenico Chiocchetti's daughter, there was no 'r' in his name so I have used this version.

The Camp 60 priest's name also causes some confusion. He was christened Gioacchino Giacobazzi and virtually all articles refer to him as Padre Giacobazzi. However, a biography of the priest, written by a man called Berardo Rossi and published in 1997, reveals that he was known as Padre Giacomo, which translates as Father James, and was most likely his ordination name.

Throughout the book, I have tried to keep to known dates, names and events where possible, but obviously some parts have been guessed at, other parts altered for dramatic effect and some situations simplified. The latter is particularly the case with regard to the offer to be 'volunteer co-operatives', made in April 1944 by the British Government to the Italians in captivity. In reality, this was extremely complex and the details of the offer changed over the following months.

Before the Italians arrived in Orkney they spent several weeks in Edinburgh, undergoing medical checks and further registration procedures. It was during this time that they were given new uniforms, which incorporated target discs, two on the jacket and one on the outside of the trousers.

Padre Giacomo arrived at Camp 60 with the Italian flag that he had saved at the last minute from a field hospital in Soddu, Ethiopia. I don't know if he hung the flag in the vestry or what happened to it after the Italians left the islands.

Coriolano 'Gino' Caprara and Primiano Malvolti spent their captivity in Orkney in Camp 34 on Burray. I liked the story about the walking stick so much that I 'transferred' both men to Camp 60. The tale about how 'Shipwreck' fooled everyone for over two years, but then gave himself away by entering sports events, is recounted as it was told to me by his good friend Gino. This includes the presentation to Shipwreck of the cup for best overall sportsman and his experience the following day, when the British camp commander ignored him as he stood to attention in his office then, without speaking, simply handed over a card upon which was written 'Quarry'!

One can only imagine the frustration endured by the men held captive in Camp 60 for so long, but the incidents of conflict that I have recounted between the Italians are not based on any actual events.

Many of the stories that may appear implausible are based on facts, such as how Domenico and his friends caught a gull and painted it to look like the Italian flag. For this action, they did indeed spend a couple of days in the punishment block. Domenico's meeting with Major Buckland during the initial stages of the chapel's creation, at which the officer thought the artist was refusing to do the work, is also documented. When he realised his mistake, he slapped Domenico on the back, saying, 'Bravo.' Major Buckland's mother had spent a frantic couple of days while he had been working, as a young man, on the SS *Cedric* as she thought he had transferred to the *Titanic* just before its tragic maiden voyage.

One of the Italians was given a ferret by a local farmer, the two men coming to an agreement that the farmer could have the skins of any animal caught. The parcels sent by Italian families to Camp 60 sometimes contained fruit and there are Orcadians today who remember being given these fruits when they were small children.

I never discovered the identity of the popular English sergeant nicknamed 'Wooden Leg'. Mr Ian McClure was the surgeon at the Balfour Hospital from 1928 until his retirement in 1962, although his interactions with characters in the book are not based on fact.

Most of the men who had been in Camp 60 are dead, but new information continues to come to light. The electrician Michael De Vitto died in 2007 in Lancashire, which I discovered only recently when I tracked down his widow, Margaret. The two met while he was in the Skipton camp and although he was repatriated in 1945, Michael returned two years later to marry her. Margaret tells her husband's story in the nonfiction *Orkney's Italian Chapel*.

Although the majority of published articles put the date of the departure of the men in Camp 60 as the spring of 1945, they left Lamb Holm on 9th September 1944 to transfer to Overdale Camp, near Skipton.

A copy of the letter from 'Tony' to the girl in the Kirkwall shop is in the Orkney library archives (ref D31/27/4), and is reproduced exactly as it was written. Also in the archives (ref D31/27) is the letter Domenico Chiocchetti presented to the preservation committee in 1960. However, this is not in his handwriting, so was probably written for him at the time by someone with better English.

By 1945, more than 150,000 Italians, who had been POWs in Britain, were still in the country. They had become an important part of the nation's depleted workforce, though most were repatriated during the following year. Many later returned to Britain to work, marry and raise families.

This book concentrates on the lives of the Italians in Camp 60, but credit should be given to the huge effort also made by civilian workers in building the barriers, who started the project more than eighteen months before the Italian POWs arrived on the islands. Tragically, several men were killed during the construction work, most of them drowned in the first year when travel between the islands was extremely dangerous.

Many chapels were built in POW camps around the world by Italians during the Second World War and although most have been lost there are still examples that exist today, such as the one in Henllan, West Wales and Letterkenny, USA. The chapel that was built under the supervision of Giovanni Pennisi in Camp 34 on the Orkney island of Burray was demolished after the war along with the other Nissen huts. It was the fate destined for the chapel in Camp 60 . . . if the demolition crew had not refused to carry out their orders.